THE PAINTING ON
AUERPERG'S WALL

Canada Council for the Arts **Conseil des Arts du Canada**  ONTARIO ARTS COUNCIL CONSEIL DES ARTS DE L'ONTARIO an Ontario government agency un organisme du gouvernement de l'Ontario  **Canadä**

We gratefully acknowledge the support of the Canada Council for the Arts and the Ontario Arts Council for our publishing program. We also acknowledge the financial support of the Government of Canada through the Canada Book Fund.

Cover design: Val Fullard

The Painting on Auerperg's Wall is a work of fiction. All the characters and situations portrayed in this book are fictitious and any resemblance to persons living or dead is purely coincidental.

Library and Archives Canada Cataloguing in Publication

Rummel, Erika, 1942-, author
        The painting on Auerberg's wall / Erika Rummel.

(Inanna poetry & fiction series)
Issued in print and electronic formats.
ISBN 978-1-77133-489-1 (softcover).— ISBN 978-1-77133-490-7 (epub).—
ISBN 978-1-77133-491-4 (Kindle).— ISBN 978-1-77133-492-1 (pdf)

        I. Title. II. Series: Inanna poetry and fiction series

PS8635.U56P35 2018   C813'.6   C2018-901523-3
                                                                            C2018-901524-1

Printed and bound in Canada

Inanna Publications and Education Inc.
210 Founders College, York University
4700 Keele Street, Toronto, Ontario, Canada M3J 1P3
Telephone: (416) 736-5356 Fax: (416) 736-5765
Email: inanna.publications@inanna.ca   Website: www.inanna.ca

THE PAINTING ON AUERPERG'S WALL

a novel

ERIKA RUMMEL

inanna poetry & fiction series

INANNA PUBLICATIONS AND EDUCATION INC.
TORONTO, CANADA

TABLE OF CONTENTS

PRELUDE

D AVID OPENED THE BOOK to the first page and read the title: *The Rescue.* The slim volume looked frail. He was afraid of cracking the spine and loosening the pages. It had been a mistake to remove the book. He should have read it right there, in Nancy's bedroom. You don't disturb the grave-yard of memories. Picking up the book was like moving a dead man's bones. Even running his eyes down the page felt like an intrusion.

THE RESCUE

I was born in Vienna on May 20, 1939, the son of Samuel Wassermann, a manufacturer of mining equipment, and his wife Irene. The Ahnenpass[1] *identified my mother as a descendant of Jews to the fourth generation. On my father's side, there was a mixture of gentiles and Jews, including an Aryan grandmother and a set of Aryan great-grandparents. But that wasn't good enough for the Nazis. An Ahnenpass with a preponderance of Jews was a death sentence.*

My uncle, Josef Wassermann, a lawyer, was married to a gentile — which made Eva Wassermann a Judenhure[2] *in the eyes of the Nazis. In July 1938, a decree was passed in the*

---

[1]The document required by the Nazis to establish Aryan lineage.
[2]Whore of the Jews.

Reichstag, requiring Aryans to divorce their Jewish spouses. My aunt complied with the law. Josef moved in with my parents. Eva visited whenever possible, maintaining a clandestine relationship with her husband.

In June of 1939, the Gestapo arrested my father on trumped-up charges of embezzlement. Friends advised my mother to leave the country immediately. The consensus was that the Gestapo would come back and detain her and Josef Wassermann as well.

My mother was reluctant to leave. She needed to stand by her husband, she said.

"Be reasonable, Irene," her brother-in-law said. "Think of the baby. Any risk you take involves the child as well. We must get you a visa for England. And I'll look after affairs here and do what I can for Samuel."

"And what if the Nazis come after you, Josef?"

"They won't touch me," he said. "They wouldn't dare. I have friends in the diplomatic corps. That's my safety net. But you must go."

My mother gave in to his pleas and started clearing out the apartment. She moved all her personal belongings to Eva's flat and discreetly sold her valuables. She needed money to start over in England. The large principal rooms of the apartment turned into echo chambers. The festive gatherings, the laughter, the animated conversations were still swirling in her memory, but the rooms themselves had become barren. The glass vitrines holding the family's crystal and silver platters were empty, the Sorgenthal porcelain sold. The fine Tabriz and Nain carpets were rolled up, ready to be put into storage. A trusted employee was to pick them up at night and drive them to the warehouse in a company van. The oil paintings and baroque mirrors that had hung on the walls had been sold at bargain prices. One or two paintings proved impossible to sell because they were the work of Jewish painters. Irene didn't know what to do about them.

Josef was impatient.

"You are wasting precious time," he said to her. "If you need cash, I'll lend it to you. Samuel can pay me back when this nightmare is over."

"No, I can't take money from you," she said. "What if you need it to get Sam out of the country? And I can't just up and leave. I must put things in order first." The truth was she couldn't bring herself to leave Vienna while Samuel was in prison. And so, while she dawdled and Josef thought he was untouchable, the trap closed on her and Josef.

In September of 1939, the Gestapo showed up at the Wassermann apartment in the Herrengasse and arrested them both. My aunt, who happened to be at the flat, held me close and pretended I was her child.

She told me the story so often, it turned into a prayer. She handed it down to me as a relic of the past, and I offer it here in the same spirit: Eva's story, in her words.

"Keep your hands off the baby," she said to the officer in command of the squad. "Ich bin eine deutsche Mutter."[3]

"So what is a deutsche Mutter doing here, visiting Jews?" the Kommandant asked. "And where is the father of the child?"

"Is this an interrogation?" Eva shot back. "My husband has been drafted. He is doing his duty, fighting for the fatherland. I am here to get my jewellery back. I divorced this Judenschwein[4] three years ago." She pointed at Josef, who was being handcuffed. "When he moved out, he took my jewellery. A pearl necklace and a diamond ring. He says it belongs to him because he paid for it. I say it was a wedding present and mine to keep. That's why I came here, to get my property back. But no luck."

"Let me get this story straight," the Kommandant said, tapping a short riding crop against his thigh. "You divorced

[3]"I am a German mother." Motherhood, Aryan that is, was a Nazi *shibboleth.*
[4]"Jewish pig," an expletive widely used by the Nazis.

this Judenschwein *three years ago and remarried? And now
you hate your ex?"*

"I hate his guts."

"Is that so? Let's see you spit into his face."

*That is how my aunt parted from her husband. That is how
they were forced to say goodbye: she spat into his face.*

"Das haben Sie schön gemacht,"[5] *the Kommandant said to
Eva, grinning broadly.*

Josef had turned ashen.

*"Now, where is the jewellery the lady is talking about?" the
Kommandant said to him.*

*Josef said nothing. He brought his hand up to his face and
awkwardly wiped his cheek.*

*The Kommandant pointed to the suitcase Josef had been
permitted to pack. It was sitting on the floor between them.*

*"So what have you got in there?" the Kommandant said,
nudging the bag with the toe of his boot.*

*One of his goons kicked open the suitcase and rifled through
it, throwing clothes and toiletries on the tiled floor of the hall.
There was no jewellery.*

*My mother came forward and quietly put things back into
the suitcase. There was silence as the men watched her bending
over the clothes, gathering up and refolding the pieces.*

*The Kommandant made an impatient gesture. "Enough,"
he said. "Move your* breiten Judenarsch.[6] He *won't need those
clothes where he is going. He'll be issued a potato sack."*

*The squad laughed appreciatively. They formed a cordon
around Irene and Josef, waiting for the order to decamp, but
the officer was in no hurry.*

*"I bet he sold the jewellery," he said to my aunt. "Those two
were getting ready to skedaddle. The apartment is half-empty.
Another day or two, and they would have flown the coop."*

---

[5]"You did that very nicely."
[6]"Your big Jewish arse."

He gave Irene the evil eye. She was wearing a pair of emerald earrings. She still didn't understand how precarious her situation was. The Kommandant raised his crop and with the tip of the cane touched the emerald on her left ear, making the pendant sway.

Irene flinched.

"Take them off," he said to her, "and give them to the lady here as compensation for the jewellery she lost."

Irene fiddled with the clasps of her earrings.

"Need any help?" the Kommandant said and nodded to one of his men. "Help the lady, why don't you?"

The man stepped forward and ripped the pendants from Irene's ears with two brutal jags that made her head snap sideways. She cried out, and immediately pressed her lips together to stifle the sound. She didn't want to give the men the satisfaction of hearing her cry. Blood was dripping from her earlobes. She kept her head down.

The Kommandant chucked her under the chin and made her look into his eyes. He stood close to her, like a lover saying adieu to his sweetheart. "Come on," he said, his voice silky, "be a sport. Tell the lady that the earrings are a present, to remember you by."

Irene freed herself from his caressing hand. There was a smear of blood on her cheek. She looked across to Eva who held the emerald pendants in her cupped hand.

"It's a present, to remember me by," she said quietly. Her face had gone rigid.

"I'll remember you," my aunt said with a toss of her head. She knew she had to give a flawless performance to carry off the show.

"There you are," the Kommandant said smoothly. "Everything in order now?"

Eva nodded, and tucked away the earrings.

"It looks that way at any rate," he said, "but we can't be sure until we have checked out the whole story, right, sweetheart?

How many children do you have?"

On cue, the baby started fussing, and Eva buried her face in the blanket and nuzzled him. "Shush, darling," she said, trying desperately to maintain her composure. "Only this one," she said to the Kommandant. "I won't be a candidate for the Mutterkreuz,[7] *I know, but I'm doing what I can for the fatherland. You have a problem with that?"*

He grinned. "No problem, sweetheart."

He turned to go but stopped when he heard someone coming up the stairs.

A gentleman in a tailored grey coat and black homburg appeared on the landing with a boy in tow — the Wassermanns' neighbour, Leo von Auerperg and his son Max. The boy stopped on the last step and stared, but the father took his arm, leading him toward the door of their suite. He knew better than to show an interest in the activities of the Gestapo. You don't tangle with the secret police. He was pulling out his keys when the Kommandant called to him.

"You are a neighbour of the Wassermanns?"

"Yes, sir."

"This woman," the Kommandant said, pointing to my aunt, "claims the baby is hers. Is that correct?"

Von Auerperg took a step toward my aunt as if he wanted to get a better look at her in the gloomy halflight of the corridor. The tension was palpable, the seconds stretching into minutes, or so it seemed to Eva as she waited for Auerperg's reply.

"I've seen them before," Auerperg said. "Her and the baby. But that's all I can tell you, I'm afraid. I'm not on familiar terms with the Wassermanns."

The Kommandant turned to Max.

"How old are you, son?"

---

[7]The Iron Cross for mothers, an honour instituted in December of 1938 to encourage Aryan population growth; it was awarded to mothers of four or more children.

"Ten, sir."

"In the HJ?"[8]

The boy shot out his arm in a precise military salute. "Jawohl, Herr Kommandant."

"Good. You know the Wassermanns?"

"No, sir. I don't associate with Jews, sir."

"Very commendable," the Kommandant said and clapped him on the shoulder. "Your father can be proud of you."

He turned to his men. "Forwärts. Marsch," he barked, and the men snapped to attention and escorted Irene and Josef downstairs.

The Kommandant cast a look back at my aunt. "I still think I should check you out, sweetheart," he said. "Maybe we can do something together for the fatherland."

Eva listened to the dull thud of the retreating boots.

Von Auerperg was lingering in the corridor.

"Go on in, Max," he said to the boy. "I'll be with you in a minute."

When the door had closed on the boy, Auerperg leaned over the banister and scanned the foyer below. Satisfied that they were alone, he said to Eva:

"You'd better get out of Vienna — you and the child."

"I don't have enough money to get out," she said.

"Let's talk," he said. "Maybe I can help you. Meet me inside St. Peter's Church in half an hour."

Eva nodded and walked stiffly downstairs. The baby had started fussing again. She went into a small café at the corner, sat down in one of the booths, and ordered café au lait. When it came, she poured a little milk and sugar into the saucer, dipped the pacifier into the mixture and managed to calm the baby. After a while she paid, crossed the Graben and entered St. Peter's.

---

[8]Hitler Jugend (Youth for Hitler), a paramilitary youth organization. Membership was not obligatory, but those who refused to join were shunned.

If I had read this earlier, David thought, would it have made a difference? Not really. He still had a lot of questions that needed answers.

I. DAVID

THE CRISIS CAME IN THE SUMMER of 2001. The breakup with Elaine had a castrating effect on him. There wasn't the slightest increase in his pulse rate at the thought of sex, in whatever position, leg over, ass first, or Kama Sutra knot. There was no swelling in his groin area, none.

The uncertainty, the lack of definition in his crotch, started with Elaine bitching about the house. It was too shabby. She wanted something that was more in tune with her executive mind and her executive salary, something that spelled success.

"Let's move to Brentwood," she said, scanning the real estate ads in the LA *Times*. "Or Pacific Palisades."

"I thought you wanted to live here, in Santa Monica. You said you liked the funky shops, the cafés, the beach. Suddenly you don't?"

"The neighbourhood is fine. It's the house that bothers me, David. If you don't want to move, let's talk to an architect about renovating, putting in an extra bathroom, and extending the back of the house. We need space to entertain."

"The space we have is perfectly good for entertaining. I don't see why we have to change anything."

She threw the Real Estate section at him. "Christ! David!" she said. "What's wrong with you? You're turning into a vegetable."

True. Arguing with Elaine left him limp, in a subhuman state. It was a winter of raised voices and bitter accusations.

The incongruity of their lives became obvious. How could he have failed to notice it before? It was fundamental. He was incompatible with women of Elaine's type: the cool intellectual, the long-legged blonde with endless energy and a knack for closing deals. Elaine knew how to network, how to put herself on the promotional track. A woman like that is a daily challenge. Match her wit, match her high- powered moves, match her minimum sleep requirements. David needed a solid eight hours of sleep. Four hours were enough to recharge Elaine.

When Elaine moved out, she packed two suitcases with personal belongings. She was in a hurry to get away. She had no use for the furniture, the dishes, the linens, the stuff that marked their common past. She was keen on leaving everything behind and starting over. She took only a dozen books and cherry-picked a few collectibles: an etching, a small rug, some knick-knacks they had brought back from vacations. It was no more than she could load into her Infiniti, but the place looked raided nevertheless. There were empty spaces where familiar things had been. It all added to David's confusion and uncertainty. He put his hand on the spot that had once held a jade Buddha. He stood before the plucked bookshelves, put his fingers into the gaps, and felt hollow around the heart.

The TV offered no escape, no mindless entertainment. Every show was about bickering couples. All love affairs ended in crimes of passion or lingering deaths. David watched the evening news with a heightened sense of alarm. The violence kept piling up. It may have started with Elaine going away, but it continued with train derailments, gang rapes, drive-by shootings, and the attack on the World Trade Center. The images of the planes crashing into the towers, the billowing smoke, the toxic cloud, the howling sirens trailed in David's head for months. Things continued to go terribly wrong, at home and abroad. Nothing but disasters of biblical proportions:tsunamis, earthquakes, war, famine, epidemics. So it came as no surprise to David that the foundations of his house began to shake, as the excavator ripped into the bungalow nextdoor, a leftover from the thirties, a teardown in real estate parlance.

Most of the properties on Wadsworth Avenue had long ago been renovated, extended, topped with a second storey, or replaced altogether. David and the old woman next door had been the last holdouts. Now his house was the only reminder of the beach cottage era. Nancy Auerperg, who won the bidding war for the double-sized lot next door, had the bungalow razed and put up a house inspired by Frank Lloyd Wright, all glass, stone, and cedar. She put in a pool and next to it a cabana with a Swedish spa.

That's what he saw from his sunroom: the back of the cabana and, at the end of his own lawn, a garden shed, a mini barn from Home Depot. There used to be a row of ficus trees marking the property line. But they were gone now. He could see Nancy Auerperg's pool shimmering through the newly planted hedge. Why the hell did she have to cut down the trees?

Well, why not? The ficus trees had monstrous, driveway-heaving roots. His neighbour had done the right thing. Maybe. Probably. Fucking doubts again.

The phone started ringing. David didn't move from his chair in the sunroom. No one called him on the landline except telemarketers, pollsters, and scammers. And now that the semester was over and he had escaped the harlotry of lecturing, there was no need to answer the phone. He was no longer on call. He hadn't shown his face in the department for three weeks, resisted doing anything: answering email, doing research, filing his overdue income tax return. He did nothing, stuck to the house fungus-like, procrastinated, delaying the walk to the ATM machine until he was down to his last dollar.

The petulant ringing stopped.

David looked at the coffee stains at the bottom of his mug and made a mental note: Put mug into dishwasher. He had a habit of rinsing it in cold water and using it over again, sometimes for days. Did everyone do that, or was it a sign of slipping standards? He winced at the triviality of his own thought. Please. Someone stop the questions in my head! He tried to rouse himself. Get a grip, David! Do something.

He got up, made himself walk to the kitchen, open the fridge, take out the bottle of Prosecco that had been sitting there since Christmas since, no shit, Christmas! He looked down on his feet, pointed them toward the front door, and gave them marching orders. He walked over to Nancy Auerperg's house, bottle in hand, a housewarming present for his new neighbour, and rang the bell. His brain was stirring fitfully. He wasn't sure what he wanted from the woman next door. It was a wish without defined object, an amorphous wish originating in the limbic brain, a vague search for someone to fill the void and end his doubts. Was Nancy Auerperg the one? The burnished gold bangles on Nancy's wrists flashed ominously as she opened the door.

He introduced himself, handed her the bottle of Prosecco, his welcome present, and she asked him in and gave him a tour of her house, pointing out, as she put it, "the palette of natural materials." She had the modernist terminology pat. She never used a generic term. The cladding wasn't stone. It was Ledge stone. The ceiling wasn't wood. It was Jatoba. The cabinets were Wenge wood from Zaire, and so on. She talked with the fluency of an architectural digest about the elegant distillation to essentials, the dynamic spatiality, the great staging areas the house offered, the rhythmic flow of rooms. Yes, the house had all that, but most of all it had a quality of trying too hard to be pure and beautiful. Like Nancy herself?

David suspected she had undergone a few nip and tuck proce-dures to bring her features in line with the prevailing esthetics, to achieve that sculpted look. He couldn't pinpoint Nancy's age. In the soft lighting of her living room, she could pass for a woman of forty, but the raised veins on the back of her hands and a hint of stiffness when she got up from the sofa pushed the estimate closer to fifty. Nancy began to slip off his mental stage. He couldn't imagine blue-veined hands unzipping him and moving down into the nest of his pubic hair. And there was no comfort in her words, her perfect tech-language, although he noticed that she slipped occasionally. She had a tendency to gush when she got off the safe subject of things and entered the dangerous territory of feelings.

"When I first saw the architect's design, it gave me a thrill," she said, stroking her arms as if to flatten goosebumps. "Even on draft paper, the house was full of drama, energy, and momentum." There was religious excitement in her voice, or at any rate, the fervour of consumerism.

"The moment I saw the plans," she said, "I knew it was a house that would give proper attention to my art."

She was right about that. David noticed the stunning effect of the afternoon light on the large, Neoplasticist painting above the fireplace. The yellow, red, and black lines had a primordial glow, and Nancy confirmed what he had guessed already. It was a Piet Mondrian. David took a professional interest in art. For the last three years he had been labouring over a book, *Objets d'Art and Their Role in Burgundian Family Feuds*, a book never to be finished, he feared, because he could no longer tell what was or wasn't playing a role in anything. The book had turned into a labyrinth of questions, ground zero for his doubts.

"My husband was a collector," Nancy said, and of course she had all the details about the Mondrian at her fingertips, the sort of information you find in auction catalogues. There wasn't a shadow of doubt in her voice as she gave David the rundown. She certainly knew what was what, how to distinguish genuine art from kitsch, authentic from fake, appearance from truth.

Now that she had moved from furniture to art, her wealth of words began to have an effect on David. There was something soothing about the rich flow pouring from Nancy's mouth like milk and honey. Maybe Nancy was on to something. Maybe that was the way to overcome doubt: to have a name for everything, fill every space in your brain with crystal-clear words, and crowd out any hesitation. And yet, something was missing from her talk. It was bloodless. Nancy reminded him of an idiot savant, someone who knew that November 13, 1974, was a Wednesday or that 134 people died in a plane crash on April 2, 1968. Except that Nancy had words at her command instead of dates and numbers. No doubt, she could tell you that an s-shaped moulding was called an "ogee" and the strip with the buttonholes on the front of a man's shirt was a "placket." She knew the difference between columns and pilasters, but when David trawled for native thought, Nancy kept a polite silence. Either she had nothing original to offer or she disapproved of intellectual engagement on first contact. Perhaps she thought it was too intimate, like sex on a first date. But even when David got to know Nancy Auerperg better, his knowledge of her life never progressed much beyond her initial autobiographical sketch.

Nancy told him she moved to L.A. from Mendocino County, where her husband had been an executive in the wine industry. He owned vineyards in California and in Austria. They used to travel back and forth a great deal, she said, until Max had a series of crippling strokes.

"Poor man," she said devoutly. "He was in a wheelchair for the last two years of his life. I miss him terribly." She put in a reverential, commemorative pause before resuming her regular, sprightly tone.

"I still go to Vienna every summer," she said. "I can't get myself to sell the condo." It was, she said breathlessly, absolutely marvelous, divinely furnished, and in a superb location, right in the centre of the city. Her voice was tinged with feelings of bereavement over the unimaginable loss of the apartment.

"If you ever go to Vienna, David, you must come and visit," she said.

"I might take you up on the invitation," he said, although he knew she didn't mean it. She was only being polite. But he really should go to Vienna. With a pang he thought of his work-in-progress, *Objets d'Art and Their Role in Burgundian Family Feuds,* and of the travel funds he had wrangled from the Department to visit the Austrian National Library in Vienna. That was before he fell into the black hole of depression, and now time was running out. The grant money had to be used before the end of the fiscal year.

"As it happens, I'm working on manuscripts owned by the Burgundian Habsburgs," he told Nancy. "They were bibliophiles. The bulk of their collection ended up in Vienna."

David hadn't worked on his book for months, but now that he had managed to leave the safety of his house, made it past his driveway and initiated a conversation with Nancy, he felt he was entering a new phase. He was coming out of his stupor. Who knows, he might resume his research and make the deadline for using the grant money.

"Fascinating," Nancy said, but didn't let her fascination run away to the point of asking for details.

"They have some spectacularly beautiful manuscripts in their collection," David said and lingered over the description of his favourite, a fifteenth-century herbarium. He told Nancy about the vellum leaves, the fine illuminations, the historiated borders, the red Morocco gilt binding and ornamental clasps. He thought she might appreciate the adjectives, the technical terminology.

Nancy listened with polite attention but had no further comment. Perhaps there were limits to her vocabulary after all.

She returned to the subject of her late husband and tried to make out that he was a scion of Viennese aristocracy. But when David asked a follow-up question, she faltered and backed away from the claim. Their conversation stalled. She looked at him, suddenly tongue-tied. Perhaps his plain T-shirt, department store khaki pants and run-of-the-mill loafers stumped her. Not a single haute couture label. It left her mind blank.

She saw David to the door, waggled her fingers at him and said, "See you," with a perfunctory little smile.

"Just call if there is anything I can do for you," David said. "Come over for a drink. Any time."

He instantly regretted his words. Why encourage Nancy? She was probably casting around for a liaison, a replacement for the late Mr. Auerperg. What if she took his invitation as a come-on? There had been a certain flirtatious tone in her voice when she told him about the Mondrian, a certain airiness in her movements, a half-hearted, fleeting play for his attention. He had given her a look meant to chill, meant to tell her she wasn't his type. Wouldn't do. Couldn't fill the void. She seemed to recognize the futility of her efforts, took a step back as if to regain her balance, kept her distance from him for the rest of the house tour, slipped into an interpersonal style, smiling at him in an amiable uninflected way. And then he spoiled it all by giving out the wrong signal, inviting her to come over.

But it's just a polite phrase, he thought, as he walked back to his house. She won't take me up on it.

NANCY DID take him up on the invitation. She dropped by the next day.

David led her into the living room, hoping it might pass for shabby chic in her eyes, but he could tell she wasn't fooled. She averted her eyes from the overstuffed sofa with the white linen throw and the old TV set. He should have given that set away years ago. By now, even the people at Goodwill might turn up their noses at the ancient thing.

Nancy kept a poker face and made no comment as she followed David and they passed through the unrenovated kitchen to the sunroom. He wasn't quick enough to steer her to the swivel chair facing the planter on the patio, which offered a floral still life. Instead, she sat down in the recliner, with the dented garden shed directly in her line of vision.

"Can I offer you a drink?" he asked.

"Just coffee, thanks. I'm watching my calorie intake." She gave him a decorous smile.

He went into the kitchen, leaving Nancy looking around the room, no doubt noticing the penumbra of dust on the furniture and the fluff on the carpet. Perhaps he should have the cleaning lady in more often.

He hoped Nancy would not ask to use the washroom. The toilet seat was up, and the porcelain rim unwiped. There was probably hair in the sink and toothpaste smears. Damn. It was too late to do anything about that now. David stood in the kitchen, embarrassed by the dowdiness of his house, the sound of the throbbing refrigerator, now falling silent with a lurch. Was the sound audible in the sunroom?

When he returned with a Scotch for himself and a mug of coffee for Nancy, she was looking out the window, past his property line, at her own immaculate lawn and the cabana, now outfitted with vertical blinds. There was a confessional look on her face. Was she about to speak up? Express her disgust with his slipshod housekeeping or his lack of taste or the cheap reproductions on the walls of the sunroom?

"I've decided to rent out the guest house," she said.

For a few seconds David was stumped. "The cabana, you mean?" He knew at once that he had said the wrong thing. It sounded as if he was questioning Nancy's choice of words. She had a perfect ear for naming objects. If she called the structure in her backyard a "guest house," it was a guest house.

Nancy ignored his interjection. She crossed her shapely legs, one heel hitched behind the other.

"I thought it would be a good idea to have someone around to keep an eye on the house while I'm in Europe."

"Whatever you do, don't put it on Craigslist," he cautioned her, "I've heard..."

"Oh, I wouldn't go there," she said quickly, as if the idea was too crass to contemplate. "The daughter of a friend happened to be looking for a place, and I thought the arrangement would suit us both. Laura is a curator at the Getty."

Nancy paused to make sure David understood the implication. The future occupant of the cabana (correction: guest house) was no ordinary tenant. The Getty was the sort of place that conferred prestige on its employees, wrapped them in a mantle of culture and refinement.

"She'll move in next weekend," Nancy said. "I'm having a few people over for dinner tomorrow, a welcome party for Laura. I hope you can join us."

She suddenly seemed uneasy. Was it over the cabana/guest house flap? The Craigslist remark? The short notice? To clear the air, he quickly said he'd come. And of course he had second thoughts the moment he closed the front door on Nancy with a final, "See you tomorrow then." He hated parties. He thought he had permanently escaped the party circuit by the simple expedient of never returning an invitation. Eventually, the neighbours got the message and stopped inviting him. And now he was caught in Nancy's flytrap, stuck with her invitation.

He tried to reason with himself. Going to a party was good for him. He needed to get out of the house. He need-ed a burst of activity in his life. But he couldn't silence the interior backtalk: Come on, David, you like your splendid isolation! Why set yourself up for a strenuous social exercise, the bloody how-are-you ritual, the name dropping, the boring travelogues, Thailand and Hawaii or unknown European cor-ners, all the rehashed anecdotes? Keeping away from people was the better choice. The only drawback was a tendency to talk to himself — internal conversations exploring the past or just musing about the human condition. That was okay when he was at home, but he needed to pay more attention to his body language in public. Sometimes a murmur got away from him, or a hand gesture. He didn't want to end up like the fellow at the supermarket who scowled at no one in particular, hollered a string of profanities, and was escorted outside by security.

The natural alternative was to talk to friends. But when you divorce, you divide up your friends as well as your property. And the friends he had made in college thinned out and dropped away. Michael, who was his best buddy for years, moved to the East Coast. Their email messages became fewer. Now they wrote once a year, at Christmas. Erin was another lapsed friend. In her case, it was a quick cut. She picked a quarrel and became a stranger after telling him: "Lose my number. I have nothing more to say to you." Lose my number? You'd expect a more literate dismissal from a librarian. With others, there were no flashpoints, only a ghostly drifting away. And Jerry died last year, during a week of face-blenching events: the destruction of the World Trade Center and the collapse of Jerry's lungs, the racing fire trucks in Manhattan and the blaring ambulance taking Jerry to UCLA Medical Center. The images piled up in David's mind, heaped on top of the other wreckage, the bits and pieces of his broken marriage. He couldn't take any more. CNN was the worst. Watching it was like playing an interactive game for which his thumbs were too clumsy, a game governed by rules he couldn't understand. David's eyes were used to history books with solid lines about done deals that were unalterable. There was no crawling tickertape at the bottom of history books, no news travelling across, dissolving on the left, and reforming on the right. There were no changing figures or call-in polls, and it was too late to cast a vote for or against bygone wars and economic trends.

He stopped watching TV and switched to porn movies, but the frantic humping and sucking of the DVD whores, their fake orgasmic moans left him flaccid. They all looked the same, and their silicone enhanced balloon breasts had no beneficent effect. He tried a live prostitute and made her bend over his crotch and work hard for her money. He had to rent a mid-sized car from Avis because the vintage sports car he bought to console himself after the divorce couldn't accommodate that kind of action. At least it worked, but the relief was temporary. Remorse set in almost immediately. He was ashamed, disgusted. He had committed a sin, not against God — David wasn't a religious man — but against his own aesthetic standards. It was an ugly thing to do. It added to the bleakness in his soul. And sex didn't change anything. The news reports were still dismal and full of dire warnings. David gave up watching TV, but he was still confronted with the articles and images in the LA *Times*, especially the gloomy op-ed pages. And Jerry's column was missing now, replaced with lifestyle articles that had no punch. He missed Jerry's witty column. He missed his camaraderie. "Come on over, David. Have a drink. How goes the battle in the trenches of academia?" Jerry was that kind of guy, all-embracing, and generous with encouragement. He was the kind of guy who hosted noisy parties that silenced the ghosts of sorrow.

The hopelessness of Jerry's condition was allegorical, wasn't it? His death was indicative of everything David felt that year when Elaine moved out, a sense of an ending, a relentless decline. After Jerry's death, he was reduced to shoptalk with colleagues, exchanging niceties with dogowners on the boardwalk, or carrying on safely boring conversations with neighbours. Time to move on, get past Elaine, past Jerry's death, and out of his daze of self-pity, he thought. So why not make a start at Nancy's party?

NANCY'S CROWD was well-heeled — stockbroker types mostly, an investment banker, a few lawyers, a software engineer, a sprinkle of people in the film industry. Money was the social lubricant, but academic credentials, preferably earned at an Ivy League university, counted for something as well. Which explained why Nancy had invited him, why she thought he fit in. But David was uneasy. He had the prickly sensation of danger, of something he should avoid or escape altogether.

The guests milled around, eddying in and out of rooms, forming little clusters, talking. Nancy discreetly surveyed the scene. She saw David stuck on the fringes, wandering aimlessly from one group to another, and came to his rescue.

"Let me introduce you to Laura Nagy," she said, putting on her warmest hostess tone. Nancy's enthusiasm for her guest of honour was palpable. She steered David across the room to the future occupant of the guest house.

"Isn't she darling?" she breathed into his ear.

But "darling" wasn't the adjective David would have used. Nancy's choice of words was off when she was in gushing mode. Laura was model-thin, achingly stylish, with adamantine cheekbones. Her beauty was of the austere kind. She was wearing a thigh-grazing black dress, glittery black ankle socks, and high-heeled pumps. The matching glittery choker around her neck reminded David of a dog collar. She was definitely not darling. She was slightly outré. A type that attracted him, dangerously. Please, God, don't let me fall for her, he thought. She's got NO written all over her face. I'm too old to suffer that kind of humiliation. But he felt a miraculous stirring as his eyes wandered over her slender body.

Nancy cheerfully slipped an arm around Laura and introduced David. The man in the grey Armani suit, who had been talking to Laura, broke for another group. Nancy lingered long enough to cement the new configuration. She managed to spark a conversation, gave David's shoulder an encouraging squeeze and moved on, resuming her duty round and leaving him to face Laura on his own.

It was hard going. He knew it would be like that. Laura was stingy with words, and he wasn't good at making conversation, could hear the drag in his own voice. Meanwhile, his brain was cross-firing questions: Where have I seen those amber cat eyes before? The narrow face framed by thick dead-straight bangs? The boyish, faintly cruel smile? Nowhere, he thought, except in my imagination. Laura was the perfect fit for his desire. She was a fantasy *déjà vu*. He couldn't resist Laura's gamine promise and struggled to keep the words going despite the cold anger in her eyes, as if she, like David, had been dragged to the party against her will.

From across the room, Nancy shot them a look of approval. Red highlights were running across Laura's dark hair like lightning. The prime colours merged nicely with the Mondrian on the wall behind her. David wondered whether Nancy used aesthetic principles in picking her guests, choosing them like design elements to show off the house to advantage.

He asked Laura about her work at the Getty. She gave him clipped answers and dodged sideways. He could see she was impatient to get away. She had no time to waste on a nondescript, thirty-something academic. She was probably looking for an art dealer or a media chief or a software entrepreneur.

Her tight-lipped answers began to sap David's energy. Or was it her voice, which had a shadow of a drawl, a slight foreign accent. Or the funereal black of her cocktail dress? Their conversation was flagging. He was about to give up when he realized where he had seen her before. Jerry's funeral! She was a fellow mourner. He suddenly remembered Laura's solemn upturned face as she was listening to the eulogy, the fish-pale colour of her cheeks and forehead, the pursed, disapproving lips. Did she, too, think that the cemetery was too beautiful and the man who gave the eulogy not eloquent enough? That his words, floating above the perfect lawn, did not match the man they were meant to describe? Still, the mourners were moved by the eulogy. They were weeping in each other's arms. Their tears at least did justice to Jerry. David and Laura had stood apart, solitary and dry-eyed.

"We've met before," he said to her. "At Jerry White's funeral."

"Ah, yes," she said, "last September." Her carmine mouth turned soft. She was about to say more, cut across the boundaries, but then she swallowed the words and lowered her eyes. When she raised them again, her face had turned to pasteboard, and her lips were a pencil-thin line refusing to divulge private information.

But David couldn't admit another uncertainty. His brain was overloaded with doubts. There was no more room for unanswered questions. He needed to know: What was the connection between Laura and Jerry? He knew Jerry's friends. He had been to many of his parties, but he'd never seen Laura until the day of the funeral. Was she a secret Jerry guarded from his friends?

"Did you know Jerry well?" he said.

"Sometimes I think I didn't know him at all," she said. Before she could say more, Nancy came by, put a possessive arm around David and asked everyone to move to the dining room. The conversations broke up. People began circling the elegant table, looking for their place card.

It was a moment of hope and fear. Please, God, don't let me sit next to the lawyer whose brain is a mash of bylaws or the jovial man who has been on a thousand cruises.

David ended up across from Laura's father, a barrel-chested fellow with a florid complexion and abundant wavy hair. Zoltan Nagy did not share his daughter's reticence. He talked volubly, with large hand movements that threatened to overturn his wineglass. His black shirt and candy-pink tie clashed with the décor of the house. No aesthetic principle could account for his presence at Nancy's table.

The caterers were gliding behind the backs of the company like dancers. Perhaps that's what they were, moonlighting dancers, impossibly lithe and elegant, weaving in and out of the room, balancing serving dishes and refilling glasses.

Zoltan was holding forth on the meaning of life. His heroic tenor carried and dominated the conversation. His ideas, it seemed to David, were a fuzzy catalogue of grammatical possibilities, a pileup of words growing at a dizzying rate. Zoltan was an analyst. Was it typical of shrinks to talk like that?

Irritation crept up on David, became unbearable. He interrupted Zoltan and said sharply: "So, what does it all mean — put in logical terms?"

Zoltan gave him a crinkle-eyed look. "You want to know what it means? Okay, I'll put it in logical terms for you. Are you familiar with the reductionist-vitalist argument?"

"Never heard of it," David said. Apparently it was part of the General Systems Theory. Zoltan spouted a great deal about the difference between the closed, purely physico-chemical processes of organisms and the open systems that import free energy from outside themselves and could, under certain circumstances, result in states of mutual dynamic interaction.

"That's a well-established phenomenon," he said. "And what is valid in behavioural sciences — self-actualization, intermingling, and re-formation — can also, under specific conditions, take place in biology." As he spoke, his hands drew arcs in the air, banking and swooping like seagulls.

"I'm afraid I don't follow," David said. "Are you suggesting that an object or a person might, physiologically, become another? That a fake Mondrian could turn into a real one, for example? Or that Nancy could turn into Laura?" Out of the corner of his eye he saw Nancy looking at Zoltan with the expectant smile of a child waiting for a magician to work his trick.

Zoltan leaned back and gave David a quizzical smile. For a moment, it seemed he had no comeback, but then he recovered and carried on in the same fluid style, as if he was quoting himself. "Let me put it this way, David. If schemes are isomorphic in regard to the underlying invariances and if all areas of reality are reduced to a single level, yes, they may become interchangeable and vertically interrelated. Isomorphy of invariant constructs is known to occur in nature in differentiated forms."

"You mean there is scientific proof for this reductionist — what did you call it?"

"Reductionist-vitalist argument," Zoltan said with a kindly smile, as if to placate an idiot. "*I* regard it as scientific proof. It is, of course, intuitive rather than mathematical, but it follows the logical deductive principles of mathematics."

"I find it confusing," David said doggedly.

Zoltan shrugged his shoulders. "Some things," he said, "are difficult to put in layman's terms. A minimum of mathematical training is required to understand the implications of the theory, I'm afraid."

Pompous ass! David looked at the rest of the table for confirmation, for support. Nancy looked suddenly flustered. There was a smirk on Laura's face, a mocking smile, which disappeared as soon as she met David's eyes. Her expression became unreadable.

The investment banker, who had been raring to hold forth and give them his economic prognostications, riffed on Zoltan's psychobabble.

"Let me tell you about the mutual dynamic interactions in the marketplace," he said.

The faces of the men around the table showed relief. Here was a topic they knew something about. Everything was back to normal: Gourmet food, vintage wine, the mellow glow of silver serving dishes, and the light patter of trade deals, travel anecdotes,and political jokes.

HE HAD FEARED the party would be a disaster, but walking home, David noticed that his lethargic mood was lifting, giving way to a tingling sensation of annoyance at Zoltan's one-upmanship, and a prick of desire for Laura, whose perfectly defined butt had entered his force field. He felt no more than a shadow of guilt when he plugged her into a mind game and bedded her down on satin. The fantasy felt good, the buzz held. The next morning he woke up with a spurt of energy.

After breakfast, he went up to his study and pulled the printout of his manuscript from the filing cabinet, where it had rested for months. He flipped through the pages and the questions and corrections he had written in the margins. Pre-empting the doubts that threatened to hobble him again, he quickly sat down at the computer, opened the file and started editing the text.

It went well until he started thinking about Laura and anxiety set in. Desire tinged with the fear of failure ran down his spine. He stopped typing. *Remember: Relax your posture. Rest your eyes every thirty minutes.* This was advice for which David had paid a chiropractor eighty dollars. Looking up from the computer screen, he rested his eyes on Nancy's backyard, on the immaculate green lawn and the glittering reflection of the sunlight in the pool, the cabana soon to be inhabited by Laura, the object of his desire and the source of renewed anxiety, both. He straightened his spine, rolled his shoulders and stretched his neck. *Most neck pain results from a head forward posture*, according to the leaflet the chiropractor had given him. He drew his neck back. Was he doing this right? *Guiding the chin with the fingertips helps to avoid an unwanted up and down movement,* the leaflet said. He retracted his chin once more, this time using his fingertips to ensure he wasn't nodding up and down. *Keep your eyes level. If the exercise is performed correctly, you will feel your chest rise.* He was concentrating on his chest, when a movement outside caught his eye. Zoltan was strolling across the lawn, heading for a lounge chair. He was wearing a Bolshevist red T-shirt that revealed a tuft of chest hair, and he was carrying a glass of orange juice.

Was it a follow-up visit or a sleepover? David squinted, trying to decide whether the pants were the same pants Zoltan had worn last night. Nancy appeared in a burst of colour, dressed in a kimono with a Bird-of-Paradise design. As she settled into a deck chair beside Zoltan, the kimono birds seemed to flap their wings, ready to take flight. Zoltan leaned forward and said something to her, moving the conversation along with a wave of his hands to give his words momentum. His mouth opened and closed steadily. His voice drifted through the open window into David's study. He couldn't tell whether Nancy had anything to say in response. He could see only the back of her head. Zoltan finished his story with a belly laugh, and

Nancy's hands went up in a gesture of pleasant surprise. Her tinkling laughter seemed to make ripples in the pool.

That's alright, then, David thought. He needn't have worried about being in Nancy's crosshairs. She had found an escort or boyfriend or whatever role Zoltan was playing there. David watched him giveNancy a half-hug and Nancy wiggle her painted toes in response and touch Zoltan's shoulder with an addled coziness. That was settled then, but the sight of the old lovers discoloured his dreams of Laura. She needed a sexier background. He turned his eyes away from the window to guard his perfect fantasies of Laura.

DAVID'S ENERGY LEVEL was holding steady. He was at his computer the next morning when a moving van pulled into Nancy's driveway. A black Mini Cooper drew up behind it, with Zoltan in the driver's seat. It was a ridiculously small car for a large man like Zoltan. Of course the vintage Karmann Ghia in David's garage wasn't much bigger, but it was the right size for him. And it was a beautiful car, which excused a lot, including the fact that he had paid too much for it.

Zoltan wriggled out from behind the steering wheel, Houdini-like, stood on the pavement dipping at the knees as if to limber up, and started giving instructions to the movers. They carted a couple of IKEA boxes into the guest house, and wheeled along a clothes rack with zip-up bags.

Nancy appeared in the backyard and bussed Zoltan on the cheek. There was a replay of the tinkling laughter scene David had witnessed the morning after the party. This time, Zoltan did a little pantomime for Nancy, capering on the lawn, waltzing with an imaginary partner.

There was no sign of Laura. No sign of the real-life Laura at any rate. Only her avatar, her effigy which was now firmly lodged in the back of David's brain. He started to worry. Were the clothes bags on the rack he had seen Laura's, or was there a change of plans, with Zoltan staying at the guest house instead of his daughter? Was Laura doomed to a virtual existence in David's head, while a reality show developed next door with Nancy in the lead? He didn't think that Zoltan was right for the role of Nancy's lover. He remembered her claim to aristocracy by marriage. She had an old-fashioned sense of class. It was surprising to see her on such friendly terms with a man like Zoltan, a shameless self-promoter, a crass type really. Of course, Nancy was a woman of a certain age, and eligible men were hard to find. And perhaps she liked Zoltan's antics. He was a showman at any rate, the kind who pulls rabbits out of hats.

David got up from his desk. Why was he so irritated by the Nancy-Zoltan scenario? Was he begrudging them a good time because he had no partner? So Elaine had walked out on him. These things happened. Relationships collapsed. He and Elaine weren't compatible. But that was no reason to resent other people having a good time. If Nancy liked Zoltan, great. It wasn't his business to judge her taste in men. No, he realized, it had nothing to do with Nancy or Zoltan. It was his desire for Laura that was making him short-tempered.

Perhaps it would be better to roll his computer desk away from the window and cut the pool deck from his peripheral vision. Or should he keep the desk where it was and close the blinds instead? He hesitated, and the indecision troubled him. Was he slipping back into his former state of morbid doubt? Half an hour later he was still sitting at the desk, wondering if he should move the computer or shut the blinds, when he heard the doorbell ring.

He craned his neck and had a bird eye's view of Nancy standing at the door. She had changed into Capri pants and was jangling the golden bracelets on her arm as if the sound of the doorbell needed reinforcing.

He went downstairs and opened the door.

"Nancy!" he said, feigning surprise, hoping that she had not seen him peering from the window. "Come on in."

"I need to ask you a favour," she said with just the right tone of polite hesitation. Her hand went up in a supplicant gesture. The golden bangles at her wrist slipped, lodging halfway up her arm.

"Consider it done," David said gallantly to make up for his uncharitable thoughts about her and Zoltan.

She patted his shoulder playfully. "Don't say yes until you've heard what it is."

She sat down on the ancient sofa in the living room, making the centre sag and the end cushions rise. Air escaped from the seams like a suppressed sigh. I really must get rid of the sofa, David thought. And the white throw as well. It looks like a dead man's shroud.

"So what can I do for you, Nancy?" he said, trying to sound hearty, although now he was afraid that he had promised too much and would be drawn into something more than he was able to do.

"I expected Laura to move in this weekend," Nancy said, "but now it seems there will be a delay, which is awkward, because we'll be leaving for Cairo in a couple of days."

We? Meaning she and Zoltan?

Nancy left the "we" unexplained. "We booked the trip months ago — a Nile cruise — and we can't possibly change the dates now." She paused, giving David a helpless look. Her mouth was shaped into a plangent "o," a mute complaint about Laura's whims and about her own predicament.

So, no Laura. At least not this weekend. David pushed down his disappointment.

"You are worried about the house? You want me to keep an eye on your place?" he said to Nancy.

"Would you?" Nancy said, looking relieved. "Actually, I'm not worried about the house. I have surveillance. The problem is the cat. Would you mind feeding Bébé?"

She sat forward and perched on the edge of the sofa, ready to withdraw the cat-feeding request if it met with the least resistance. The cushions billowed and sighed.

"I'm so sorry to impose on you," she said, "but it's only for a few days. Laura has decided to visit her mother in Hungary. Zoltan encouraged her, you see. He wants Laura to get in touch with her roots, and this is the only week she can get away from her job."

"Not to worry," David said. "I'll feed the cat and keep the burglars at bay."

"You are a darling," Nancy said and air-kissed him. "I knew I could rely on you. And it's so important for Laura to understand where Zoltan is coming from. Last chance to see the old Hungary, you know. Once it becomes part of the European Union, it will change forever."

"And Zoltan wants his daughter to see the old country in its original, wretched state?"

Nancy gave him a breathless, fluttering laugh, and immediately became serious again. It wasn't a laughing matter. "Zoltan broke up with his wife when Laura was a teenager," she said. "He got custody and emigrated. It was a bitter divorce, and there are scars. Laura hasn't seen her mother in years, so she's a little apprehensive about the visit."

Nancy weighed the sentence down with a pause and let the story go. She didn't want to develop the Nagy saga beyond the Hungarian background, the divorce, and the suspended mother/daughter relationship. Just a few factoids. This wasn't about Zoltan or Laura after all. This was about her house. And her cat.

"If you have a minute, David, I could explain the security system to you."

He followed Nancy across to her immaculate house. The Mini Cooper had disappeared from the driveway. She showed David how to disarm and rearm the security system. She took him into the stainless steel kitchen and showed him the cat pantry, initiated him into feeding times, and explained the workings of the state-of-the-art litter box. The "LitterMaid," as Nancy called it, was a handsome cedar cabinet with a chute on top and a plastic bag suspended underneath. It needed emptying only every two or three weeks, Nancy said. There was really nothing to do, but just in case, she showed him where she kept the operating manual.

To divert their thoughts from the nasty business of the LitterMaid, Nancy suggested drinks on the patio. At the sliding door, David stopped and, for a second, saw the deck chair by the pool in a double exposure: himself superimposed on the image of a bull-necked Zoltan. Was Nancy playing musical chairs with them? No, really, he had to wean himself from indulging in this kind of thought. It was all straightforward, a neighbourly transaction. Nancy was asking him to pet-sit while she and Zoltan were away.

"What does Zoltan do with his patients when he takes a vacation?" he asked, pulling back into the realm of practicalities. "Are they supposed to put their phobias on hold, or does he refer them to a substitute shrink?"

"I have no idea," Nancy said, keeping her eyes on the tray with the drinks, fully occupied, apparently, with setting down David's glass.

"But that wouldn't work, would it?" he mused. "Say you are midway through exploring your messed-up childhood or your dysfunctional marriage, you'd have to start all over again with the new shrink. The replacement shrink, I mean."

"I really don't know," Nancy said in a strained voice. She would have wrinkled her brow if Botox had permitted it. "In any case, it's not a problem at this point because Zoltan is between assignments."

Between assignments, as in "unemployed?" Taking a Nile cruise seemed a little extravagant for an unemployed man. Unless, of course, Zoltan was independently wealthy. Or Nancy was footing the bill.

"I thought Zoltan was working at a treatment centre in Malibu," David said, unwilling to let Nancy off the hook. "That's what he said to me at the party."

"At the Hope Center," she said, "but he had a falling-out with the director over methodology. He thought the Center was too lenient on celebrity clients. Britney was there for a week, you know, and they allowed her out on shopping trips. The place was ringed with paparazzi after that. Things came to a head when Zoltan was offered a spot on TV to talk about rehab. The board vetoed it — something about a confidentiality clause."

"I can see that there might be a problem, a conflict of interest," David said.

"Oh, of course it would have meant walking a fine line," Nancy said. She had found her stride again and gave him a gleaming, super-white smile. "Zoltan could have handled it. That wasn't the problem. The problem was the Executive Director. He thought he should be the one in front of the camera. He was upset because Zoltan had been asked to do it. Naturally, the media want someone with pizzazz. They don't want a dry, clinical lecture. They asked Zoltan because he has the human touch. He knows how to engage people, but they never gave him credit for that at the Center." Nancy looked aggrieved on Zoltan's behalf.

"I hope he finds something more suited to his talents," David said, trying to keep the irony out of his voice. TV shrink? Ladies' escort? Director of recreation?

"He has other projects," Nancy said airily. "I just read the first draft of his novel-in-progress. It's fascinating."

"Zoltan is writing a novel?"

"Science fiction," she said. "About a biologist who develops a method of shedding old age by transferring it to a clone. The clone then goes through the aging process on behalf of the donor, if that's the right word."

David could see Nancy taking an interest in remedial cloning as a way to maintain youthful looks.

"I think it's an amazing idea, absolutely marvelous, don't you think?" she said.

"A little too esoteric for my taste," David said.

"I'm not very good at explaining the story. You should read the manuscript. I'll ask Zoltan to give you a copy."

David begged off. "I'm hopeless," he said. "I've never been able to follow science-fiction plots. I think I lack the requisite imagination." He finished his drink and stood. "Give Zoltan my regards. I wish him the best of luck."

AS SOON AS David got home, he googled the Hope Center. Why am I doing this, he thought as he hit "Enter." It was small-time snooping, despicable greasy behaviour. But Zoltan's name was inseparably linked in his mind with Laura's, and the memory of Zoltan's incomprehensible babble at the party meshed with Laura's enigmatic smile. David thought of her with a rush of desire. He had already googled the Getty and found only a short listing for Laura that told him no more than her title, "Curator," which he knew already, and the number of her extension, which he could have gotten through the switchboard. Would a background check on Zoltan provide more clues? He wasn't even sure what he was looking for.

A click-on series of images on the website of the Hope Center showed a resort-like complex, a woman in a white lab coat giving a PowerPoint presentation, and a group of people in designer gym clothes doing aerobics. Another click brought him to the mission statement. The Center endeavoured to treat the whole person, taking into consideration his/her special needs: "We promise security combined with luxury and comfort." Zoltan Nagy was still listed as a team member. He had degrees from Vienna and Berkeley, but no publication record popped up, at least nothing of a scholarly nature. Apparently he was the author of a memoir entitled *The Rescue*. Rescue from what? The dreary economics of Hungarian communism? David felt faintly curious about Zoltan's life story, which included fathering Laura after all, but the book wasn't listed on Amazon.com. He considered putting in a special order at the local bookstore, but his recent bout of energy was coming to an end. His desire to go out and do things was waning. He was settling back into sloth mode, no, worse than sloth mode. He no longer had the strength to read the paper. He decided not to renew his subscription to the *LA Times*. No more international calamities, no more natural disasters. He decided to stick to the local daily, *The Santa Monica Daily Press*, even though it meant going to the corner to pick up a copy. Local crime, city council squabbles, and entertainment news was all he could handle. He missed Jerry. His talk had been like CPR. He knew how to keep the pulse going. Maybe it was the professional skill of a columnist. Was that the difference between the two of them, the difference between an academic and a journalist? Or the fact that Jerry was gay? No, that was irrelevant. *Gay is the new straight,* Jerry wrote in his column. *Forget about the old stereotypes, the hedonistic, transgressive, radical ethos* (But it fits you, Jerry!). *The politics of coming out are shifting. There is no more need to change or assimilate to fit into the mainstream.*

"And that's a good thing?" he said to Jerry.

"Well, it's a little sad. The edgy times are over, but that's what we wanted, after all, to be like everyone else," Jerry said.

So, gay wasn't the point. The difference between them was the difference between certainty and doubt, Jerry's wide-open arms and David's need to hold in his breath. Before David could figure it out — Should you be friends with a gay man? Was it okay to like Jerry's slim-hipped boyfriends? — Jerry started dying. His eyes faded to a washed-out blue. He became painfully thin. His laugh shrunk to a sardonic grin. He stood, leaning on the back of a chair to steady himself, and looked at David with his newly colourless, appraising gaze that said: You are healthy, you lucky bugger. What's your reason for being depressed?

Right. No reason. Except the spine-crushing doubts, the constant questioning of his thoughts, his methods, his worth. Doubts were tightening David's throat, whispering to him. He was back where he had been before Nancy's party, before the dream vision of Laura. He spent mornings in the sunroom, holding on to his empty coffee cup, looking at the hedge separating his property from Nancy's and thinking of the trees that had been there, still expecting them to be there. He made himself turn away and look for something real, staring at his garden shed, trying to memorize the shape of the aluminum siding and the location of the dented spots. He had given up working on his book. The footnotes were strangling him. He tried to rally and rekindle his ambitions, but there was no answering call in his mind. His insides had gone blank. Going upstairs and switching on the computer required too much effort. It had turned into an expedition on the scale of climbing Mount Everest. And Nancy's backyard offered no diversion. She and Zoltan had left for their vacation the night before.

David dragged himself to the kitchen and contemplated Nancy's set of keys hanging on a hook next to a striped potholder. A sense of obligation took hold. The thought of Bébé starving stirred him into action.

He went next door and did a duty round, crossing the conversation pit in Nancy's living room, presided over by the Mondrian. He schlepped upstairs. More art of the significant kind. A small collotype of a landscape, impressed with Klimt's signet in metallic ink. A sculpture that looked like a Picasso. In the master bedroom, a black-and-white photo (of the late Mr. Auerperg?) signed by Karsh. In the hall, two landscape photos by Ansel Adams. David checked the other bedrooms — mostly abstract expressionism. He looked into the gleaming bathrooms and noted a whimsical bird by David Hockney.

Everything was in order, as far as he could see.

Back downstairs, in the kitchen, he opened a tin of cat food and watched Bébé crouching over her dish, scarfing down the food, her body tense, her tongue flicking rapidly.

He reached down and stroked her sleek coat. Some of Bébé's animal energy passed through his hand like a galvanic current, an electric sizzle. His pulse came to life. He went out into the backyard and stood at the edge of the pool, looking at the shimmering reflection of the cabana: Laura's future home. He became aware of his stepped-up heartbeat, sensed a certain disquiet springing up. He had noticed it before. The sloth mode was peaceful, spurts of energy brought anxiety.

I'll take the Karmann Ghia for a spin, he thought. It was an unfailing remedy for anxiety — a calming drive, a cruise along Montana to watch the latte-sippers in the sidewalk cafés, then over to San Vicente, past the coral trees, and back home to the quiet of Wadsworth Avenue. Then maybe something halfway between work and indolence, like buffing the car. The garnet red finish was beginning to dull a little on top, but the biscuit interior was still perfect, and all the accessories were original down to the spotlessly clean ashtray. David knew his admiration for the car bordered on fetishism, but beauty had that effect on him, whether live or cast in steel. It made him prayerful, at one with the cosmos. It was the only way to restore inner peace.

He cast a final look at the pool and was about to leave when it occurred to him that his guardianship over Nancy's house included the cabana. He fingered the set of keys, debating the propriety of inspecting Laura's space. If the set contained a key to the cabana, Nancy meant him to check it. If not...

There was a key. David felt a riff of anxiety — or was it a voyeur's thrill — as he unlocked the door and surveyed the space, a large open room with an alcove, cool and mysteriously sombre in the half-light of the shuttered windows. He turned on the lights and furtively took stock, looking for clues to Laura's life. The rattan seating arrangement with the melon green pillows, the close-up art photos of blooming cacti, and the tribal carpet covering the terracotta tiles were probably Nancy's. They reflected her interior decorating spirit. There was a Barcelona settee in the alcove, intended for an after-sauna siesta but set up as a bed now. The computer desk and shelves on the far wall had probably come out of those IKEA cartons the movers had delivered. They were made of pressed wood with a white finish, the kind you assemble with a screwdriver. He could see the clothes rack in the hallway, hung with square-shouldered bags. The content might be revealing, but he couldn't get himself to unzip them. The gesture seemed too intimate, even fetishist.

What was on view didn't yield as much information as David had hoped. There were no signposts to Laura's past. No travel souvenirs, no books whose titles might reveal her interests.

No books! David realized. Wouldn't you expect a curator to have a wall of art books? Maybe there was more stuff to come. His thoughts were blanked out by the sound of footsteps on the gravel path — had he left the gate open? David heard the scraping of boots on the patio, saw a shadow darkening the doorframe. His heartbeat speeded up. Burly intruder. No, uniformed man. Cop. Cops. Two of them. A flash of a badge.

"Are you the owner?" the front man said, sizing up David with a quick glance. His black sunglasses gave off a menacing glint.

"I'm a neighbour," David said. "The owner asked me to check the property while she's away." He held up Nancy's keys to validate his claim. There was something in the officer's polycarbonate, UV-resistant stare that turned David from an innocent man into a person of interest.

Why were the cops here? Had he set off an alarm? Breached the security when he entered the cabana? Perhaps he'd touched one of the paintings in the house by mistake. Were they wired? If so, Nancy should have warned him. But he had disarmed the security system. Wouldn't that take care of everything?

The officer gave him the steady look reserved for suspects.

"I live next door," David said and pointed in the direction of his house, becoming aware of the flaking paint on the clapboard siding of his sunroom. A board had come loose under the eaves.

"Next door?" the officer said. "What's your name?" He pulled out a pad and noted down the information. If it wasn't for the gun, you could have taken him for a TV repairman or a guy from a cable company. Same type of uniform. Short sleeves, shirt open to the second button, undershirt showing through the V, tools of the trade hanging from his leather belt. Okay, that was the giveaway: a holstered gun, handcuffs, and an electronic gadget — a metal detector? A taser to jellify your muscles?

"Can we ask you a few questions?" the officer said and went on without waiting for David's answer. "When have you last seen or spoken to Laura Nagy?" His colleague was standing by silently, twitching an incipient Latino mustache, keeping an eye on David, ready to jump him if he tried to bolt.

"Laura Nagy? Let me see. Wednesday night."

"And she told you to take care of the property?" the officer said, leaning forward, straining to look into David's eyes. The outline of a bulletproof vest was showing under his uniform.

There was a moment of confusion until David sorted out the misunderstanding.

"No, not Laura Nagy," he said. "The owner, Nancy Auerperg, asked me to drop in and feed her cat. Laura is her tenant." How to explain the whole complicated story to a cop, that Laura was supposed to house-sit, but now she wasn't? "Mrs. Auerperg asked me to take care of things until Laura's return from her vacation in Hungary. Is there a problem?"

"Miss Nagy has been the victim of a mugging."

David blinked. In Hungary? "When was that? Where? Is she hurt?"

"She is under medical care," the officer said. "Have you seen any unusual activity around here in the last few days?"

"Nothing unusual," David said. "So is Laura okay?" That was a stupid question to ask after being told that she was under medical care. He corrected himself. "I mean, where is she now?"

The officers exchanged looks. Were they assessing his sanity? Gauging the value of the information he was asking for?

"You can contact the UCLA Medical Center for information," the front man said.

Laura was not in Hungary then. She was at the Medical Center.

The second-in-command stepped up, boots clanking on the tiled floor. "Mind if we have a look around?" he said.

"Do you have a search warrant?" David said. The words were out of his mouth before he could stop himself, an old bit of TV dialogue stuck in his brain, something from *LAPD: Life on the Beat.*

Was it his imagination or did the officers' eyes harden?

"If you are uncomfortable with a search...," the second-in-command said.

"There is nothing out of order here, as far as I can see," David said apologetically.

"That's okay," the front man said, shutting his notebook and tucking it away. "If you notice anything unusual, people loitering, that sort of thing, give us a call." He handed David a card. "The phone number is on here."

When they were gone, David reset the security system and went back to his house. He rummaged through the blue bin for yesterday's local paper, which he had not had the courage to read, and found the article almost immediately: *Mugging at Santa Monica Place.* That must be it. *Security officers were called when an employee of Macy's found a woman unconscious on the floor of the ladies' room.* He skimmed the article. Wallet, credit cards missing. No arrest. Victim has no recollection of the attack. *There were no obvious signs of physical trauma. Doctors suspect that the assailant drugged his victim.*

David dropped the paper back into the bin. He was no longer in the mood for taking his Karmann Ghia out for a spin. He needed something more effective to cope with the anxiety puddling in his stomach like acid rain. The bad news had jumped the barrier of the TV screen and gone 3D. He could no longer confine it to the media. There was trouble next door. It was making its way through the hedge, breaking into his

house, and slamming his body with a bone-deep impact. The
news of the mugging left David knocked out and breathless.
He slumped into his easy chair in the sunroom and took up
an issue of the *Times Literary Supplement*, hoping the reviews
were dry enough to mop up the inner mess.

I MUST GO and visit Laura in hospital, he thought. It was the
decent thing to do, an extension of the duties he had taken on,
like looking after Nancy's house and pet. No, not a duty. Don't
kid yourself, David. You want to see Laura, you are desperate
to see her, talk to her, touch her. His desire for Laura was so
strong it ripped through the weariness of his depression. What
was he waiting for? He was waiting for the feeling of unease to
go away. There was something distasteful about Laura sharing
mental space with hospitals, with images of surgeons in green
scrubs and staff wearing Crocs, the plastic bedside chairs, the
steel contraptions with gauges and tubes, the fluorescent lights,
the smell of disinfectant. Clean was good, of course, but sterility
was disheartening. No, don't lie to yourself, David. It wasn't
the sterility or the IV tubes or the disinfectant. It wasn't any
of those things that made him uneasy about visiting Laura. It
was the memory of Jerry lying in a hospital bed in that same
Medical Center.

"The fact is, I am dying," Jerry said, looking up at him from
the bed, white face on white pillow. The dark circles under his
eyes gave him a vulnerable softness, but his voice had a hard
edge. "Let's call a spade a spade, David," he said hoarsely.
Right. Let's call a spade a spade. David's objections to hospitals
weren't aesthetic. They were visceral. He didn't want to walk
through the lobby of the hospital, go up in the gurney-sized
elevator, walk past the nurses' station and be reminded of
Jerry's gaunt face and wasted body.

I don't want to get Laura mixed up in these memories, he
thought. I don't want to see her lying in a thin-sheeted bed
jaundiced by neon light, with an ID bracelet on her wrist. I want

to see her the way she was at Nancy's party, her mouth a little petulant, holding herself very upright, hard and unyielding and tempting all at the same time.

And what was he going to say to Laura when he got to the hospital, how was he going to explain his presence there? I came because Nancy told me to look after the house and its contents? The question of what to say to Laura put a stranglehold on him. For the next hour, he could not move. He sat rooted in the sunroom with the unfolded *Times Literary Supplement* on his knees weighing him down. He couldn't pull his ass out of the chair or his foot off the floor. He had to give himself detailed orders, the kind you find in operating manuals. How to move your body and get from A to B, from his house to the hospital. Get out of the chair, David. March to the garage. Back out the car. Drive to the Medical Center. Park the car. He did, although the Karmann Ghia didn't belong in a hospital parking lot. It was an insult to its beauty.

Walking into the Medical Center, he had a sudden glimpse of himself reflected in the glass door, a man of no qualities with a polite half-smile on his face. That was what others saw, so unlike the David who suffered doubt, who was filled with angst and who procrastinated, who couldn't rally his body or his spirit, the man who stayed in hiding. No, David kept a serene face. Who wants to put his raw and bloodied soul on display for all to see?

He found Laura's room, knocked, entered, allowed his eyes to move slowly upward from the vinyl floor past the first, empty bed, to the woman lying on the bed by the window, to her face. It was as bad as he had feared. She wasn't Laura at all. Her complexion had gone from milky white to ashen. She had lost weight. Her cheekbones were protruding, giving her face a sharply sculpted look. The emaciated face, the shadowy eyes of a dying man. No! Her amber eyes weren't shadowy. Don't get those memories of Jerry mixed up with her. Still, he couldn't deny it. Her eyes had lost their flintiness.

"How are you, Laura?" he said. He had been afraid of that first meeting of their eyes, the first exchange of words, but his question came out natural after all, banal but natural.

"I am fine, thank you. And how are you?" She didn't sound natural. She looked dazed. Did she suffer from the same problem as David, was she in a video mash-up-confusion as well, trying to sort out the complexities of life? No, she was in worse shape than David. She sounded like someone reciting English for Beginners. The look in her eyes was blank, as if she couldn't be bothered to remember him, didn't want to recognize him.

This was going to be even more awkward than he had feared. He pulled up a chair and sat down, uninvited. He couldn't think of anything more to say. He was too dispirited by Laura's stiffness and by the room itself, which tinkled with frozen time, the memory of Jerry, once fearless and a volcanic life force, suddenly silenced. David remembered how Jerry lay on the hospital bed, his long finely-tapering fingers resting on the blanket, no longer capable of gestures.

David forced his attention back to the woman on the bed, Laura.

"I read about the mugging in the local paper," he said. "I wanted to see how you are doing."

She smiled at him wanly. "I'm on the mend," she said. "The results of the toxicology tests have come back. It is xylene poisoning."

"What's xylene?"

"A type of solvent, but the doctors don't know what to make of it." They couldn't explain how a mugger could overpower a person with xylene, she said. There was no quick way of administering it.

Her accent was stronger than David remembered. She was dragging the words out, as if she wanted to make every syllable count. Was it the effect of toxic shock? A reversion to childhood, a throwback to the time when she came to the States, when English was a foreign language to her?

"You are in touch with Zoltan?" he said.

She shook her head. "I can't get in touch with him. He is on a Nile cruise, I think, or maybe back in Cairo. I have lost the information. I don't remember the details."

"I can help you with that," he said. "Nancy left the contact information with me."

"Excuse me," she said. "This is embarrassing, but I have forgotten your name. My memory is spotty, you know. It's the effect of the toxins, the doctor says."

So it was toxic shock. That explained her vacant look.

"I'm David," he said. "Nancy's neighbour. We met at the dinner party last week. Nancy told me you were going to Hungary and asked me to feed her cat until your return."

"Oh, yes," she said quickly. "I did not make it to Hungary, as you can see. I'm sorry I didn't recognize you, David. It feels dark in my brain."

Dark in her brain? Was that a metaphor, or was it that she couldn't think of the right phrase? David felt sorry for her being stuck in some neurological limbo. He knew how it felt to be at a loss for words. Depression had that effect on him. The breakdown of his marriage, the death of Jerry, the world news — each catastrophe cut into his supply of vocabulary, curtailed his sentences, lengthened the pauses between words.

"The last time I was in here, I came to see Jerry," he said. "I still miss him. I imagine you do, too."

"Jerry?" she said, twitching her shoulders as if she wanted to shake off the name. "I do not want to talk of Jerry. I cannot." She no longer looked helpless. A glint of the old Laura was back in her eyes, recalcitrant, pushing him away.

"Sorry," he said. "I don't know why I brought up Jerry." He was flustered. Why mention death to a convalescent? The empty bed beside Laura's was bad enough. It, too, suggested a permanent absence.

"I should be going," he said. "I'm tiring you." Again he felt he had said the wrong thing. He no longer knew what was appropriate. He wished he had the gift of chit-chat, for this occasion at least.

He pushed back his chair.

"Don't go," she said. "It is nice to have company. I am bored here, but everything is an effort. To read. To talk."

"I can imagine," he said, settling back. "I guess I should do the talking."

He would have preferred the perfect accord of silence with its large space to think and imagine, but she said "Yes, talk to me," and he obediently launched into conversation, brought out sentences of an indeterminate nature. He wished he could be gossipy and tell her tabloid crazy stuff, inane stories to make her smile, but he could think only of serious words, the kind that weigh a person down. He carried on nevertheless. It was clear that Laura wanted words, any words, to replenish her vocabulary, to make up for what the toxic shock had destroyed. She looked at him with concentrated attention, her lips slightly parted, expectant, taking in everything he said. She was grateful for every word, grateful when he offered to phone Zoltan on her behalf and come back the next day for another visit.

"THAT'S BIZARRE," Zoltan said when David reached him at his hotel in Cairo and told him of the mugging. David pictured him in a red T-shirt, the one he had been wearing in Nancy's backyard, imagined him acting out shock, throwing up his hands, opening his eyes wide. There was static electricity on the line, and Zoltan's voice came across the phone with an echo. *Bizarre... Bizarre...*

"A case of being in the wrong place at the wrong time," Zoltan said. "None of this would have happened if Laura had gone to Hungary as planned, if she hadn't changed her mind at the last moment."

"What do you mean, 'changed her mind'?" David said.

There was a pause as Zoltan let the echo die down. "She phoned me from the airport and said she couldn't go through with it. She was feeling panicky about seeing her mother. She didn't tell you she cancelled the flight?"

"No, I had no idea. I thought Laura had missed her flight because of the mugging. She didn't say anything about cancelling her trip. She has no recollection of what happened on the day she was mugged."

"I'll book the first available flight and get back to L.A."

"No need to change your plans," David said quickly. "Everything is under control." He gave Zoltan a quick rundown, medical bulletin style: The crisis point had passed. Laura's condition was improving. She was on a sodium-free diet of carbohydrates and gaining weight. Gaps remained in her memory, and an odd stiffness in her language, but her blood count was up. The kidneys showed signs of recovery.

"That's good to know," Zoltan said, "but I'd better get back."

"When were you supposed to come back?"

"On Monday. Nancy and I were going to fly to Vienna tonight. I'd planned to stay with her for a couple of days."

"Well, then it's not worth changing your arrangements. I can look after Laura until you are back."

"That's too much trouble…"

"No trouble at all."

David wanted to take care of Laura. He wasn't sure of his motives. The pull Laura had on him was no longer erotic or romantic. It had turned into something more complicated, one of those messy human interactions that was hard to define. Maybe it was pity for Laura tangled up with memories of Jerry. Or maybe the afterglow of the attraction he had felt for Laura when he first met her and looked into her cat eyes had turned into sympathy for the diminished version of Laura in the hospital bed. He still felt the occasional lurch and tightening of the crotch when he looked at her, but the frisson was caused by a simulacrum, the woman at the party with NO written all over her face, who had given him a look of dismissal. The Laura at the hospital was different, softer. Illness had mellowed her and melted her reserve. The edge was gone from her voice. Perhaps they could be friends. He needed a friend. In any case, the hospital visits seemed to improve his mood. They got him out of the house, out of his slump.

He went back to the Medical Center the next day and told her about his telephone conversation with Zoltan.

"He was going to come back on the first available flight," he said, "but I told him there was no need to change his plans. I'd look after things here until Monday. I hope you don't mind."

"No, I don't mind," she said. "Let him have his holiday. He cannot help me here."

Right. Her father couldn't help her. When you are no longer a child, can anyone help you?

He patiently listened to Laura's slow speech, her meticulously crafted sentences, phrases put together from the remnants of her memory.

"They will discharge me on Saturday," she said. "Dr. Mahler tells me I am well enough to leave the hospital."

"I'll pick you up," he said.

"Thank you. That is very kind of you, but I could take a taxi." Her voice was hollow, full of submerged vowels. She gave him a rueful look full of regrets, as if the mugging had been her fault and could have been avoided.

"No, that's okay," he said quickly and repeated his offer. "I'll pick you up. Do they want you back for checkups?"

"I have one appointment for next week. They want to see how the medicine works. And Dr. Mahler says it is important to do mental rehab." She choked on "rehab" as if she was unsure of the pronunciation. "I must talk, Dr. Mahler says. I must read books to bring back the language, but everything tires me out."

"Do you want me to read to you once you are home? We could make it a routine. A lesson a day, you know."

"Yes, I would like that. Perhaps we could read poetry. It is good to get back into the rhythm of the language."

On Saturday, he drove Laura home. She passed her fingertips over the leather interior of his Karmann Ghia and said,
"Nice." He had a sudden sense of intimacy, wanted to feel her
fingertips on his arm, on his cheek, on his neck. She was very
quiet, almost as if she had changed her mind and didn't want
to go home. Or didn't want to go to her *new* home. Perhaps
that was the problem.

"This isn't a good time for you to move," David said.

"Move?" she said. Perhaps she had forgotten the word or
some of its connotations.

"Move from your old place to Nancy's guest house," he said.

"No, that is fine," she said, "I need my own space. I was
sharing an apartment with Zoltan, you know. Or have I told
you already?"

"No, you didn't tell me." He noticed she called her father
"Zoltan." Did therapists encourage offspring to call them by
their first name to blur the paternal relationship and make it
seem more like friendship? Or was it the other way round, and
did their children opt for first names because they wanted to
put distance between themselves and their therapeutic parent?

"Could we stop somewhere to buy food?" Laura said. The
illness had darkened her voice, given it a deep, almost hypnotic
resonance. He rather liked the new timbre.

At Vons, she wandered the aisles as if she had never been to
a supermarket. She picked up a pomegranate, turned it in her
hand, brought it up to her face — to smell it, to get a closer
look? — and put it back. Her hand hovered over the grapes,
withdrew. She trawled the dairy section, stopping, bending
forward to read the labels. Did she need to refresh her memory
about the names of everyday things?

In line at the checkout, she keenly watched the transactions.
In the parking lot, she looked on with alert eyes as he put the
bags into the car. Every movement seemed a revelation to her.
It was as if she had to relearn life.

They pulled into Nancy's driveway and walked through the

gate to the cabana. He unlocked the door. She stood on the threshold and scanned the space.

"Do you need help with anything?" he said.

She looked at him uncertainly. "I think I must get organized."

Her eyes were sending him away, but he hovered.

"Let me help you put the groceries away," he said.

The galley kitchen in the hall off the front room was equipped with a toaster oven, a small fridge, a microwave, and a coffee maker. David worked silently, opening and shutting cupboards and drawers, putting the groceries away haphazardly, under Laura's watchful eye.

"I see you haven't unpacked your books yet," he said, waiting for her to explain the absence of books. He expected her to say something like "They are in storage" or "They are in the closet," if there were closets in the further reaches of the cabana. But she said nothing. She gave him a blank look, as if the lack of books had just occurred to her.

"Would you like me to bring over some books?" he said, taking both of her hands, pulling her toward him, into a hug of undetermined quality, fatherly-friendly or copping a feel, he wasn't sure. She offered neither resistance nor cooperation. It was a strangely bloodless embrace, a trial touching of bodies.

"Would you like us to start reading tonight?" he said.

She hesitated.

"We could read Brecht together," he said.

"Brecht? That would be nice." The confusion in her eyes cleared. "I left my books at the apartment," she said. "There is not enough space for them here. Besides, this is not a permanent arrangement. Nancy wanted a house-sitter for the summer. But now you had to do the house-sitting for me."

"Not a permanent arrangement?" he said with a twinge of regret. "You mean, we are only temporary neighbours? In that case, we have no time to lose. Why don't you come over to my place when you are settled in? I'll make us dinner, and afterwards we'll read Brecht."

THEY MOVED FROM the dinner table to the sofa. Unlike Nancy, Laura was the right fit. Her body was too light to make the cushions sigh. And she did not seem to mind the dowdiness, taking the room in with the same wondering look she gave to everything.

"How old were you when you came to America?" David asked to break the silence Laura had carried with her from the table to the sofa. The silence surrounding her threatened to spread to him. It wasn't an uncomfortable silence, but David thought he should break it up, as a therapeutic measure. She was under doctors' orders to practice speech.

There was a delayed response to his question, as if she had to calculate the number of years first. "Thirteen," she said.

"And you wanted to be with Zoltan rather than with your mother?"

She considered the question. "Maybe the choice was for America more than for Zoltan." Her speech was clunky, as if the toxins had rusted not only her speech but the whole narrative machinery. She sighed, exhausted by the effort of speaking or by the difficulty of his question. She chewed her lip, becoming for a moment the Laura he had met at the party, her eyes distracted, her mouth impatient.

"My parents came to Austria from Hungary in fifty-six," she said, "but they weren't happy in Vienna. Zoltan wanted to move on to the promised land." She laughed ruefully. "That's what he used to call America. 'The promised land.' My mother wanted to move back to Hungary. She is a poet, you know. She needs to live within earshot of her native language. I mean..." Laura waved her hand. "I can't explain it. It is too complicated."

She slumped and gave David a helpless, suffering look.

David lost his footing in the marshy terrain of Laura's eyes. Images collided in his memory, of the cool sophisticate at the party and the tired woman on his sofa, who had aged more than the passage of two weeks could justify. There was a mur-

muring dissonance, a consequence perhaps of the confusion in David's mind.

"I shouldn't be asking you questions about the past. We should concentrate on the present."

"That is what Zoltan says. A few years ago, he wrote his memoirs. To put the past behind, he told me, and get on with the present."

"And now he is writing about the future. He's working on a sci-fi novel, isn't he?"

"He has not told me about that," she said. "Or perhaps I do not remember."

"It's about rejuvenation, about staying young and healthy by shifting your old age to a clone," he said, and a crazy idea came into his mind, a connection between Laura's weariness and the plot of Zoltan's sci-fi novel. Had Nancy shifted her surplus years to Laura? He pulled himself up sharply. Nonsense.

"Oh, but that is..." She searched for words. "Silly," she said. "I am not interested in such constructions. Let's read Brecht."

She reached for the volume of Brecht's poems on the coffee table, opened it and ran her finger down the list of contents. "'In Memory of Marie A.' Do you like that?"

Brecht's poem about a kiss on an autumn day, under a young plum tree. Was that a wise choice?

He took the book from Laura's hands and read of a cloud in the sky, incredibly white, incredibly far away, of a lover's face long forgotten.

I only know: I kissed her once,
Would not recall the kiss
But for the cloud,
So white, so far away.

Laura's eyes were solemn, full of grief for something lost, her memory perhaps.

He turned the page and read the next poem: "Changing the Wheel."

I sit by the roadside.
The driver changes the wheel.
I do not like the place I have come from.
I do not like the place I am going to.
Why with impatience do I
Watch him changing the wheel?

Laura had sunk back on the sofa with her eyes closed. Was she concentrating or getting tired of his reading? David put the book down and observed her closely, silently, like a thief stealing a forbidden pleasure. He studied her small perfect ears, the dark fringe of her eyelashes, her whey-coloured cheeks. There was a pale scar on her chin. He hadn't noticed it before. It was visible only now that she was leaning back, a scar on the cusp between her chin and throat. It took away his breath. He felt endangered suddenly, burdened with unexpected affection. It must be a trick, he thought, an illusion brought on by Brecht's poem. He needed to sort this out: Had Laura caused the unmistakable warming around his heart, or was it the poem? He listened to the silence between them, the harmony of their breathing and remembered their eyes meeting at the cemetery, at Jerry's funeral. Two solitudes. We are both in need of friends, he thought.

Laura's eyes fluttered open.

"Sorry," she said. "I stopped listening. That line about the cloud — 'very white and terribly far above us' — reminded me of a painting in my grandfather's study: *Herbstwald.* Autumn Forest. I used to look at it while he read Grimm's fairy tales to me. I imagined that the castles and the giants and the witches were right there in that forest, under a great billowing cloud." She stopped and bit her lip as if she had said too much, as if it was too intimate a story. The sadness in her eyes deepened. "I thought about the painting and drifted off. Sorry."

"No need to apologize," he said. "I guess my voice put you to sleep. Maybe we should think of something more interesting than reading poetry. Like organizing a homecoming party for you."

She shook her head. "No party. No. I don't want anyone to see me in this state." There was something solitary and troubled in her voice. She reached up to her head and ran her hand through her hair, which had grown ragged at the edges. The red streaks had faded, had washed out. Only a pink glow remained. She was wearing a roomy T-shirt and jogging pants. It made her look suburban. He hoped the change wasn't permanent.

"But people will understand," he said.

"No, I don't want a party, I don't..." She stopped and bit back the words.

She is holding something in her heart, David thought, something she won't allow to pass her lips. Her reticence was like a barrier. He feared he could neither go back and desire Laura, nor go forward and be her friend. He could feel the doubts moving in like a fog bank, grounding his brain.

ZOLTAN RETURNED bright-eyed and punchy as if he had just won a poker game. He phoned David. "I'm at Laura's," he said. "Come over, let's celebrate her recovery."

He welcomed David at the door. He was playing host in Nancy's absence.

"She's still in Vienna," he said. "She'll be back in two weeks."

He took David through to the backyard, plunked a bottle of Johnny Walker on the table by the pool and went in search of glasses and ice cubes.

Laura was sitting at the edge of the pool, dipping her toes into the water, shallow-splashing. She barely looked up when David came into the backyard and gave him only an absent-minded wave of her hand.

Zoltan returned with the glasses and served them drinks. He was full of loud, fall-off-your-chair jokes.

"Smile," he said to Laura. "Life is good."

She got up and joined them at the table, still unsmiling.

"Come on, Laura, what's eating you?" he said and chucked her under the chin.

She pulled away, refused to get into the party spirit.

For David, the afternoon had a sad finality about it. Was Laura feeling it as well? It was the end of their togetherness. David was no longer needed. Zoltan was ready to take over and look after Laura and Bébé.

"Thanks for being a friend to Laura," Zoltan said and kept talking, fighting David's moodiness and Laura's silence. He moved deftly from one topic to the next. What we need is innovative thinking, he said, offering them an array of dazzling futuristic ideas: jacuzzis for pets, chicken coops on apartment balconies, cross-country skiing on sand, subdermal scannable IDs, water sommeliers who tasted and rated tap water.

"You know what's limiting our creativity?" he said. "Information technology. It reduces our imagination to what can be represented on the computer in patterns of ones and zeros. It works on us like genetic engineering. In the long-run, all knowledge will be reduced to multiple-choice boxes."

"You exaggerate," David said mildly.

Laura looked down on her hands and said nothing.

Zoltan stirred his drink and started up again.

"I'm not exaggerating," he said. "But you can't fight progress. It's going to happen, whether you want it or not. You have to deal with it, and here's my solution for people who don't want to waste their time, who don't want to get lost in the cyber jungle: trend hunting."

"Trend hunting?"

"The majority of web traffic comes from search engines, right? People need a pathfinder, someone directing their hunting expeditions." He raised a prophetic finger. "Today, we have personal trainers," he said. "Tomorrow. we'll hire personal content managers, someone who will identify your taste direction, or shape it, who will dowse for cool if that's what you want."

"Are you considering a career as a personal content manager?" David said.

Zoltan wrinkled his brow. "Not me," he said. "I'm an ideas man. I leave the execution to others."

That was unexpected. Zoltan admitting to limits. At Nancy's party, in the soft reflection of the silver serving dishes, he had looked omnipotent, a producer, a facilitator, a man capable of pulling off anything. Out here on the patio, in the bright sunlight, he looked shabbier and hairier. The hem of his T-shirt was unravelling, his sneakers decaying at the toes. His gut was pronounced, but in spite of his bulk, he refused to be anchored to the spot. He was vibrating with the energy of his ideas.

Laura ran her finger over the rim of her glass mechanically, clockwise and back again. She had withdrawn into an opaque wordlessness and was once again the reserved woman David remembered from the party, only thinner and less stylish.

Zoltan finally ran out of steam and stopped. His eyes were on Laura, probing, as if he, too, was trying to remember what she looked like before her illness, as if he, too, had to get to know her again.

David emptied his glass and stood. "I'd better get back to my work," he said vaguely. It was time to let Zoltan take over the poetry readings and the grocery shopping and the cat feeding, and for David to return to the default position at his desk, transcribing the manuscript.

He went back to his house, determined to stay out of Zoltan's way, but his thoughts wandered across the fence with surprising frequency. He was suffering from withdrawal. He missed the caretaker role. He missed Laura, the other Laura, the cool woman at Nancy's party.

Every afternoon, he forced himself to sit down at the computer and work on his book, inserting words, taking them out again, rewording a footnote, rearranging a sentence here and there. The computer desk was still angled to take in Nancy's driveway and backyard. David couldn't keep from watching the comings and goings next door. Zoltan usually pulled into the driveway at dinnertime, carrying bags of takeout food, and left again around nine. On Saturday, there was a new development. When David sat down at his desk, he saw that Zoltan's car was already parked next door. Zoltan himself appeared in the driveway. A furl of belly-flesh showed between the belt of his jeans and the hem of his dryer-shrunk T-shirt. He walked around the Mini Cooper and out of David's field of vision.

A moment later, the doorbell rang. He answered the door. It was Zoltan. David waved him in.

"Coffee?"

"Sure. Thanks. As long as I'm not interrupting anything."

David went to get two mugs.

"Milk?" he shouted from the kitchen.

"Hold the milk. Double the sugar," Zoltan shouted back.

They sat in the sunroom, clutching their mugs. David couldn't figure out why Zoltan had come over, what he wanted. He seemed to have run out of original ideas. He got caught in dead-end sentences. David refused to help him along. A creeping annoyance took hold. Zoltan was too big for the room and too restless. His incessantly moving elbow was rubbing the tufted upholstery of the swivel chair. It was meant for a mid-sized man who didn't fidget.

Zoltan put down his cup and reached for a piece of the carrot cake David had brought from the kitchen. He failed to navigate the distance between plate and mouth, dropping crumbs on the way, eating with a ravenous appetite to make up for the gap in conversation.

Why had he come over? What did he want?

Zoltan swallowed the last bit of cake, eyed the plate as if

he wanted to give it a lick, and announced with incongruous formality: "I've accepted a position as counsellor at UC Irvine."

"Congratulations," David said and decided to keep to one-word answers from here on in, to make Zoltan go away.

"I've rented a place in Irvine," Zoltan said. "Laura is coming with me. She's taking a leave of absence from the Getty. She needs time out."

Whose idea was that? Laura needed her own space. That's what she'd said. Had Zoltan overruled her? David's resolution to keep to one-word replies wilted.

"When are you moving?" he asked. He was thinking of Laura, how to keep in touch when she was no longer next door.

"I've already moved my stuff to Irvine," Zoltan said. "And Laura is packing up as we speak." He gave David a prompting look that was hard to resist.

"What about Bébé?" David asked, obeying the prompt.

"That's the problem. It's a bit of a commute from Irvine. I hate to bother you, David, but would you mind taking over again? Nancy will be back in a couple of days."

David nodded mutely. He wished he hadn't made it so easy for Zoltan. Laura could have stayed a few days longer, until Nancy's return. She could have taken care of Bébé. What was the hurry?

As if sensing David's resistance, Zoltan said: "We really need to settle in and establish a routine before term starts. Otherwise, it will be hard on Laura. She tires easily. We don't want a relapse."

He reached into his back pocket and dangled Nancy's key ring. David meekly held out his palm to receive it.

"Thanks," Zoltan said. "I really appreciate it."

Casting about for something to say in the awkward silence that followed, it occurred to David that he had never asked Zoltan about his vacation.

"I never got around to asking," he said. "How was the Nile cruise?"

"Alright I guess." Zoltan pushed away the empty cake plate and waved his hand, as if he wanted to erase the memory of the cruise. "I'm not keen on that sort of thing. The cruise was Nancy's idea. She thought it was the perfect set-up for writing. I think she told you that I'm working on a science fiction novel. She is very supportive of my work, but I write best at home, alone, out of the sunlight. Splendid vistas destroy the concentration." He gave a self-deprecating laugh. "Nancy wanted to pamper me, but I wasn't in the mood for luxury. I had to think about the rest of my life, make up my mind. Do I take up writing full-time or find another job as a counsellor? But one can't always be thinking of one's career. Nancy had her heart set on the cruise, so I went along. I think it was good for our relationship."

He trailed off, waiting for an encouraging question, but this time David held firm and refused to be cued.

"Does the Great Systems Theory come into this?" he asked instead. "The reductionist-vitalist argument?" He couldn't hide the irony in his voice.

Zoltan erupted in a belly laugh. "Oh that," he said. "I made that up on the spot. I got bored with the huckster talk around the table and thought I'd inject a little bafflegab into the proceedings. You had me cornered at one point, and if you had pressed me, I would have owned up to whole thing. I was waiting for you to call my bluff."

"You should consider a career on stage, Zoltan," David said. "You are a first-rate actor. You had me completely fooled. I even googled you afterwards to see whether you had written anything on the Great Systems Theory. All I found was a memoir: *The Rescue*."

"Is that thing still floating around in cyberspace?" Zoltan said.

"I looked for a copy, but Amazon doesn't carry the book. Is it out of print?"

"It started out as a pamphlet. I wrote it for Max — Nancy's husband — after he had a stroke. When he passed away, Nancy had copies run off and handed them out at the memorial service. She wanted people to know that Max and his father saved my life."

"They saved your life?"

"The Nazis deported my parents in 1939. I was saved only because my aunt, who had Aryan papers, claimed I was her child. The Auerpergs, who were our neighbours in Vienna, realized what was going on and went along with the cover-up when they were questioned. That sort of thing took courage — a courage worth commemorating. You know what happened to people who collaborated with Jews? They were deported, together with their protégés."

"I see. And how did you end up in Hungary?"

"My aunt took me to Hungary. She had relatives in Budapest. But after the war, things went from bad to worse. The Russians closed the border and imposed their regime on the country."

"But you studied in Vienna, isn't that what you told me?"

Zoltan gave him a quizzical look, and David realized his mistake. Zoltan had told him nothing. He had read it on the website of the Hope Center.

"I escaped to Vienna during the Hungarian Uprising in '56," Zoltan said, "and the Auerpergs took me in. I wrote the pamphlet as a tribute to Max. He was like an older brother to me. Later, I wrote the story up properly, with names and dates, and shopped it around to publishers, but no luck. They either wanted me to jazz up the narrative or said the book was too short and needed more historical background. In the end, I published it myself. It's not that I was desperate to see my name in print. I just wanted to go on record."

"If you have a spare copy, I'd like to read it."

Zoltan put up his hands in a gesture of helplessness. "Nancy was unhappy with the longer version. I ended up trashing the print run. I didn't want the book to come between us. Relationships are difficult enough, without dragging in history."

"She didn't like your interpretation of history?"

"You could put it that way."

"But everyone is entitled to his own views," David said, lapsing into his lecturer's voice. "There is no such thing as The Historical Truth."

"Derrida, and all that — I know," Zoltan said. His voice picked up. He wasn't going to be lectured by David. "But Deconstruction is old hat. Philosophies aren't what they used to be, have you noticed? Plato stayed on top for a millennium. The Enlightenment lasted two centuries. Marx kept his grip on the communist movement for a hundred years. Derrida and Deconstruction are already fading. I give them another five years, tops."

"And after that certainty will return?" David said. If so, it was too late to do him any good. Deconstruction had worked its insidious poison on his brain. It would be a long time before he could say again with total conviction: What I see is what I get. In the meantime, he was stuck with doubts and best-guess scenarios.

"I don't know about certainty in the philosophical sense," Zoltan said. "But as far as the historical truth is concerned: I know what happened to my parents. They died at Dachau in a typhus epidemic. That's documented. And I have my aunt's word for what happened in Vienna. She told me the story of their deportation so often, I know it by heart. We could have recited it together. But for Nancy it wasn't about the historical truth. It was about family, about the Auerpergs. She was loyal to her husband, and she didn't think I'd given him and his father enough credit for what they'd done. She was unhappy about certain details, about a painting my aunt sold to Max's father and shouldn't have. Or perhaps it was the other way round, a painting Auerperg shouldn't have bought from her. It's a complicated story." He shrugged.

"Stories involving heirlooms are always complicated," David said. "I'm working on a book about the Burgundian Habsburgs in the fifteenth century. It involves a lot of family quarrels over *objets d'art*. There were feuds about who was going to inherit what. Greed, jealousy, intrigue, forgery, murder. You name it, and there is a Burgundian case story to illustrate it."

"No murder in this case," Zoltan said. "Jealousy maybe. But I'm not going to quarrel with Nancy over something that happened half a century ago."

"And so you decided to leave the past alone and write about the future?"

Zoltan grinned. "Science fiction is a great genre. You won't hurt anyone's feelings speculating about the future. You can tweak it to suit your taste. Or rather, I tweaked it to suit Nancy's taste. I'm writing this novel for her."

"Have you made her a character in the book?"

He thought for a moment. "In a way," he said. "You could say Nancy is the heroine searching for eternal youth, and I'm the mad scientist trying to find a way to make it possible. But now I'm thinking of changing the storyline. The idea of rejuvenating the body isn't futuristic enough."

"You mean, there's no need to transfer your physical imperfections to a clone when you can have cosmetic surgery instead?"

"Right. There are ways to reshape the body, but no one has developed a procedure for reshaping experiences. You can't shed them or transfer them to another person, not yet anyway. Although Hollywood is trying to provide that experience. Why do you think action movies are such a hit with young males? Because they crave the excitement of action. They are hungry for a high-risk life, for the adrenalin high of fighting the enemy. Their own lives are so boring. Nothing exciting ever happens to them. They are bus drivers or mailmen working the same route week after week. They shelve products at Walmart all day long or sit in a cubicle looking at figures on a screen. I myself have the opposite problem. I've had some frightening experiences in my life, adventures I'd like to forget or shuffle off."

For a moment, David thought Zoltan might tell him of those adventures, but he only wrinkled his brow and capped the confidential talk, moving from the particular to the general. "Now that's a subject for a futuristic novel," he said. "The protagonist gets rid of painful experiences by shifting them to a clone. Or simply sheds whatever he no longer needs or wants by selling it to the highest builder. A Craigslist of old experiences, if you want."

It was a vintage Zoltan speech. He was a futurist, always a civilization ahead of everyone else. He gave David a victorious smile and handed him the coffee mug balanced on the empty cake plate. He was getting up to go when Laura appeared at the sliding glass door. Her thin figure was backlit, sharply outlined by the bright morning light, dark and luminous at the same time. She waved, and David let her in. She was wearing a black T-shirt and Lycra shorts. The black outfit gave her a crow-like appearance.

"I've finished packing," she said to Zoltan, "and I wanted to say goodbye to David." She reached up, untangled a red rubber band from her ponytail, scraped her hair back from her forehead, and put the elastic back on. A few loose strands kept dangling behind her ears. She did not look well. Her face was pasty.

She turned to David. "So long, then," she said. She avoided his eyes and focused on some point below his chin instead.

"Good luck," he said, bending forward to kiss her on the cheek, but she failed to turn her head, and his lips touched the corner of her mouth, while her outstretched hand bumped into his stomach. It was an awkward goodbye: half New World peck, half Old World handshake.

"It was nice to have you as a neighbour, however briefly," he said, stepping back.

"Yes," she said, giving him a limp smile.

"I'll see you around," he said, realizing at the same time that he probably wouldn't.

"Yes," she said again. Her lips stayed parted as if she wanted to say more and couldn't because her supply of words had dried up. He tried to read her thoughts in her eyes, but she put on a mask of anonymity, keeping her words and her thoughts from him.

"Okay, let's get your things into the car," Zoltan said with determination and started for the door.

David watched them cross the driveway, Zoltan solid, hand-paddling, Laura hiding in his shadow, a starveling little girl. He tried to tie down his feelings, his coming and going affection for Laura. Would he miss her, or was he glad to see her go? When Laura was helpless, he answered her silent call for help. He wanted to coddle her, to take care of her. But he preferred the pre-hospital Laura, the one with the cold reserve in her eyes, the one with the eccentric fashion sense and clipped speech, the woman who fitted seamlessly into his erotic dreams. Perhaps it was best to let go of Laura, both Lauras.

TIME SLOWED TO a crawl for David after Laura's departure. He was once again Bébé's caretaker, but Nancy's house was peopled with ghosts now: Laura, dark, silent, sylphlike. Zoltan, voluble, his hefty body weighing down the elegant patio chairs. Zoltan's memoirs were floating in the air, nudging David's brain with bits of information, enough to pique his curiosity, not enough to satisfy him, leaving him hanging, wanting to know more than the few words he had been offered in passing. About the Gestapo raid. About Zoltan's rescue. About the painting that was sold and shouldn't have been sold. David's mind drifted to another fragment of the Nagy saga, Laura reminiscing about a painting in her grandfather's study, *Herbstwald,* an autumn landscape, a stage for the fairy tales he told her. But that must have been another painting and another man because Zoltan's father died before Laura was born and her maternal grandfather, if he was alive, would have been left behind in Hungary. Or was that another dark corner of the Nagy family history?

David wondered about the memoir Zoltan had peddled and failed to sell to a publisher. Was it confined to Zoltan's rescue from the Nazis, or did his gratitude to the Auerpergs carry on into the postwar years, to his flight from Hungary to Vienna and the hospitality they offered him? Because it was the sequel that David was interested in. Was there any mention of Laura in Zoltan's memoir?

An idea struck him: Nancy might have a copy of the book. While Bébé was crouching over her food, David searched the bookshelves in Nancy's living room. He tried to tell himself that his search was no different from looking for historical sources in an archive. Maybe that was the definition of a historian's job, probing the lives of others. But he couldn't suppress a twinge of bad conscience. He was sticking his nose into other people's business.

He checked the titles of the books on the top shelf. They were devoted to art. He skimmed the books arranged at eye level, but he saw at a glance that they didn't have the right shape for a memoir. They were coffee-table books, the hefty kind, display-sized. The lower shelves held a medley of books on history, biography, literary classics, and travel books. The Morocco leather spines were the only common denominator. He remembered reading somewhere that interior decorators bought that type of book by the yard to give a warm red and gold glow to a room. The bottom shelf contained a row of paperback novels, the kind sold at airport stores, thick with shiny textured covers, but no copy of *The Rescue*. It was a hopeless search, really. Why would Nancy keep a copy of the book if she disapproved of it?

He went back to the kitchen. Bébé had finished eating and rubbed against David's pant leg. He reached down, stroking her absent-mindedly. She escaped from the kitchen and dashed upstairs in a sudden display of nervous agility. He followed her lead. Nancy might have a copy of the short version of *The Rescue* at any rate, the one handed out at her husband's funeral. He searched the bedrooms and found the memorial pamphlet in the most obvious place for a woman who had played the devout widow for him — on Nancy's bedside table. On the cover page was a black-and-white headshot of a patriarchal-looking man: Max Auerperg, 1929-2000. David picked up the pamphlet and saw a slim volume underneath. *The Rescue* — disapproved by Nancy but preserved nevertheless, out of decorum because it was signed by the author? "For Nancy with love, Zoltan," it said below the title.

David sat down in one of the chintz-covered chairs and turned to the first page, but it didn't seem right to sit in Nancy's bedroom and read a book he had ferreted out by going through her things, a book of which she did not approve. It seemed a double violation of decency. He decided to take the book back to his house, to his study, the place where he did research. Because this was historical research, he reminded himself.

Later, sitting at his desk, he opened the volume gingerly, afraid of cracking the spine and loosening the pages. For all he knew, it was a unique copy, the only witness left to Zoltan's composition, a purloined copy on which he did not want to leave any traces of his guilt.

He began reading. He expected to hear Zoltan's voice, long-winded, complex, delivering some sort of Freudian analysis, but the account was plain. The facts were hard enough to take, and Zoltan understood: The suffering of the innocent is diminished by what is merely circumstantial.

Zoltan's name at birth was Samuel Wassermann. His father was arrested first. His mother was preparing to flee to England, but she waited too long and got caught in a Gestapo raid. Zoltan was saved because his aunt, Eva, pretended he was her child, but it was impossible to maintain the lie. Someone was bound to rat on her sooner or later. She had to get out of Vienna. Leo Auerperg offered to help her. Let's talk, he said. They met at St. Peter's Church.

David put the book down. If he had known all that about Zoltan earlier — well, what difference would it have made?

None. He still had a lot of questions that needed answers. He read on.

It was a weekday. The church was deserted. Her steps were ringing on the flagstones, bringing a faint echo from the cupola. Von Auerperg was kneeling in one of the pews at a side altar lit by a single candelabra. With his hands covering his face, he looked like a man in deep prayer. She sat down in the row ahead of him, the baby in her lap sleeping fitfully.

"Thank you for offering to help me," she said to Auerperg, turning her head, speaking to him over her shoulder.

The pew creaked faintly, as Auerperg leaned forward and whispered, "I've been thinking. You need cash. Could you sell some of the things in the apartment? I remember seeing an ormolu clock on the mantelpiece, and a Fabergé egg, and a Waldmüller over the fireplace — was it a Waldmüller? And what about the Pettenkofens and the Hobbema? They are worth a great deal."

"They've all been sold. The money has been deposited in an account in Switzerland, but I don't know the details. Josef took care of everything. We thought the information was safe with him."

"And there's nothing of value left?" he said.

"Only the Persian carpets and a painting by Liebermann: Herbstwald. *He has been blacklisted by the Nazis. Irene couldn't find a buyer, or maybe she didn't try hard enough. It was her favourite painting, you know. She loved* Herbstwald.*"*

David stopped, confused. There it was. The painting Laura had mentioned. *Herbstwald.* Autumn Forest. But the time frame was wrong, wasn't it? Laura could not have seen it in her grandfather's study. She might have seen *Herbstwald* later when Auerperg owned it. But he wasn't her grandfather. Was Laura's reminiscence a fantasy born of longing? Was it a false memory or a neural malfunction?

He turned the page.

"I tell you what," von Auerperg said. "I'll buy the carpets and

the Liebermann from you. I'll move the stuff to my property in the country. I'll give you,well, I don't know... whatever I can scrape together in a hurry."

"I can't sell them to you," she said. "They belong to Sam and Irene."

There was a pause, in which the baby set up a wail. Von Auerperg said hurriedly: "If anything happens to the parents, the little one is the heir. So you'll be acting on his behalf."

"I suppose so," Eva said, cradling the child in her arms. "I guess I can't worry about legal niceties now. I'm between a rock and a hard place."

"Yes," he said. "It's a tough situation. And you understand: I'm taking a calculated risk buying the stuff and moving it out of the apartment. You'll have to give me a receipt predating Sam's arrest. Can you fake his signature?"

"I couldn't do that. I'll give you a receipt in my own name."

The baby was settling into a crying jag. Von Auerperg sighed. "That will have to do then."

"And how will you get the money to me? I'm afraid to go home in case the Gestapo checks up on me. Honestly, I don't know what to do," she said, wiping the baby's snotty face with her handkerchief. They were both inconsolable.

"It's probably best for you to go back to your sister-in-law's apartment and stay there for the night," Auerperg said. He was talking fast now. The child's bawling unnerved him. "The Gestapo isn't likely to go back there after they've made the arrests. Tomorrow, we'll see. My secretary is looking for someone to mind her mother. The old lady had a stroke, and her maid quit. She said she didn't want to clean up after an imbecile who soils her pants. I'll talk to my secretary. Her name is Liese Meisel. Phone her tomorrow morning. Maybe you can work something out with her. She needs a live-in maid. You need a place to stay. And I could get the money to you through Liese."

He got up.

"*Make up your mind,*" *he whispered urgently.* "*I have to go. I don't want to be caught talking to you here.*"

"*Alright, then,*" *Eva said.* "*I'll go back to the apartment. I just hope there's some milk there for the child.*"

"*I'll come by later and bring you some milk,*" *he said.*

My aunt and Liese Meisel came to an arrangement. Liese would do the food shopping. Eva would look after old Mrs. Meisel and do the cooking and the cleaning.

"*What's the little boy's name?*" *Liese asked.*

"*Zoltan,*" *my aunt said. It wasn't wise to tell Liese my real name. I was named Samuel after my father, but that was a giveaway. It meant I was Jewish. No one else used Old Testament names in Vienna.*

"*I'm afraid I can't offer you any pay, only room and board,*" *Liese said.* "*You understand that I'm doing this as a favour to Mr. von Auerperg. He says you are in some sort of trouble. On the run from a husband who beat you up — something like that, right? He said you didn't want to talk about it, but you were scared of him. You don't want him to know where you are.*" *She gave Eva a questioning look.*

"*That's right,*" *Eva said.* "*I need to keep out of his way.*"

"*Well, that's not a very nice situation,*" *Liese said.* "*What if he finds out where you live and comes after you? What if he makes a scene at my place? What will the neighbours say?*"

"*That's why I'm prepared to work without pay,*" *Eva said.* "*I appreciate the risk you are taking.*"

"*As long as you appreciate it,*" *Liese said.*

Von Auerperg kept his word. He sent Eva a package through Liese. Just some clothes of my late wife, he told his secretary. An envelope with money was folded in with the clothes. It was less money than Eva had expected but sufficient to buy a birth certificate for the child and a death certificate for a man named Andras Nagy that turned Eva into a widow. In return for the money, she sent Auerperg a receipt signed with a squiggle since she was between names. It was a letter of thanks, she told Liese.

What could have offended Nancy in this account? Auerperg's offer to buy the Liebermann and the Persian carpets seemed humane, even if the transaction was legally questionable. So what if his motives weren't entirely altruistic and he got a bargain? Eva and Zoltan got the better deal. They escaped the long arm of the Gestapo. And where was the Liebermann now, David wondered. Did Auerperg sell it or was it still in the family? Nancy might be able to answer those questions, but David couldn't ask her, or she'd know that he had been nosing around her bedroom.

A feeling of unease crept up his spine, a tingle of shame at doing something surreptitious. He had an irrational fear of being caught and humiliated. He no longer had the peace of mind to give Zoltan's book a leisurely reading. He started skipping pages. The sooner the book was restored to its place in Nancy's bedroom the better. What if she sprung a surprise on him and returned early? What if a cab pulled up this very moment? He would have to explain. She would know that he had rummaged through her belongings. Idiot, he said to himself, paranoid idiot, she's due back tomorrow. You've got all the time you need to give Zoltan's memoirs a thorough reading. But he couldn't get rid of the feeling that he was a voyeur, had no right to look at a book that was deeply personal and didn't belong to him.

No, he argued with himself, Zoltan didn't mean it to be private. He had been looking for a publisher. He meant to describe a moment in history, a subject that concerned David. He was a historian. It was his professional duty to keep himself informed even if, after Derrida, the historical truth was unknowable because the life of the writer had no parallel in the reader's mind and could therefore not be absorbed. The experience remained outside his ken, forever abstract. Zoltan was right, he realized. To understand another man's experience, a mechanism was needed to clone it and make it your own. David's own life, an American life, quiet and privileged, was no preparation for understanding Zoltan's experiences or those of his aunt and the upheavals of life in Vienna, 1939. The words in Zoltan's memoir touched his optical nerve but did not enter his bloodstream.

With diminishing hope, David skimmed the next chapter of *The Rescue*: Eva moving from Vienna to Budapest, the shabby apartment there, the ration cards, the postwar years with the Iron Curtain descending and shutting Hungary off from the West, the revolt of '56, refugees trudging through the snow toward the Austrian border, Zoltan among them.

The narrative switched to the first person, and David slowed down over the account of Zoltan's flight to freedom in '56. He was riding in the back of a van. Cars, trucks, and refugees on foot clogged the road leading to Austria.

The van came to a halt, Zoltan wrote. *We were out of gas. Someone helped us push the vehicle to the side so that others could pass. We joined the refugees on foot, carrying what we could. Someone said that the border with Austria, that crack in the Iron Curtain, was about to close. Someone else said the Russians had searchlights trained on the no man's land separating Austria from Hungary. There were rumours that the Russians had mined the tract along the border, that it was an impassable marsh now that the snow had turned to sleet. You couldn't get across to Austria because the Russians demolished the bridges. No one knew what was true, what wasn't. We fanned out cross-country, individuals and little family groups. An old man limping along beside me said the Russians had bloodhounds, trained to sniff you out. Everyone's guilty to the dogs, he said. They can smell your fear. But I saw only a sheepdog circling a bleating flock. The sheep moved slowly across my field of vision, flanks rubbing, filling my nose with the smell of dung and wet wool. No mines, I thought, at least not where those grey-faced sheep are. The ground was marshy, though, too soft to sustain the weight of an adult. My boots sank in and made a sucking sound. I belly-crawled the last few hundred yards toward the barbed wire, where someone had cut a hole and thrown logs across the narrow canal that marked the border.*

I slid along the makeshift bridge and was in Austria. There was a long line of Red Cross ambulances, army field kitchens, buses provided by a disaster relief organization. Each of us, who made it through, got a mug of hot tea and a bread and butter sandwich. We sat down wherever there was space to sit down. People slept on chairs with blankets and hats pulled over their faces and feet propped up on their belongings. I had abandoned my bundle crossing the marsh. I brought only myself across the border.

David hurried on to the last chapter. He was no longer reading line for line. He was just trawling for Laura's name, looking for capital Ls and keywords like "marriage" and "birth," but Zoltan's post-revolution private life was apparently beside the point. The Zoltan on the pages of the memoir was a historical figure, an emblematic casualty of racial politics and postwar manoeuvring. His studies at the University of Vienna occupied a few lines. His move to California was squeezed into the epilogue, a paragraph to cap the story.

David shut the book and patted down the cover. The first twenty pages wanted to open and fan out, betraying his selective reading. No doubt, his fingerprints were on the margins of the pages. The paper was stamped with his DNA, bore permanent traces of his secret borrowing.

It was best to go back to Nancy's house at once, return the volume, and slip it into its old place under the memorial pamphlet. He shouldn't have taken it away in the first place. He should have read it in Nancy's bedroom, standing up. He should have put it back immediately after reading it, exactly where he had found it, under the pamphlet. He tried to re-member whether the edges of the pamphlet and the book had been flush. Would Nancy notice the difference? He might have to confess everything to her in the end.

BACK HOME, DAVID tallied his gains. What had he learned about Laura from reading *The Rescue*? Nothing. That she had fantasies or false memories about her grandfather and a painting that belonged to him? David felt a historian's frustration with the inadequacy of his sources, the gaps in Zoltan's story. The period that interested him — his life in Vienna, Laura's childhood — were missing from the account. They weren't relevant to Zoltan's subject: his rescue, Auerperg's courage and goodwill. The solution, he realized, was to go to location in Vienna and track down the sources in person.

Thinking of *The Rescue* as a document and of unravelling Laura's story as a research project made him feel better about the whole enterprise. His skin stopped radiating heat, and the nervous tingle in his spine abated. His conscience no longer nagged him for snooping around in Nancy's bedroom or in Laura's past. He was on solid ground. Historical research was his profession, something he knew how to handle. It was a matter of developing the right methodology, of approaching his meandering feelings for Laura in a critical manner. His desire wasn't prurient, he told himself. It wasn't a subdermal irritation, an urge coming up from the reptilian part of his brain. It was a professional interest, a genealogical inquiry. His feelings for Laura were vague like an unidentified fever, disturbing like a badly stitched scar. But his interest in Laura's family history was a defined field, subject to method and ratiocination. So why not combine his planned visit to the manuscript collection at the National Library in Vienna with an inquiry into the history of the Nagys?

Once David sat down at the computer and put his fingertips to the keyboard, he saw his way clear. There must be documents in the archives of Vienna relating to Laura's grandparents, the Wassermanns. Their art collection must be traceable. In *The Rescue,* Auerperg mentioned Waldmüller, Pettenkofen, Hobbema. Those names by themselves might not produce useful leads — they were ubiquitous in the history of eighteenth and nineteenth century art — but he had one specific piece of information: Liebermann's *Herbstwald*.

He googled Liebermann and scanned the results — biographies of the artist, images of his paintings, recent sales. *Herbstwald*. The image of an autumn landscape under a cloudy sky popped up on his screen. Was this the landscape Laura's eyes saw while she listened to someone telling her fairy tales?

Offered for sale. The words entered David's mind like a flash flood. The painting was for sale in Vienna, at an auction house called the Dorotheum. *Herbstwald. Est. value 400,000 Euros*, he read. The painting that changed hands and saved Zoltan's life. David saw his research trip turning into a pilgrimage to the shrine of an auction house, to lay his eyes on the miraculous, life-saving *Herbstwald*.

And who was the owner of the painting now? Could it be Nancy? Was she the seller?

When Nancy returned the next day, David had his questions under control and distilled into a research project and a travel plan. He walked across the driveway to return Nancy's keys, hoping to catch in her eyes an afterimage of Vienna, the city of wonders. She did look wonderfully reconfigured. She seemed to have shed a few years. The lines of her body had shifted, giving her a more streamlined appearance.

"How was Vienna?" he said, suppressing the real question: Who put the Liebermann up for sale? Had Nancy inherited it from her husband?

Nancy gave him a flawless smile. "I had a great time," she said. "I love Vienna. You should come and visit. You'd enjoy the parks, the architecture, the concerts, the museums…"

"I've been thinking about it," he said. "In fact, I checked out flights for next week. They have incredible last-minute prices."

Nancy gave him a distracted look. Was the information too generic for her? Was she searching her mind for a list of trans-atlantic airlines with service to Vienna? Lufthansa. Austrian Airlines. Swissair.

"I'm planning to do research in the National Library in Vienna," he said. "I think I mentioned to you that I'm working on a manuscript. A fifteenth-century herbarium."

"Oh, yes," she said, recovering her composure. "You did mention it. Vellum. Illuminated. Historiated borders. It sounded lovely. I wish you had told me earlier that you were going to Vienna. You could have stayed at my apartment, David, but I'm having a new heating system installed, and everything is at sixes and sevens. Bad timing, I'm afraid."

"That's okay," he said. "I've booked a hotel." Reasonably priced and in the right location, near the church where Zoltan's aunt had met with Leo Auerperg. In his head, David had mapped out a historical walk, a step-by-step reconstruction of Zoltan's rescue, an outline of Laura's prehistory. It included a stroll down the Herrengasse in search of the café where Eva had fed the baby, and a stop at St. Peter's, where she had concluded her bargain with Auerperg.

"Oh," Nancy said. "Oh, that's alright then." She trailed off, looking at him in wonder. The newest procedure seemed to have erased all lines around her eyes and left her with the wide-open look of an ingénue, permanently surprised at the wickedness of the world.

DAVID PACKED HIS carry-on with a flailing energy. He was impatient to grind through the three days separating him from the date of departure. He arrived at the airport too early, paced the lounge, seethed through the abbreviated night on the plane, and had no time for jet lag after landing in Vienna. He was unwilling to rest, but once he was in his hotel room, he could not shake the torpor of exhaustion. He lay down on the bed, fully dressed, meaning to get up shortly and check out the city's nightlife. Instead, he slept fitfully through the night, through a series of stop-motion dreams with fenced yards, blind alleys, and groaning beasts.

Quite possibly his dystopian dreams were inspired by the

view he had glimpsed from the window. His room looked out across a narrow lane at the curved back of St. Peter's. The grey stucco walls of the church were claustrophobically close. When David opened his eyes at dawn, he saw, through the sheer curtains, two baroque stone angels writhing in a slow dance of religious intoxication, calling on God with lips parted in moaning exultation. In the first moments between sleeping and waking, he mistook them for live performers, and even when he hitched himself up to a sitting position and turned a steady eye on them, they remained precariously balanced in their shallow niches, in danger of falling off their pedestals, it seemed to him, and shattering on the pavement below.

He checked the time: It was too early for breakfast, too late to go back to sleep. At home, back in L.A., he knew how to steady himself with a routine, with the morning ritual of coffee and local news. Here, nothing kept his heart from playing a drum solo of nostalgia for the past, another man's past. Studying the lives of others was a kind of avoidance, he thought, something to keep him from thinking about his own life, which was sad but lacked the heroic quality that made sadness bearable. Art had the same effect on him. Beauty like heroism made life bearable. Studying artworks, especially illuminated manuscripts, was a way to keep depression at bay, he thought. It removed the third dimension and flattened all grief. But there was no artifact at hand here in his hotel room, no manuscript whose beauty might placate his mind, whose vellum pages might soothe his anxiety. He had to wait, sit still in an upholstered chair, whose flowery pattern annoyed him. He closed his eyes against the print above the bed, another floral assault on his senses. He had no way of dealing with the impatience humming in his brain like a tuning fork. He was at the mercy of the local time zone.

It took a solid breakfast of bacon and eggs to bring order to the jagged disarray of David's inner life. The fatty acids had a settling effect, and he was ready, finally, to embark on the historical trail, the story of Zoltan's rescue. First stop: St. Peter's.

David had planned to sit in one of the pews and savour the atmosphere, but a mass was in progress, and a sandwich board at the entrance told visitors in three languages not to loiter and disturb the devotions of the faithful. All he could do was stand at the back and look down the centre aisle of the nave leading up to the main altar. The pews were crowded. The nave was brightly lit with chandeliers, shining a searchlight on the congregation, probing their consciences. The priest at the altar genuflected and lifted up the host. The altar boys in lacy surplices tinkled their bells. It was a ritual to banish all ghosts and admit only God's Truth.

David had barely set foot on the historical path, and already his progress was impeded. Already he had come up against the conundrum of Truth. How could he find truth here, in this baroque confusion, where painted columns seemed to jut out, and turned flat against the palm of his searching hand? Where the touch of a master's brush had changed hard plaster into soft flesh and created a dizzying, curlicue movement the eye could not arrest? David ducked out of the church, fled the house of illusion.

But even in the street, he felt unsteady, a time zone traveller. His life was distorted, wrenched from its context and twisted into something touristy and fantastic. A horse-drawn carriage passed him, with a coachman wearing a top hat, pointing out the sights to his fare with a furled whip. Their heads turned to the right and left, following his whip pointer. David longed for familiar American sights, the square shape of high-rises, the names of chain stores, the L.A. vernacular, but he was surrounded by classical façades, unfamiliar words on striped marquees, and the lilt of Austrian voices. The newness of the impressions was exhausting. Time to hit the refresh button and switch to his default project, the Habsburg collection. The manuscripts were David's escape route to a familiar world, to a reality he could recognize, a world in which he could claim competence. He wanted to be comforted and enjoy the peace of reading words written long ago, in a time of certainty.

The solution was to spend the remainder of the day in the manuscript room of the National Library, doing conventional research, the kind that was like a mother tongue to David, so familiar it calmed the heartbeat. He needed time out from the Nagy project, and the National Library provided the pure atmosphere conducive to restful contemplation — and the hope that the past could be brought into the present. On the marble stairs leading to the reading room, he saw a clerk carrying from the vault a pile of rare books and manuscripts. He lugged them on his back in a hod that looked like something a peasant might have used for hauling firewood long ago. And yet the receptionist who renewed David's library card was firmly anchored in the present. Her office was state-of-the-art. She made him look into a camera connected to her computer, punched a few keys, waited for the machine to spit out a plastic card, and handed it to him for signing. David replaced his old card, a laminated piece that had taken on the curve of his wallet, with the new one that bore his instant photo, the photo of a man looking like a rabbit on the run, surprised and red-eyed.

He filled out the requisition slip for the Habsburg manuscript, put his things into a locker, as instructed, bringing with him only a writing pad and a sharpened pencil. Then he waited in the hushed reading room, where the air conditioning was at the glacial level required for the conservation of historical artifacts. He watched the three other readers in the room, bent over their books with myopic concentration, and felt at home, one of a small, like-minded community.

The walls of the reading room were lined with shelves containing reference books, largely unused now that a computer had been installed in one corner and the data contained in bibliographies and encyclopedias could be had at the click of a mouse. On impulse, David walked over to the computer, typed in "Dorotheum," the name of the auction house where the Liebermann was offered for sale, and double-checked the viewing times. Next, he clicked on the auction catalogue and zeroed in on *Herbstwald,* until the Liebermann painting filled the screen, dissolved into blotches and turned into a Rorschach test. Yes, what did it all mean?

Out of the corner of his eye, David saw the archivist on duty signalling to him. He logged off. The manuscript he had requested was waiting for him at the counter. He signed for it, returned to his seat, and a few minutes later, was looking at the Burgundian Herbarium, set before him on foam supports to protect the fragile spine of the codex. With a contented sigh, he embarked on the sacred ritual of dealing with the past.

THE NEXT MORNING, invigorated by the hours he had spent at the library breathing in the spicy air of parchment and old books, David resumed his research into the Nagy family saga. This time, he avoided the risk of getting lost in a maze of baroque angels and arcane ritual. He decided to confine himself to the modern age and go after the secular places in Zoltan's story. It was too early to go to the auction house and view the Liebermann. Instead, he walked down the Herrengasse, slowed to look into the shop windows of high-priced boutiques, admired the classic façade of the Palais Modena, lost himself in the aisles of a fancy delicatessen, recalled his purpose and began looking for the café where Zoltan's aunt might have fed him sugary milk to stop the infant's crying. There was an abundance of possible locations. Vienna had a high ratio of cafés to street corners. David stuck his head into one or two places. He wasn't sure what clues, what commemorative traces he expected to find — shadows on the wall, echoes of a mewling child, vibrations of a trembling hand? The first two cafés were too modern to evoke the war years. In the third, he found the stage he had been looking for. The Café Hawelka was dark and filled with the inertia of tradition. Its wooden floors smelled of wax. Newspapers, clipped to bamboo frames, were hanging from coat pegs by the door. The atmosphere was a heady mix of warm bodies, smoke, and ashes. A lanky waiter in a red vest took David's order and brought him an espresso, setting the tray on the table with a sweeping motion. The foaming black liquid eddied dangerously close to the rim of the cup, barely resisting the centrifugal force. The movement had something mesmerizing about it, pulling David into the past. The set was right. It could have been circa 1939, but the atmosphere did not gel. The patrons had a contemporary look, and the dialogue was all wrong. Someone at the next table was talking about a rock concert. *In the mosh pit...some sort of gigantic...drone heavy*. The snatches of conversation undercut his mood.

David checked his watch. The auction house would be open by now. He paid and walked on.

The Dorotheum was in a street of antique shops that gave the appearance of being permanently closed. Their interior looked dark and deserted. The sculptures and gold-framed paintings on display had a patina of dust. But the auction house was a going concern. It occupied a large building, museum-like in its architectural glory, with banners trailing from the upper storey announcing the next auction date. David entered the white, vaulted foyer and made his way through the crowded galleries, looking at the paintings on display and reading the tags. He was getting close to the core of *The Rescue*, the part Nancy had found so distasteful, the transaction involving the Liebermann painting. It seemed more than a coincidence that a Liebermann was being offered for sale, here, so close to the scene of the historical transaction. It seemed fated. David felt a shiver of anticipation, of something momentous about to happen. LIEBERMANN — the name was printed on a small card taped to an empty spot on the gallery wall where the painting was supposed to be.

HERBSTWALD BY MAX LIEBERMANN
HAS BEEN WITHDRAWN FROM SALE

David felt a sudden drop in air pressure as his expectations collapsed, a pain in his ear as if someone had slammed a door shut and left him in the dark, fighting for breath. The essential clue was missing. Why had the painting been withdrawn from sale? He looked around for an attendant, someone who could explain the circumstances to him. And there was Laura! No, his mind was playing him a trick. How could it possibly be Laura? It was a woman who looked like her. Or was it Laura after all? His mind went into overdrive. He set off in pursuit, following Laura's avatar through the corridor to the exit. By the time he reached the street, she was half a block ahead, walking briskly. Her coat fluttered like the garments of St. Peter's saints. She seemed to be tapping out a message on her high-heeled pumps, an imperious "Follow me," leading him back to the Herrengasse. She quickened her pace and made it to the other side of the street just before the lights turned red. David broke into a run and was about to cross recklessly, when a man put out his arm and wrenched him back.

"*Sans lebensunlustig? Sehns net, dass' rot is?*" he asked David in broad dialect.

David could barely make out his meaning. Something about crossing against the light. "Are you suicidal?" Is that what the man said?

Halfway down the street, the woman who looked like Laura stopped and pulled out a set of keys. Her saw her profile. There could be no doubt. It was Laura. Every detail matched the image in his mind.

By the time the lights turned green, she had disappeared, passed through an imposing oak portal, a portal large enough to admit a coach and four. A square entrance had been cut into it, sized for pedestrians.

David hurried after her, put his hand on the doorknob and found it locked. He stepped back and looked up at the façade, expecting what? Expecting Laura to appear at a window and wave to him? The building was one of those stately complexes built at the end of the nineteenth century, with rows of windows crowned by little triangles, netted to keep the pigeons from roosting there. Beside the entrance was a wall-mounted intercom. There were no names, only apartment numbers and codes that were of no use to David because he was missing that piece of crucial information. The number of the apartment was just one of many things he did not know. A terrible uncertainty took hold of him. He could no longer tell the time or the season, whether he was moving or standing still. He could no longer think. A volcano of doubt exploded in his chest, leaving uncouth holes, dark grottoes, and clefts where his heart and lungs were supposed to be. He had difficulty breathing as he walked back to his hotel, troubled by a stitch in his side, the pain of longing for certainty.

He wanted to turn back the clock and feel the reassurance of his former convictions, the density and overwhelming stability of The Truth — the what-you-see-is-what-you-get kind of truth. But doubt had taken root in his system, entered his bloodstream, corrupted the oxygen supply, leaving him short of breath. He was stuck with doubt.

II. LAURA

FROM HER DESK, LAURA COULD SEE the Getty Museum garden, bowl-shaped with a pond at the centre, a garden that was, like her life, in transition, in need of improvement. There was too much empty space. The newly planted trees didn't offer enough canopy, and the blooms were too sparse. The bougainvillea was only halfway up the trellis, leaving the iron crown at the top bare, black spears silhouetted against the honeyed travertine of the museum walls. The walls, too, needed something more, like the patina of time. They were so new, so bland, the eye slipped off them. There was nothing to hold the interest.

The phone buzzed.

"Laura Nagy," she said, hoping for something that would hold her interest.

"How are you, dear?"

Oh God, not her.

There was no need for Nancy to identify herself. Her voice was instantly recognizable, breathy, floating the words on a cushion of air.

"Laura, darling," she said, "I have bad news. David Finley spotted you in Vienna." She emphasized *you*, leaving a pause, allowing Laura to substitute another pronoun: him/her/them? "He came back from Vienna yesterday and phoned me right away. I'm sure it was Laura, he said. Not possible, I said. She's back at the Getty. I talked to her yesterday."

"Nancy! Why would you say that? It contradicts everything Dad told him: that I was moving with him to Irvine, that I was taking a leave of absence from the Getty. I'm sick and tired of living the lies the two of you concoct, the charades you expect me to play."

"I beg your pardon, Laura? I didn't concoct any lies. I told David the truth."

"And now he'll be hounding me for answers."

"Laura, darling, be fair. This whole thing wasn't my idea. On the contrary, I thought it was deplorable, and I told Zoltan so. Why are you blaming me for everything? It's still about Jerry, isn't it? Deep down, you think it was my fault."

"Don't bring Jerry into this. I won't go there."

"Fine," Nancy said. "I don't want to get into an argument." Laura could hear her drawing in her breath, imagined her lips compressing into a thin line so that the words came out pinched: "I just wanted you to know, Laura, so you can handle the situation accordingly."

"Thanks," Laura said and hung up. It was a messy situation, exactly what she'd been afraid of, but there was no use discussing it with Nancy. She was an airhead.

"How can you stand Nancy?" she said to her father when she saw what was going on between them. "She's such an airhead."

"I think she's delightful," he said, "but you are too young to understand the charm of innocence."

"I understand the charm of innocence," she said, "but it should be reserved for children."

"On the contrary," he said. "I admire Nancy for holding on to it, in spite of everything."

I wish he found someone else to admire, Laura thought. I wish he hadn't involved me and Nancy in his ridiculous scheme, in his fantastic idea.

Laura wanted more excitement in her life, but not the kind that was her father's specialty, the zany kind. She should have said no, refused to have anything to do with his crazy games.

She looked at the stack of catalogues on her desk. They had turned into a cement block and become impenetrable. Her concentration was gone.

I always pick the wrong man, she thought. Zoltan, to begin with. You don't pick your father of course, but I had a choice: I could have stayed with mother. She made us call her *anya*. She made us speak Hungarian at home when we were children. She wanted to shut out Vienna and its German sounds, was homesick for the dark, velvety sounds of Hungarian. I could have stayed with *anya*. Would that have been better than staying with my father? No, I was thirteen. I wanted to go with him to America and live on the wealthy side of the world where kids had skateboards, ghetto blasters, and Commodore 64 computers. I wanted to learn English, the language that contained all the words in the Top Pop Songs Chart. I wanted to get away from *anya*'s poetry cloaked in Hungarian, a language that had no connection to anything, a language that was unsuited to dating, a language full of ornamental rhythms and old-fashioned courtesies. But most of all, I wanted to be myself, not one of a pair: Laura and Cereta, Cereta and Laura, the interchangeable Nagy sisters, dressed in matching outfits. *Anya* enjoyed it when people got us mixed up, until we revolted and insisted on being individuals.

Opa Auerperg was the only one who never treated us as a unit, who unfailingly knew who was who even when we wore identical outfits, who had memorized our little souls. He was our substitute grandfather because we didn't have one of our own. He wasn't the cuddly grandpa type. He was more like God the Father, or a hero on a pedestal: steel-blue eyes, square chin, bold nose, and gold-capped teeth that became visible on the rare occasions when he laughed. Leo von Auerperg was born, bred, and by natural inclination an aristocrat. He bestowed his attention on me like divine grace, a favour freely given to redeem my life. He made me feel like the chosen one. Merit had nothing to do with it. I could never have earned his love.

It was a gift magnanimously given and gratefully received, and reverently observed, like his instructions. His first commandment: One child at a time. Only one of us was admitted to the inner sanctum of his study on any given afternoon. He quoted Grillparzer to me: "*Erträglich ist der Mensch als Einzelner...*"

Man is bearable only as an individual.

"Why?" I said.

"*Im Haufen steht die Tierwelt gar zu nah.*"

In a crowd, he behaves like an animal.

"Like the buffalo you dreamed about?" I asked him.

"Yes," he said. "Like an animal in a herd."

Opa Auerperg had a recurring nightmare in which he was in the midst of a stampeding herd of buffaloes. Their hooves churned up the ground and filled the air with thick brown dust, he said. He couldn't breathe. He was afraid of being trampled to death. He told me his nightmare story the way other grandfathers tell a fairy tale. After a while, I forgot that the buffalo dream had anything to do with him. It was like something out of a book, became a tableau of illustrations. A darkened prairie sky, the hollow drumming of hooves, the musty smell of buffalo, a jostling mass of shaggy beasts.

"It started after the Gestapo took away your grandmother," he said. "Sometimes, I dream of her walking down the stairs, flanked by soldiers, with the Kommandant bringing up the rear. She is wearing a green, lacy dress, calf-length. Her hair is shiny black, piled on top of her head. There is blood gushing from her ears like a geyser, spilling over her neck, over her shoulders, running down the front of her dress in a jagged pattern of rivulets, but she takes no notice of the bloody river. She looks straight ahead as I pass her on the stairs. The Kommandant stops me. He asks me something, but I can't take my eyes off your grandmother and miss his question. When I ask him to repeat it, there is a rushing sound, like water. It's the blood, I realize. It's cascading down the stairs, roaring like a waterfall. I can't make out what the Kommandant is saying, and I'm afraid I'll give him the wrong answer. I try to walk away, and suddenly I realize it's me they are escorting down the stairs. They are taking me instead of your grandmother. The staircase is so dark I can hardly make out the steps. I lose my footing and stumble. The staircase has expanded into a huge cave, or maybe it's the nave of a church. The men of the Gestapo are casting up strange shadows, like serpents, undulating shapes. I realize they *are* serpents — the Gestapo men have turned into scaly monsters. I can't run away, my legs are paralyzed. They open their hinged mouths, saliva oozing out, dripping on me. They are about to sink their fangs into my throat when I wake up with a jolt."

I thought Opa Auerperg's dream was better than any ghost story.

"You should write that down, Opa, and make it into a book with illustrations."

"Laura, have you ever had a nightmare?"

I searched my brain for images of thrashing bodies, full-throated screams, phantasmagorical snakes. Nothing.

"I don't think so," I said. I felt small and insignificant beside him. I had never been visited by an important dream. "Are you scared when you wake up from the nightmare?"

"No, just sad."

I remember Opa Auerperg's dream story the way I remember movie scenes: cut to, pan to, dissolve to. A cinematic version of my grandmother's arrest. I wanted a part in her story, a heroic part, even if it meant I had to die.

Cereta and I liked play-acting, but she preferred contemporary scenes. We took turns pretending to be each other's pet. Cereta was my shepherd dog. I patted her head and took her for a walk around the living room on all fours. When I said "Heel," she heeled and licked my hand. When I said "Sit," she sat on her haunches and looked at me with soulful eyes, her head tilted to one side. Then I patted her and said, "Good dog," and she yapped pleasantly. Sometimes, we pretended to be cats. We humped our backs and hissed at each other and clawed the air, but she was always the more plausible cat. She had more theatrical talent than I, especially when it came to playing pets, slaves, and victims. She was good at licking hands, making pleading sounds, staggering around wounded to the heart, and sinking to the ground, lifeless. She enjoyed playing scenes, I just went along. I wanted a real pet, but *anya* said she couldn't deal with dog barks or cat hair. And I think she wanted to be the heroine in our lives. There was no room for another. Once or twice, Cereta and I put her into our play. Enter "Zoltan" and "Livia," but neither of us was keen on playing our mother. We couldn't think of any good lines for her. We moved stiffly, didn't know what to do with our hands, and the scene folded for lack of dialogue.

After Opa Auerperg told me about his nightmare, I came up with a new scenario.

"Let's do a snake fight," I said to Cereta.

"Like in Opa Auerperg's dream?" she said.

She knew! I was disappointed. I thought I was the chosen one, the exclusive keeper of Opa Auerperg's nightmares. I felt betrayed. I wasn't special after all. He had told Cereta about the Gestapo snakes as well.

"So which part of the story did you like best?" I said, covering up the jealousy souring my blood. "The fang attack? The blood spurting all over the green dress?"

"He didn't say anything about a green dress."

"He didn't tell you?" I savoured my victory. I was unique after all.

I liked Opa's rule of "one at a time," I relished my solo time with him. I didn't like his other rules: No running and no jumping in his apartment. And no noise. When it was my turn to visit, we sat at his lacquered mahogany desk — a behemoth of a desk with brass legs in the shape of lion paws — and looked at the cartoons of Wilhelm Busch and his stories for children, which came with a moral. Do not play with matches. Do not tease your friends. Treat animals kindly.

Sometimes Opa said, "Read on by yourself, Laura. I need a little rest," and moved from the desk to his easy chair, leaned back and closed his eyes. You couldn't call it napping because his body remained ramrod stiff. His eyes seemed to watch me from behind closed lids. His lips parted as if he was going to tell me a story, the spellbinding story of his dreams.

This was my time to be a heroine, to defy Opa's instructions and skip forward in the volume of Busch' cartoons to less edifying stories. In one, a young man was steadying a ladder for a girl picking apples. He looked up her skirt and said rude things to her. In another frame, he came home drunk, late at night. He sat down, his head drooping, and the candle on the table set his hair on fire. It came out by the fistfuls, making him look like a mangy dog. But in the next frame, his hair had grown back. He was in the garden shed with the girl, kissing and petting her in a dark corner. There was no moral to the story.

I told Cereta about the garden shed. We developed a storyline, acting it out under the blanket, at night. It was the story of a young man seducing us and wanting to get his hands between our legs. Sometimes, we let him get away with it. We took turns being the naughty young man, who touches the girl's crotch, trying to find the forbidden pleasure spot and to wriggle a finger into her hole.

Such smutty scenarios were unthinkable in Opa Auerperg's elegant flat. The Louis Quinze sofa in the drawing room kept you upright in mind and body. Above the sofa, in a place of honour, was an oil painting in a gilded frame: Liebermann's *Herbstwald*. When Dad dropped me off at Opa Auerperg's apartment, he stopped and gave the painting a searching look, as if he couldn't believe it was genuine.

"Why do you keep looking at the painting like that?" I asked him one day.

"It used to be in my parents' place," he said.

"You remember that from when you were a baby?"

"No, I was too young to remember. Aunt Eva told me about it."

"But you always say: Don't believe in hearsay."

He smiled. "Okay, you win, Laura."

One day when I came to visit Opa, the painting was gone. In its place was another landscape, an alpine scene with snow-capped mountains. Liebermann's *Herbstwald* had been moved to the study and was hanging above Opa's desk now.

"Why did you move the painting?" I said.

"I like the alpine landscape better," he said. "Which do you prefer, Laura?"

Liebermann's *Herbstwald* was a jungle of blurry green foliage with generous splurges of red. Everything was soft-edged. The brush strokes kept you guessing: Was that a person on the path leading into the wood? A child bending over? Or just a smudge, an unevenness in the canvas? The greens and reds were faded, as if a great weariness had overcome the artist. The autumn in Liebermann's painting was permanent, with no possibility of renewal, of spring refreshing the colours. It was a sad painting, but I felt a familial connection to it.

"I like the painting of the forest," I said to Opa. "Dad told me it was in his parents' apartment once."

"That's right," Opa said. "I bought it from them."

"Why did they sell it?"

"They needed the money to escape the Nazis."

"But they didn't escape."

"Your father did. His aunt took him to Hungary."

The Liebermann painting was the last of my grandparents' possessions, the last material proof of their existence. Can't you buy it back? I said to Dad. I don't have the money, he said.

One afternoon, when Opa Auerperg nodded off in his chair, I went up to the painting and ran my fingers over it. I wanted to feel its texture, but then touching didn't seem enough, and I picked at a blob of paint in the left-hand corner of the painting and scraped off a fragment. The chip got stuck under my nail.

I reamed it out and was looking at the chip when Opa sighed, the kind of long sigh a man makes waking up, but it sounded as if he had caught me and was sad because of what I'd done. I panicked and swallowed the paint chip.

He opened his eyes and fixed them on me. "What are you chewing, Laura?"

"Nothing."

Guilt has etched the scene on my mind. I still remember his probing eyes, his slightly raised eyebrows, the lines forming brackets around his mouth, when he asked me what I was chewing.

When Opa Auerperg died, the visits to his apartment ended. It was strange to know that the rooms were still there, in the building on the Herrengasse, but out of my range, like something that had slipped sideways. Cereta and I made detours on our way home from school and looked up to the third floor, at the row of windows that belonged to Opa's apartment. I had a choked-up feeling when I turned into the familiar street. I pictured the apartment empty, the furniture gone like Opa Auerperg himself, but if there had been a change, it wasn't evident from the sidewalk. The curtains were drawn close, as they had been drawn during Opa's lifetime. Direct light was bad for his paintings, he said. Opa's son, Max, had emigrated to California. We expected him to sell the apartment, but he decided to use it as a *pied-à-terre* for his family. They spent their summer vacations in Vienna. The first time Max and Nancy asked us to dinner, I was absurdly afraid of going to the Herrengasse, of seeing the apartment desecrated by new inhabitants. I wondered what it would be like without Opa Auerperg.

It was more or less the same. Nancy had done some redecorating, but nothing drastic. Freshening up, she called it, as if she had to get rid of a stale odour. It was comforting to see Thea, Opa Auerperg's old maid, who was back for the duration of Max's visit. She was moving around stiffly, at her usual, glacial pace, dressed in her black maid's uniform and wearing laced-up canvas boots. She said her ankles needed support because the job kept her on her toes all day. I still missed Opa, but the Americans had brought us a consolation prize: their son Jerry. He was our age, a ginger-haired boy, looking fey, except when he laughed and showed an impish gap between his front teeth. Cereta and I both fell in love with him at once.

After dinner, I excused myself and went out into the hall. Instead of crossing to the washroom, I stopped in front of the wardrobe. It was a hulking piece, polished to a sheen, darkly glowing, with a scalloped frieze along the top. I caught a glimpse of myself in the mirrored doors, looking worried, afraid of being caught in a place where I had no business to be. I opened the door of the wardrobe slowly, inch by inch, to mask the creak of the turning hinges. Opa's winter coat with the Persian lamb collar was still there. I felt a sudden, violent yearning and buried my face in the sleeve, breathing in the tobacco and lavender smell.

When I came back to the dining room, Thea was serving coffee. My moment of nostalgia came at a price. Cereta had slipped into the seat next to Jerry and was trying out her English on him. *The cat. The cat on the mat. A black cat is on the mat.* Jerry was laughing. It had been a mistake to leave Cereta alone with him. We were competitors for Jerry's attention, and she was in the lead now. When Thea served us hot chocolate in gold-rimmed cups, Jerry said he didn't like chocolate, and we, too, pushed away the treat. We were no longer children.

When Jerry came to visit our flat, I kept a wary eye on Cereta. We showed him our room and shared with him the secret of our games. We invited him into our blanket tent, and gave him an athletic performance, tumbling like clowns. We allowed him to be the ringmaster, following his hand signals. Jerry knew only a few words of German, but that didn't bother us. We made up dialogue for him and put words into his mouth. All we wanted from him in turn was his accommodating body, his willing fingers, his butterscotch smile.

At first, we were apprehensive about his visits, embarrassed about the dreariness of our flat. It was a comedown from Opa Auerperg's apartment. All our furniture had plain edges. There was nothing curlicue or gilded. The pictures tacked up on the walls were black and white, a rotating number of abstracts *anya* painted on large sheets of construction paper. She drew the same thing over and over again, variants of whirling, spluttering galaxies, explosive natural catastrophes, produced night after night. There were days when we woke up to wads of construction paper draped over the living-room furniture, slightly puckered at the edges, shiny black where the ink was barely dry. On rare occasions, *anya* used indigo blue. Once, she did a green and black combo and tore it up before it had a chance to dry. It isn't me, she said.

Anya painted only at night. She was sluggish during the day but had an awakening at dark, a mysterious transformation of werewolf dimensions. She allowed no one to witness her metamorphosis. Painting is a private thing, she said. She hung the pieces on the wall reluctantly, at Dad's prompting, and took them down again after a few days, adding them to the stack she kept under their marital bed. She left the walls bare for long periods of time until Dad humoured her into another "show." It's so hard to do, she said. It's my soul. You don't put your soul on display.

Her soul? I followed the arcs of black droplets, the swishing strokes across the construction paper.

"What is it *really*?" I said. "I mean, what's in your soul?"

"*Az érzéseimet. Gondolataim,*" she said tersely, refusing to give explanations. The Hungarian words hung over us like a black storm cloud: *Her feelings, her thoughts.* Anya closed her eyes and ears to Vienna, wouldn't expose her soul to the jab of German vowels and consonants, didn't allow them to pollute the insides of her mouth and ruin her Hungarian vocal chords. She spoke a few words of English with Jerry, but we could tell she was uneasy. She would rather preserve the Hungarian configuration of her lips and mouth, and leave him to us.

When Jerry left Vienna at the end of July, and we were by ourselves again, the summer began to drag. There was nothing to do. Cereta and I were tired of being each other's pretend-lovers now that we had experienced real love. We were glad when school started again and scheduled our lives for us. At home *anya* spread ennui by her very presence, lounging on the sofa in the living room, limp and somnolent, or wearing a suffering look. Listening to LPs was the only daytime pleasure *anya* allowed herself. When we came home from school, she told us to do our homework at the kitchen table and closed the living-room door on us. We could hear the desolate strains of *Bluebeard's Castle* starting up. We recognized it at once. It was *anya*'s favourite record and her favourite composer: Béla Bartók.

"The torture chamber," I said. The Armory. The Treasury. I identified each scene by the orchestral arrangement. Distant brass chord swept over us. "The Kingdom."

"You know what she's doing in the living room, don't you?" Cereta said, as the music took on an air of dread and foreboding. "Dancing, all by herself."

We sneaked up and opened the door a crack. The sound of trilling flutes hit us full force. We were in the castle's secret garden now, when Judith asks Bluebeard if he loves her, and for a microsecond we saw *anya* swaying to the music. Then she saw us, stopped dead, and turned down the sound.

"What do you want?" she said, frowning, blinking, trying to blink us away, but we had seen the expression on her face. It was all screwed-up and dreamy. The LP was still turning, and Judith's muted voice was like an echo of *anya*'s dreamy smile: *Do you love me?*

Did the ink splashes on construction paper represent dances, arms moving, and body swaying to Bartok's music? Was there dancing in her soul?

It was hard to tell, but we knew the reason why all her paintings were black. *Anya* was unhappy.

"I don't know why I bothered going to university," she said. "You don't need a degree in Hungarian literature to make beds or boil potatoes."

"You could read us your poems," Dad said.

She waved him off. Her discontent made us feel guilty. It put us all under an obligation to cheer her up. Cereta and I weren't very good at it. Most evenings it was Dad who was on caper duty. He spun records and played air guitar. No *Bluebeard* for him. He put on Chubby Checker: *Come on, let's twist again like we did last summer.* He did fancy footwork and sang along: *Do you remember when things were really humming.* "Let's dance," he said to anya, but she shook her head. "Don't be ridiculous, Zoltan." On Sundays, Dad played chef. He served us with exaggerated flair and spoke with a faux-French accent: "Thees is why Michelin geeve me three stars." It was easy for a kid to like Dad. He had stories to tell when he came home from the personnel department of the AMA, the Austrian Mineral Administration, where he worked in the Personnel Department as a counsellor. What do you do working as a counsellor? we asked him. I solve people's problems, he said.

"Everyone at AMA is a character," he said, telling us about the woman with the one-inch nails painted cardinal red, whose problem was hitting the keys of her typewriter, and the manager, whose problem was an itchy scalp and who scratched his head so hard that dandruff rained down on his desk.

"Eew, gross," Cereta and I said in unison, but we couldn't get enough of the flakey stuff.

That was one reason why I chose Dad over *anya*. He was entertaining. The other reason was Jerry. I jumped at the chance to go to California with Dad. When the question came up, I was first past the post. Can I go with you, Dad, can I? I left

Cereta no choice. One of us had to stay with *anya*. We couldn't all desert her. It would have been indecent.

That night, under the blanket tent, Cereta refused to play. She was angry with me. It was unfair. Why should I be the one to go to California with Dad? Why not Cereta? Because she likes to play the victim, I thought, but I didn't say it. I offered to flip a coin. Heads, I go. Tails, I stay.

"Okay," she said.

I feared for my fate, but the coin toss confirmed my choice, that manifestation of a desire which took its definitive shape when I put it in words and said, "Can I go with you, Dad?" Cereta acquiesced to her bad luck. "It's my miserable, wretched…" She groped for adjectives and couldn't think of any words matching the enormity of her bad luck. "It's just stupid," she said weakly and broke down in tears. She already knew: She was tops at play-acting, but in real life I had the upper hand. I was the dominant one. Cereta was younger, not much younger, admittedly, but she was born after me and was smaller at birth than I. Clearly, I had the first run on the nutrients.

"We'll come back," I said lamely, refusing to put a consoling arm around Cereta, keeping my distance in case her bad luck was catching. I didn't want her tears wetting my shoulder. "We'll come back, or he'll bring you and *anya* over. They'll make up eventually."

Cereta nodded and wiped away her tears, but neither of us believed in the possibility of a reconciliation. Dad had stopped clowning around in the evening. He left *anya* stewing in her funk. It was a sure sign that their marriage was over. Cereta didn't say that *anya* had been her second choice, not to her face. She didn't tell her that she would rather have gone away with Dad, and *anya* didn't ask. It was a done deal. Cereta took the credit for being loyal. I accepted the blame for deserting her. Now I wonder whether she enjoyed playing the loving, caring daughter the way she had enjoyed playing pet and licking my hand. But I suspect that *anya* held the leash so tight that

Cereta couldn't stop playing pet even when she got tired of it.

Of course I suffered punishment for winning the coin-tossed lottery. I paid the price for my cosmic good fortune. As soon as we got on the plane, I felt wretchedly lonely. With a queasy despair, I realized that I needed Cereta after all. Without her, one side of my being was exposed to rough weather, to the raw winds. But Jerry was waiting for me in California. He provided the lee side. He was still malleable, allowing me to graft my lonely self onto his mind and inject my wishful thinking. We acted out the story of teenage sweethearts. He did what I asked him to do, almost as if he preferred me to himself. He was equally good at playing the male or the female lead. He had a hairless chest, long lashes and a ripe mouth, and he had no trouble switching roles. We became a secret society of two, flushed with complicity. We became best friends, no, best lovers, no, we coalesced into something indefinable.

The scenes we played were nothing like the elaborate fantasies I had constructed with Cereta under the blanket tent. The plain façades of the buildings and the square layout of the streets in Mendocino did not inspire baroque tales. We ended up playing ourselves, but not our ordinary, everyday teenage selves. We gathered up bits and pieces from fan magazines to transform ourselves into sexy Hollywood stars. We became Laurabeth Taylor and Jerry Rock Hudson. I was an avid reader of tabloids detailing the scandalous lives of movie stars, and of nature magazines with alarming or pathetic stories about exotic people in exotic places. I scanned the fashion magazines at the hairdresser's salon for haute couture fashions and designer homes. They were the props of my fantasy life. I loved glossies for the revelations they offered page after page, and the tabloids for the fodder they supplied for scenes. I no longer confined them to a blanket tent. Jerry and I acted our scenes in the backseat of his car, or in Max Auerperg's book-lined study, which was silent and dark beyond the halo of the reading lamp on the desk. It was our safe house. We knew we would never get caught there because Max was at the office during the day, and the creaking stairs gave us advanced warning of anyone's approach. Besides, hearing Nancy or the maid moving around downstairs gave us a thrill, and we rubbed against each other rhythmically, in sync with the vacuum gliding back and forth over the carpet in the living room below. The possibility of discovery, however remote, and Jerry's willingness to run the risk excited me.

I didn't tell Cereta about those trysts. I felt sorry for her. I had Jerry, and she had nothing. Worse than nothing: She was stuck behind the Iron Curtain. After Dad and I moved to California, *anya* decided to go back to Hungary. She couldn't write poetry in Vienna, she said. The sound of the German consonants clogged her mind. Cereta put on a brave face. I think that was the role she took on, the girl with the brave face, when she wrote that it wasn't so bad, that the Iron Curtain was lifting. There were tourists in Budapest now, and special stores that had everything, where they accepted only foreign currency. *And so we can use the dollars Zoltan sends us*, she wrote. She had started calling Dad "Zoltan" after the separation, to document the distance between them, the thousands of miles, or maybe she let *anya* write the script for the scenes she was playing, because I think at some point she turned into *anya*'s mouthpiece. She didn't rename me. She still called me "Laura," but her letters had nothing familiar about them. They were official communiqués, a sort of diplomatic exchange dictated by *anya*.

I was a free agent. I didn't even show Dad the long letters I wrote back, but I self-censored. We couldn't get through to each other. Although my letters were handwritten, they were like the xeroxed sheets people sent out at Christmas then. One-third was sincere, one-third was bragging, and one-third was complaining to atone for the bragging. I complained because I didn't want Cereta to feel that she was missing out on all the good things. I wanted her to know: I was suffering, too. I complained about Dad picking me up from school in his beat-up Chevy and bear-hugging me in front of my friends. *He is so embarrassing,* I wrote. *And those stupid T-shirts he wears, with corny messages. Make love not war. He's hopelessly stuck in the sixties. And his girlfriend (groan!) laughs like a hyena.* Sometimes, Cereta and I talked on the phone, but calls were worse than letters. Nothing meaningful could be said with Dad standing by and waiting his turn.

When I saw Cereta again, we were no longer teenagers. I had finished my second year at university and was backpacking through Europe on a youth hostel budget and a Eurail ticket that went as far as Vienna. Hungary was still locked behind the Iron Curtain, but I got a 48-hour visa. The three of us, *anya*, Cereta, and myself, met in Budapest, and again I had the feeling that Cereta kept to a prepared statement, that she was *anya*'s mouthpiece, literally, because my Hungarian had atrophied, and Cereta supplied instant translations. She was proud of her language skills. She was studying English and German and was going to teach high school, she said.

It was *anya*'s idea to meet in Budapest rather than in the small town where she and Cereta lived.

"She didn't want you to see how we live in Hollókõ," Cereta said. She abandoned the translator's role and became herself once we were alone. "She didn't want you to see the wretched house we've rented, with watermarks left on the wall from the time the river flooded, and the old stove, and the jerry-rigged electric lights.That is what you call it when it is not done in the approved manner, right? Jerry-rigged."

"Right."

"It sounds like Jerry's name. Fits him, I guess." She looked at me slyly. "Do you think he is gay?"

"Where do you get that idea?" I said.

Cereta shrugged. "I'm guessing. I'm reading between the lines of Zoltan's letters. Is that how you say it? 'reading between the lines'? I don't think he likes you dating Jerry."

"He doesn't like me dating Jerry because he thinks of the Auerpergs as family. It's like incest."

"Incest?"

"Not literally," I said, impatient with Cereta's attempt to turn our talk into an English lesson. "But never mind Jerry. Tell me about Laszlo." Laszlo was Cereta's boyfriend.

"There is not much to tell. I should have brought a photo of him. I will send it, but he is not photogenic." She wrinkled her brow, unsure whether "photogenic" was an English word. "He is an accountant, or maybe you say, bookkeeper. He is serious about our relationship, but I am afraid to bring him home and introduce him to *anya*."

"Why?" Because she might turn into a wax doll in *anya's* hands and become unrecognizable to a visitor?

"Because she is so strange," Cereta said, "and the house is — I don't know what to call it in English — shabby? She does nothing about the house, to make it better. All she does is write poetry and listen to the radio. She got into trouble with the workers' council, but even they cannot make her go out and work. They had to give her a disability pension."

A poetic bent is a disability, I thought. It disqualifies a person from living in society. When the three of us met in Budapest, *anya* gave me a book of poems: *Versei* by Livia Nagy. It was a slim paperback with a shiny cardboard cover depicting a chaotic abstract, an unravelling ball of twine. I wondered about the jacket design. Was it one of *anya's* soul paintings?

LAURA PUSHED AWAY the memories, turned from *anya's* soul paintings to the images on her computer. She moved the catalogues on her desk, shifting from the extracurricular thoughts back to the task at hand, trying to establish a neural connection between her brain and the email correspondence on the screen, between her eyes and the descriptive text under the images of paintings — dimensions, medium, provenance. The signals remained weak.

She couldn't do any work. It was hopeless. She had to deal with the lies first, her father's ploy, Nancy's contradictions. David Finley was bound to be suspicious. A pre-emptive strike was necessary.

She thought of David at Nancy's party, looking endearingly rumpled, the type of unstyled man she wanted in her life, with a judiciously set mouth and eyes that promised to calm the waters. Of course, it was possible that the rumpled jacket was only a front, and that David was going for a certain look. Blasé? Undercover? Some of Jerry's friends were into that, going neutral to confuse the narrative. Perhaps David was gay, in which case it wouldn't have worked between them anyway. She needed more from a man than companionship with luminous moments. In China, she read, women narrowed down the number of potential husbands by height, blood type, and zodiac sign. Wish it was that easy to establish compatibility, wish I had a list to check off, she thought. What are my criteria anyway? She would have liked to talk to David that night at Nancy's party and explore the vibes he gave off, but it wasn't the right time. She was on stage. She had to watch for cues and was reduced to automatic nods. She couldn't afford to be sidetracked by a man. She reverted to the steely voice she first used long ago when she was vulnerable and had to take precautions against unwanted attention, a voice that had somehow established itself in her psyche, so that she could bring it out any time it was needed. Talking to David, she may have sounded more discouraging than she meant to be. But she wasn't herself that evening. She was a character in the crazy scheme her father had hatched, a vintage Zoltan scheme that was zany, risky, and likely to fail. She was in a pretend game, but unlike the skits she and Cereta had played as children, this one wasn't her production. It was Zoltan's sketch, and the lines didn't suit her. Or perhaps she no longer enjoyed pretend games. Then, at dinner, David challenged Zoltan over the Something or Other Theory. It was another

Zoltan moment. He blustered. He gave David a bully smile and relished every second of their sparring match, she could tell. *Thees is why Michelin geeve me three stars.* She was rooting for David. Only she couldn't let on that she was on his side. She couldn't risk familiarity.

She picked up the phone and punched in David's number. There was a good chance he wasn't home during the day. It was easier to leave a message than to talk to him in person. The phone kept ringing — ten rings before switching to the answering service.

She got as far giving her name before he cut in.

"Laura! How are you?"

She pictured David's lips, his clean-shaven face, his grey eyes myopic behind silver-framed glasses giving him a slightly weary look, his calming presence, but his telephone voice didn't fit that image. It was too eager. Laura had rehearsed a speech for an automatic voice, a message to follow the beep. She had rehearsed answers to complicated questions — about moving to Irvine and back again, about cutting short her leave of absence. She wasn't prepared for the simple question, "How are you?" She stumbled over "I'm fine" and didn't know how to go on from there.

"I've just come back from Vienna," he said. "I could have sworn I saw you there."

She tried to smile convincingly. They say you can hear a smile on the phone. "Well, it wasn't me."

"She looked like you."

She didn't answer. She was afraid of blowing her cover.

"Why don't you come over?" he said into the ensuing silence and pressed on, fighting her hesitation. "I'll make dinner for us. How about tonight? Are you free?" And before she could answer that question, he stumped her again, adding a teaser: "We could read Brecht, you know."

Read Brecht? Is that what they had been doing?

She could hear a smile lifting his voice, upending the coda

of the sentence and turning it into a question 'you know?' She hesitated, but there was no sense in putting him off. She would have to face him sooner or later and get past the Vienna incident.

"Okay," she said, breathing out half a sigh. "You're on. When do you want me to come?"

IT FELT LIKE battling amnesia. Laura looked around furtively, speed-reading David's furniture. They had met here, she reminded herself. The room was untidy and rumpled like David. This time, she was sure he wasn't trying for urban blasé, wasn't deliberately hiding the clues. There was no artful elevation of rubbish to *objet*. Everything was old except the leather sofa, which looked newish — factory-distressed rather than sat on a hundred times and roughly used. It was bulky and of a colour that didn't go with anything — hunter green. It was the kind of furniture you might see in a chiropractor's office or in the lobby of a Super 8 motel.

"How do you like the new sofa?" David said.

So it *was* new.

She made a noise, sipping air in small quantities, breath turned to sound, something that could be interpreted as yes, no, or maybe, something noncommittal. She had no idea what the old sofa looked like, whether this new one was an improvement.

"You don't like it," he said. His voice was resigned, as if he had expected a whipping and was glad he got away with discreet noises. "Maybe I should have consulted you before I bought it."

"Why me?"

"Because you have a sense of style," he said. "Well, it was in abeyance for a while — after your stay in the hospital — but you are back in form now." He gave her a hungry look and reached for the armrest of the sofa, as if he had to hold on to something to restrain himself from reaching out and touching her. "The red highlights are back at any rate," he said.

What was that supposed to mean? What happened to the

highlights at the hospital? She lowered her eyes, moved them out of the danger zone, decided to say nothing, to go for the safety of silence.

He poured her a drink.

"Dinner will be ready in a few minutes," he said.

She didn't follow him into the kitchen. In other circumstances, she might have leaned against the counter and said flirty things, or melancholy things — she was more inclined toward melancholy at the onset of an affair. But none of this was possible because she didn't know what point they had reached in the plot, didn't know what lines had been said or still needed saying. Had their lips touched? Did she know the feel of his arms, his chest? She was caught in a maze of simulation, weighed down with an oblique version of herself, a woman who may or may not have possessed the object of her desire.

He brought two plates and set them on the table. He had already put out placemats and wineglasses and paper napkins, and now he lit two candles.

"Beef à la Campagne," he said, making air quotes, apologetic because the dish was deli-bought, upended onto plates, and microwaved, but it really didn't matter. Laura couldn't concentrate on the meal. She had to multitask — make conversation, listen, stand sentry over the past, take stock of what was in the air, write herself into the unfolding story. There was no time to think about food. She barely touched the meat on her plate. She cut off a piece and manoeuvred it around, the way she wanted to manoeuvre the conversation. When David started talking about Jerry, she felt a momentary sense of relief. At least it was a topic she knew something about, but the same purple cloud of uncertainty was hanging over her head — how much of the story had been covered already?

"How did you and Jerry meet?" he said.

That's a question she would have liked to ask him but was afraid to, in case the topic had come up before.

"We met in Vienna," she said, and told him about Opa Auerperg. She dropped the name casually, feeling her way, searching the medium of his eyes, waiting for his reaction. Perhaps she had already told him about Leo Auerperg. If so, she was ready to retreat and say, "Oh, of course, we talked about him before." She waited until he said "Opa Auerperg?" with a large question mark before she told him of her ersatz grandfather, of his buffalo nightmares, of Thea the maid with the laced-up boots, of the hot chocolate served in gold-rimmed cups.

"And how does Jerry come into this?" David said.

Was it possible he didn't know? That he had been told nothing at all?

"Jerry was Max Auerperg's son," she said. She could hear the unease in her own voice. Did her hesitation carry? Was the tremolo audible to David?

"You mean, he was Nancy's — no, wait, that's impossible. She isn't old enough."

"Her stepson. Nancy was Max's second wife."

"But Jerry's name was 'White.'"

"That was the byline he used for his column. It was his mother's maiden name."

"It's embarrassing how little I know about Jerry," David said. "I considered myself a friend, one of his many friends…" he said, as if the number of Jerry's friends diminished his own importance, downgraded his friendship to also-ran, and excused his ignorance.

"He always had a lot of friends," she said, "even as a boy. It was easy to love Jerry. I fell in love with him the moment I saw him." Privileged first sightings, destined to be permanently lodged in the brain. "I couldn't help it." *We* couldn't help it. *We* fell in love with him. She wasn't sure whether to bring Cereta into this, whether to let David know about her sister now or weave her name into the story later. She was afraid of saying her name and unleashing a ghost, allowing Cereta to play shadow games in David's mind.

"I did all the talking," David said. "That's why I never got to know Jerry. I was terribly needy when I met him. It was the time after Elaine — my wife — left me. I was looking for an antidote, a cure for depression, so I took up jogging. I wanted a jogger's high, a breakthrough into joy, or failing that, the early morning camaraderie among people doing stretches on the boardwalk."

He looked at Laura hoping she would understand, but unsure he was explaining it the right way.

"That's where we met, Jerry and I," he said. "On the board-walk. We started talking in-between knee lifts and butt kicks. At first, it was hard for me to make conversation. I couldn't look into people's faces. So, I kept my head down and con-centrated on my legs."

He had concentrated on the rhythm, on synchronizing the bending of his knees and the opening of his lips to expel words, any words, about the weather, the lack of decent food on the pier, the newest gadgets for runners. Small talk was all he could manage at the time.

"Jerry was in great form," he said to Laura. "He had enough wind to keep up the joking while I was huffing along beside him. I remember him so well: ebullient, windblown. And I out of shape, stunned by depression. The need to spill came later. That's when I talked and talked until I was out of breath, and we stopped and watched the seagulls swooping down on a bag of Doritos, or caught up in a current of air, screeching. 'Look,' I said, 'they're flying backward.' 'You wish,' he said. 'You can't go back, don't you know?' He was serious that time. But most of the time, I did the solemn talking, and Jerry supplied the light entertainment. You know the loopy humour he could put on, the I-can-blow-bubbles-with-my-spit kind?"

Oh, she knew that charming nervous energy. His sweet sting. Why was she thinking of him with the mysterious longing re-served for a lover when Jerry had caused her only pain? Why not make room for someone else like David? Pain, she realized, had more staying power than love.

"I was looking for comfort," David said, "and Jerry's anarchic kind of fun dulled the pain. He was playing macho one minute and giving me a limp wrist next. He was all things at once. Being with Jerry was like watching a non-stop cabaret."

"He knew how to swivel his antenna, if that's what you mean by being all things at once," she said, decoding Jerry's game, making a beginning, taking the first step on the road from there to here, from Jerry to David. Dispel the myth. There was nothing comforting about Jerry's receptiveness. He was like a pillow on which your head left no mark. "He was willing to listen and to play along, but he was never comforting. I don't think Jerry was into providing comfort. Or support. On the contrary…" She broke off.

Jerry had kept everyone in the dark. His plasticity was faultless, his opinions be-my-guest generic. Laura could never get an answer to the question, "What do you think?" He was waiting for her judgment and smiled it back at her. That's one thing you could count on: Jerry's white smile. He synchronized his mood with yours. He was on your side. Disagreement was something he had buried long ago, hidden away under a carapace of inscrutability. He had been hurt too many times because he was different. He no longer exposed his skin, not to her, not to anyone. He covered himself with layers of other people's opinions. Jerry's column was well named: *I'm Only Asking*.

"On the contrary — what?" David said, forcing her to complete the thought and fill in the blank.

"He needed comfort himself," she said. She thought of Jerry's pale blue eyes, his washed-out ginger hair, his soft unused hands. You wanted to protect him from seeing or hearing anything harmful, from being touched by sorrow. "He was thirteen when I met him in Vienna — my age, but I instantly wanted to take care of him, look after him, make him my pet. Even later, when he lost that innocent, vulnerable look, when it was clear that he could fend for himself, he never struck me as someone you could lean on."

"He disappointed you?"

"It wasn't disappointment. It was a misunderstanding."

He looked at her kindly. "You didn't know he was gay."

Not in high school, when they kissed and fumbled in the car. Not in university when they set up house together. Not when they stopped having sex, because, he said, he was into yoga and meditation, incense and the occult.

"For a long time, I didn't."

Didn't know, or didn't want to know? Sex started up again in a vertiginous curve. They went from celibacy to sex-shop novelties, dolphin-shaped dildos, Donald Duck-headed condoms and porn videos. Jerry turned into a voluptuary and demanded exotic moves, Kama Sutra positions, cherry knot skills, as if he was daring her to say no. Their sex life became surreal, then dropped off the edge. Silent nights returned after Jerry discovered a passion for workouts, weight belts, barbell cable rollouts, bench presses, computerized bicycles. Biceps on Monday, triceps on Thursday. His arms became muscled, super-ripped, his chest like plate armour.

"And how did you find out?" David asked.

At the beach, with the afternoon sun shining from the southwest and glinting off the water. She was sitting in the sand, on a beachtowel with a shell and crab pattern, watching Jerry as he slipped the surfboard into the water, pitched forward on it, paddling, heading out toward the surf, where a dozen guys were rocking up and down in the swell. She watched them bobbing, taking stock of the surf, deciding the wave didn't have it, letting it pass. Another swell approached, and suddenly everyone was up. Jerry made his move. He was riding the face of the incoming wave, riding over the foam top, continuing sideways, the spray from the wave in his back. She felt a rush, her heart pounding to the beauty of the surf, to the beauty of Jerry's body. She was watching him with possessive pride as he came in, triumphant. She smiled. He smiled back with a radiant, love-ya look, and then she realized that he was looking past her. His eyes had moved on and settled somewhere behind her head. She turned, and looked up at a young man, G.I. Joe perfect, bare-chested, wetsuit peeled down to his hips, flapping against pumped-up thigh muscles. She saw the answering smile, the gaze holding steady. In that moment she knew. The memory was imprinted on her mind, together with the pattern of the beach towel on which she was sitting, the position of her fingers at that moment, splayed over a yellow crab on a sky-blue background. The shock turned it into a whirlpool, giving her vertigo, reeling her into a void.

"He came out to me, but not all at once. At first, he was skittish," she said. "Once I understood, once I was sure he was gay, we split up. He didn't come out publicly, not while his father was alive. After his death, he no longer cared who knew he was gay, but he did care who knew of his former life, when he had played straight. He wanted to shake all witnesses, cut us all adrift. I didn't see him for some years. When I ran into him again, a year ago, he wore layers of clothes, corduroy jacket over sweater over woollen shirt.But he couldn't camouflage his illness. I saw he was rail-thin. At first, I thought he had gone on another yoga binge, then I saw his eyes and knew."

Jerry's eyes had turned merciless. There were jags of anger and longing in them, as if he had run out of patience and wanted his due from the world *now*. He looked haggard, bone-weary from the hard work of dying. His voice, too, had changed, was stripped of modality, flattened. His shoulders sagged under an unseen burden.

"There was something jarring about his eyes, like broken glass," she said.

Jerry had waved to her and said hello in a smoky croak. The rough pull of his breath was like a beggar's plea for a handout of air, the currency of life. He was such a wretched sight, she teared up. Are you crying for me or for yourself? he asked. For both of us, she said.

"Was Nancy at the funeral?" David asked.

"No, she didn't go. She never got over Jerry being gay."

I can't go, Nancy said in her breathy voice. I can't stand looking at those friends of his! I'd rather remember him the way he was, she said and broke off, leaving the unpleasant bits unsaid. And Laura, too, wanted to do away with the unpleasant bits. She wanted to remember Jerry the way he was before AIDS ravaged him. The way he looked in a snapshot taken at a party, wearing a blue shirt and a seersucker jacket. Tasselled loafers. No socks. He was sitting in a caned chair, one leg flung over the arm of the chair, fussing with the garnish of a Mojito, a sprig of mint floating on an ice cube.

"Let's not talk about funerals," she said to David.

They had moved to the green sofa after dinner. David was running a finger along the edge of the coffee table as if rubbing a magic lantern to conjure up a life-sized version of Jerry. She put out her hand to stop his hand and the memories. Somewhere between getting up from the table and leaning back on the green leather sofa, she realized that she didn't want to share David with anyone. Not with Jerry. Not with Cereta.

The cocktail napkins sat on the table, crumpled paper tee-pees beside plates of half-eaten food. David hadn't bothered to clear the table when they moved to the sofa. There was silence between them at last. They sank into post-dinner laziness. He made no move to turn on the lights even though the sun had gone down and the room had turned a dusty mauve that gave an antique patina to his face. In the sparse light of the candles, he looked at her with dilated pupils, like a junkie.

She felt the gentle pressure of his palm as he took her hand. She turned to him. Their lips touched as if by accident. A sudden smile caught fire, and she laughed. She saw her path clear when he put his arms around her. The past receded through a tunnel, looking small and far away. The present came in view, like a mirage: David's arm around her shoulder, the almost accidental kiss, the smile. She had to pace herself, take it in slowly, deliberately, or the present might remain a shimmering mirage and never congeal into anything solid.

"Let's read Brecht," she said. "That's what you said to me on the phone. 'We can always read Brecht.'"

"We can if you feel like it, but I think we're done with the rehab, the mental gymnastics. You've recovered your memory. The words are back, the pitch, the rhythm. We don't need Brecht, do we?Unless you are missing the cloud, so white, so far away."

"The cloud?" she said, uneasily. Was this a quote?

"The cloud that reminded you of the painting in your grandfather's study. *Herbstwald.*"

He paused as if waiting for an explanation, an answer to a test question. At least that's what it sounded like, but she didn't know what he was after. When had they talked about the Liebermann painting? In what context?

"At the time I thought you were confused," he said. "I didn't realize that you meant Leo Auerperg. That you thought of him as your grandfather. Who owns that painting now, by the way?"

"Nancy," she said, keeping it short. She wanted to steer away from the contentious subject, but David was stuck on it. How much does he know about the dispute, she wondered.

"I googled the painting," he said, "and discovered that it was up for sale. In fact, I went to the auction house in Vienna where it was supposed to be sold. That's where I saw the woman who looked like you."

He waited. She realized he expected her to repeat her denial, to tell him again what she had told him on the phone: No, you were mistaken. That wasn't me. But she couldn't do it. She was afraid to step on quicksand and be sucked into a bottomless pit of lies.

"I'm here now," she said. "Isn't that good enough?"

He pressed her close. "Good enough," he said and kissed her. It was a natural movement, as if they had done it before, weeks earlier. Perhaps they had. She stiffened as their lips touched, conscious that she did not know how far they had gone. In the chaos of the past, the unknown past, his kiss felt right, but a tiny doubt remained. What kind of love was this? Another move in an endless series of replacements? *Anya* exchanged for a father, Cereta exchanged for Jerry, Jerry exchanged for David? Metamorphoses, stretching in a long line, from Vienna and the blanket tent to the backseat of a car, and now to David's bedroom.

Stop thinking, she told herself, as she followed him upstairs. She desperately wanted to live in the moment, to see David's bedroom for what it was, not an object of comparison with bedrooms she had slept in or the generic beds of TV commercials or hotel rooms with crisp white sheets. Keep your eyes open, she told herself. Look. It's a lived-in, slept-in bed with indentations made by David's body and a too plump pillow which will give you a crick in the neck. A bed with a story not yet told, with a past that was unimportant because together we will invest it with a new story and transform it into our bed. A shared memory was building up at this very moment, as they undressed, suddenly awkward, lovers on a long diet of self-pleasuring suddenly confronted with the need to work out the old-fashioned man-woman thing. They were lying side-by-side, looking up at the ceiling, searching their brains for a synthetic imagination to bring their bodies together. She turned to him tentatively, felt the flicker of his tongue, the definition of his cock, his fingers on her breasts, the taste of licked skin. She pulled back in sudden fright, but he clung to her. A feint of yields and lunges brought them together in a rhythmic delight she did not want to end, and she startled herself with a cry of ecstasy. But too soon the dusky heedless pleasure dissolved, and her thoughts were back. She could not shut them out. They were like sunlight seeping through closed shutters, stealing through the narrow interstices between the slats. I am alright, she told herself — I didn't mention Cereta to him. But if she was alright, why did her skin feel too tight, why was she fighting the urge to get up and escape? She closed her eyes and willed herself to stay beside David, making her presence felt a little longer, and David gratefully enveloped her in his arms. His hand passed over her cheek, slipping down to her chin, tracing the contours with his fingertips.

"I thought I saw a scar on your chin," he said into the darkness. "Isn't it odd how light and shadow can play tricks on your mind?"

Her eyes fluttered open. "A scar?" she said and remembered when it happened. Summer camp. And to whom it happened. To Cereta, who slept in the upper bunk. She climbed down, missed a step, smacked her chin on the edge of the bed, and started crying. Laura put a protective arm around her sister. She felt the wetness of Cereta's blood on her fingers, searched for a handkerchief, and pressed it against the cut. Smeared memories. A fog of words. Cereta's scar.

"It's strange," David said. "I remember a scar that doesn't exist. I follow a woman who looks like you but isn't you. Am I losing my mind?"

He laughed. She kept very still in his arms, saying nothing, allowing time to elapse before slipping out of his embrace, out of this tricky doppelgänger situation.

In the shower, she luxuriated in being alone with her thoughts, admitting that she was guilty, that there was nothing wrong with David's mind. The scar existed. She had noticed it herself when she saw Cereta again this summer. It was like seeing herself in a time warp, the woman she might have been, left behind and altered by the East European air. When she picked up her sister at the airport, they no longer looked alike. The scar wasn't the only distinguishing mark. Cereta looked foreign, even though she had modelled herself after the photo Laura sent her, even though they had the same haircut, the same red highlights, even though they were twins. She still did not look like her double.

Cereta's English was perfect, and yet Laura found it hard to understand her. It was not so much the words, but what was behind them. A foreign current was running through Cereta's thoughts. You'd think their identical genetic makeup guaranteed mutual understanding, but perhaps California living had modified Laura's DNA. Would I understand Cereta better if I had grown up in a small town, she thought, in a house with damp and discoloured walls? If I had lived with *anya*? Would we be more alike then?

She turned off the shower, turned off Cereta's voice in her head. But after she had kissed David good night and she was driving home, the voice was back. Her father's crazy scheme, the lies, the new complications she had brought on herself tonight blew up in her brain like a storm. She wanted to close her mind against the onslaught, shut the door against the flurries, but something caught in the door, refused to be pushed back, flapped in the wind. Unfinished business. The day when she picked up Cereta at the L.A. airport — was it only six weeks ago? It seemed longer because it was more than a matter of earth rotations. It was a shifting of poles.

SIX WEEKS AGO, at the terminal, she and Cereta had embraced and kissed perfunctorily.

"I've brought you something," Cereta said as if she could not wait to get it off her chest, as if she had been given a task that needed discharging at once before she could be at peace and think of anything else. "A message from *anya*."

She pulled a folded sheet from her purse. No envelope. An open letter?

"A poem," Cereta said. "She was pissed off — is that what Americans say? Pissed off because you didn't come. She wanted to read the poem to you. It is less potent in writing, she said. She was afraid the words would not lift off the page. That's what she said." She gave Laura a wan smile as if to apologize for speaking *anya*'s lines in a language other than her own, as if she was unsure that the translation could match the original.

Laura glanced down at the folded sheet, at the closely spaced writing on the outside. Hungarian words. She puzzled out the meaning of the first line.

Poems are such fragile things, Laura, so easily flattened, so easily... She frowned.

"What does the next word mean?" she said to Cereta. Her knowledge of Hungarian wasn't up to her mother's vocabulary. It was a poor, second-hand thing acquired unwillingly, at *anya's* insistence. It was a doomed seedling of a language, stunted, and pulled up by the roots when she left Vienna years ago.

Cereta took the sheet of paper from her hand and translated the rest: *so easily drowned in ink. I wanted to read the lines of my poem to you, to launch them with my voice, watch them cross the divide, from me to you. You should have come to me, Laura.*

"Then comes the poem, but you will need a dictionary to read it," Cereta said, refolding the page and handing it back to her. "And even with a dictionary, I don't know if it will make sense to you."

"Have you read it? What's it about?"

"No idea. It's cryptic, like all of *anya's* writings."

Laura unfolded the sheet and looked at the title of the poem. "Rape III"? No, that couldn't be right.

"Rape?" she said. "Is that the meaning of the word?"

"Yes, that's the title. But rape of the environment or of a person? Is it factual or metaphorical? I cannot tell you."

Laura read out the first line. "*Leopold is a manufacturer of* — of what?" She didn't know the next word.

Cereta supplied the rest of the line: "*Waste water treatment.*"

"Leopold? Is this about Opa Auerperg?"

"Perhaps, but I no longer even try to understand *anya's* poems."

"Could you translate it for me?" Laura said, as they made their way to the luggage carousel.

"I will write it out for you in English," Cereta said, "but I doubt it will help you. You should have gone to Hungary and talked to her yourself."

Laura was coming to the same conclusion. It was a mistake to give in to her misgivings and cancel the trip. You can't go on denying your mother even if she is a lunatic. Even if you had no words in common. There was touch after all, and gestures more eloquent than words.

"Why didn't you stick to the original plan?" Cereta said. Her voice was dense with suppressed accusations, as if the whole situation was Laura's fault. "It was supposed to be an exchange. I come here. You go to Hollókõ. That was the idea, wasn't it?"

Yes, that was the idea: Laura departs. Cereta arrives. She takes a taxi to Nancy's place, picks up Laura's ID from the cabana, and makes her way to Santa Monica Place, the stage of the fake mugging. She is found unconscious on the floor of the public bathroom and taken to the hospital for treatment. It was a crazy scheme.

Still I should have stuck to it and gone to Hungary, Laura thought. What if someone saw the two of them together at the airport? Why run the risk? She knew why. Because she had a shamanic desire to see her double before handing off her identity.

"Yes, it was supposed to be an exchange," she said to Cereta. "But it wasn't my idea."

"You agreed to it."

"Dad twisted my arm."

"I'm glad he arranged it. I needed time out."

"Time out?" Laura said. She tried to keep her outrage down and out of her voice. "I thought it was an emergency, Cereta. Couldn't you have had time out in Budapest or in Vienna, without putting me at risk?"

They were standing at the carousel, watching the luggage sliding down the chute. Cereta looked up surprised. "You used to like making up stories," she said. "You used to like adventures."

"Not this kind of adventure. You make it sound as if it were fun. It's a scam, and I could go to jail for it. I only did it because Dad insisted that you need treatment. He made me believe it was a medical emergency. It had to be done here and now."

"I need treatment, yes," Cereta said.

Examinations. Tests. Drugs. The question of who was going to pay for them was on Laura's mind when her father first raised the subject of bringing Cereta over, but she was reluctant to ask. It seemed mean and insensitive to talk about money when her sister's health was at stake. And she didn't want to embarrass her father. Nancy would have offered to pay. She was generous with money, but he was touchy on that point, the fact that Nancy was wealthy, and he was not. Money was briefly mentioned, almost like a slip of the tongue, before he presented her with the "perfect solution" — an exchange. It sounded so innocent when he said it. Cereta needed treatment, Laura had insurance coverage, an exchange would solve all problems. It sounded so ordinary, like an au pair arrangement.

Cereta spotted her bag and picked it off the carousel. She had arrived with one small bag. She needed no luggage, really. Laura's identity was waiting for her, fully equipped.

They headed across to the garage where Laura had parked her car.

"I need treatment *and* I needed to get away from *anya*," Cereta said.

So that was Cereta's sickness. She had been playing *anya*'s slave for too long. She had no more lines of her own. She was no longer herself. She had turned into a ghost and needed to borrow Laura's persona for a while, go through the necessary larval stage, regrow her soul, emerge and return to Hungary as her newly grown self — Cereta.

She had made mistakes. A six-week holiday in Laura's skin would set her back on the right path. "It was a mistake to marry Laszlo," she said. "And another mistake to move back with *anya* after I found out that he cheated on me, but I didn't know what else to do. I am at the end of the line with him." She shot Laura a look to see if the "end-of-the-line" idiom worked, then stowed her bag in the car and got in beside Laura. "I want a divorce," she said. "That's why I moved back with *anya*. I had nowhere else to go. I will stay only as long as it takes to sort things out." She drew a breath and continued as Laura started up the car. She kept the words coming. Perhaps they were words she couldn't say to *anya* and had had to keep in storage until now. The monotous flow of Cereta's words merged with the noise of the car engine. She was absorbed in her story. "Laszlo was using me," she said, "making me do secretarial work when I came home from teaching. He said there was too much work for one assistant but not enough to hire a second one." She paused as if to look for road signs in her life that could point her to the truth. "The truth is, he was screwing his assistant and letting her get away with a lot. She spent her time at the office primping or playing solitaire, and I had to take up the slack. I want to get out of Hollókő. The only thing that is keeping me there is necessity. And maybe I should say, *anya*. She is good at manipulating people. She has given me a giant guilt complex, you know. She constantly talks about killing herself. I'm afraid she will do it one day, and I will blame myself because I was not there to help her. But really, how can I help her? She is depressed. I told her to take medication. She does not want to. She says antidepressants inhibit her creativity. Screw her creativity! I can't take it anymore."

"Your vernacular is very good," Laura said.

"My vernacular? What do you mean?" Cereta said.

"*Screw her.*"

"Oh, that," Cereta said. "I heard that on British television. But really, I can't stand living with *anya*. It's worse than living with Laszlo. I will move when Hungary becomes part of the European Union when I can work anywhere in Europe. I will go to Vienna. Or London. Or come back here to L.A. Zoltan will sponsor me."

Laura could hear the threat in her voice. The threat of competition.

She paid at the exit of the garage. Cereta watched her put the card into the slot, and the amount due light up.

"Everything is automatic here. It will take a long time for Hungary to catch up," she said as if they were through with the topic of her flight from Hungary and the scam arranged by Zoltan.

But Laura was unwilling to let her off the hook.

The bar lifted, and she eased into the airport traffic.

"Dad made me believe it was absolutely essential for your health to come here," she said, resurrecting the topic. "That it was a done deal. I couldn't back out, couldn't refuse to co-operate. He railroaded me into this crazy plan. I should have stood up to him. I'm taking an enormous risk here, Cereta. I hope you understand that."

Cereta kept her eyes on the traffic, on the car in the next lane, on the L.A. cityscape, the office buildings, the fast-food places, the on-ramp to the highway. She refused to understand anything or owe Laura anything. "You think I'm not nervous?" she said. Her voice was belligerent. "Let's go over those names and places again, in case someone asks me."

For the rest of the trip she rehearsed being Laura.

In Santa Monica, Laura turned into the cavernous city hall garage, deserted because it was Saturday, and parked next to her father's Mini. That's how they had worked it out. She turned off the ignition and handed Cereta her purse. It was the surrender of her identity. Cereta offered up her purse in exchange.

"So what are you going to do while I'm here?" Cereta said.

"Dad left me his car," Laura said, pointing to the Mini. "Mine has to stay put, obviously. I'll go to the cabin and stay out of sight."

"That is his car?" Cereta said. "It is very small. I thought everyone drove a large car in California. On the highway there were so many, ah, what do you call them? Soofs? And so many Audis and BMWs."

"They are called 'SUVs'. And Dad isn't rich, you know."

"Then he should stop sending money to *anya*. She does not appreciate it. She wastes his money."

"On what?"

"She donates his money to causes."

"What causes?"

"Save the whales, empower women in Africa, what do I know? Or she buys up kitsch and burns it 'to keep it from blighting homes,' that's what she says. She did the same with the compensation she was offered by the company that caused the chemical spill — the chemicals that made me ill. She wouldn't touch the money. She told them to give it to Greenpeace."

It was time for Laura to go. There was a plan to implement, but she could not get herself to open the car door and walk away. She was mesmerized by her sister's words, the secret markers they contained, clues to a past she had chosen not to live. She was looking for links, for patterns, something that twinned the two of them, made them interchangeable. Perhaps *anya* was that link. Or was she the one who set them apart, the mark that distinguished the captive from the escapee?

"You are going to the weekend house in the desert? 'Zoltan's folly' — that is the nickname, right?" Cereta asked, as if she was checking a fact sheet for details to memorize, to have at her fingertips when playing Laura. "Why do you want to be in a primitive place without the nice things you have here in the city?"

"Zoltan likes roughing it," Laura said. "I don't. But the cabin is the ideal spot in the circumstances. Remote. Isolated. I won't run into anyone I know."

"And what will you do there?"

"Catch up on my reading. Catch up on my life. Too bad I

didn't bring along a Hungarian dictionary. I could have translated *anya's* poem."

"I will translate it for you. As I said. But you should go now, Laura."

Yes, she needed to get away from here where someone might spot the two of them together, but she didn't move. There were so many questions left to ask.

"Tell me," she said to Cereta. "Whose idea was this charade, yours or Dad's?"

"I don't remember how the conversation went exactly. I think it was Zoltan who came up with the idea when we talked on the phone. So don't blame me. If you need a scapegoat, blame Zoltan. Maybe I planted the idea. Is that the phrase, 'plant an idea'? But Zoltan did not object." Cereta had her hand on the car door, ready to step out and begin her life as Laura. The purse gave her a certain authenticity. "Zoltan wanted to see me," she said.

Laura shook her head. Is that why he had made her run this risk, to see Cereta? It wasn't plausible. "He could have visited you in Hungary," she said.

Cereta took her hand off the car door. She wasn't going. Not yet. She was standing her ground.

"No, it wasn't a question of visiting me in Hungary," she said. "He wanted to see how I react to America. Not as a tourist, but experiencing the system, you know? To see how it would change me. He said I have to run the gamut of American life. Just me. Without you being around."

Laura recognized the desire, the longing to stand alone, to break loose from the sister bond and be unique. Perhaps they were alike after all.

"Without anyone to model myself after," Cereta was saying. "I think he wanted to study me in isolation." She smiled. There was a lipstick smear on her teeth, as if she had tasted blood. "As an exhibit in the case of Nature vs. Nurture," she said, and broadened her smile into a rueful laugh. "I think

Zoltan takes a clinical interest in me. Not like a father, more like a psychologist." She had her hand on the car door again, getting ready to launch the test run of Cereta in America. "And, on the other side there was *anya*, waiting for you," she said reproachfully. "She wanted to see you."

"Not out of any clinical interest, I take it."

Cereta pursed her lips. "You are making a joke of this, right? But I will answer you seriously. No, it is all about the inner truth for *anya*. She wanted to tell you the truth in person. That's what she said to me."

"Tell me the truth about what?"

"The truth, whatever it is for her. Don't ask me, Laura. It is not up to me to tell you. When you changed your mind and cancelled the trip, *anya* felt you played a dirty trick on her."

Because when she let go of one slave, she expected a replacement?

"Because she wanted to tell us both at the same time, you see. To me before I left, and to you when you arrived. So, instead she put it in writing. She handed me the 'Rape' poem and gave me a second copy for you, because she wanted to treat us exactly the same." She smirked. "Like identical twins. Because we are identical twins."

"Why didn't you ask her what the poem means?"

"I asked, but she said everything was right there, contained in the words. She had nothing to add. You know what she is like — obstinate. God forbid she should make things easy for anyone."

"But you see her every day. You must have some idea of what's going on in her mind."

Cereta shrugged. She got out of the car, clutching Laura's purse, her new ID. Laura got out as well.

"Don't you want to know what it means?" she said to Cereta. "Aren't you even interested in what she has to say to us?"

"Not really. I'm living with *anya*, and I am tired of her and her cryptic poems and her 'truth.' I see her every day, as you say. I have to listen to her every day. I hear a lot about the meaning of things, what the trees tell her, what the clouds tell her. The mould on the walls speaks to *anya*, you know. Be glad you don't have to put up with her and her mysteries. The poems are just like her paintings. You remember her paintings?"

"Of course I do. The swirls, in black and white." She wanted to keep on talking in spite of the risk of being observed. What if someone who knew Laura saw her here in the garage with her copycat sister? No matter, she had to know what Cereta thought about those paint swirls. Decoding them seemed crucial information all of a sudden, a message explaining everything, tying up the loose ends of her life.

"You remember when we asked her what they meant?" Cereta said. "And she said: my thoughts, my feelings. That's the kind of answer you get when you ask about her poems. So, yes, I did discuss this 'Rape' poem with her, and she said it was her vision. She said that's what she read in Aunt Eva's eyes."

They stood in the windy garage. Cereta faced her defiantly.

"Does that answer your question?" she said before walking away, to the mall, to play her part in the charade.

THAT WAS SIX weeks ago. When she arrived at the cabin, Laura had a strangling sensation in her throat, a knot of fear about being alone with her thoughts, alone in the shadeless desert, in a place unforgiving and hostile to human needs. But she rallied before her thoughts could thicken into something more sombre and took a tactile comfort in lugging canned food and bottled water from the trunk of Zoltan's car into the house. She stashed them away under the kitchen counter in columns and rows, restful patterns keeping her mind balanced. She cleaned the house, wiped the accumulated dust from the table and chairs, and put fresh sheets on the bed. And at night — she had been afraid of sleepless nights — she settled into the silence of the cabin and found that sleep came easily after all, blacking out worries. The next morning, she looked around and adapted to her makeshift home. She gave up ambition and sank into good-enough. She let the images of perfection fade from her mind — the sculpted bodies, the curated art shows, the brightly spun inspirational messages, the faith-like dedication expected at work, the faked collegiality and creditable counterfeit of warmth and interest, the rooms with the staged look. She folded her hands in her lap and looked with relief at the imperfections of the unstaged cabin, the calming effect of necessary objects. Slowly, the crispness she felt when she was in the city, the tautness of her skin, a kind of allergy against required perfection, went away. Her skin felt roomier. She had a sensation of well-being, of safety, of having survived a catastrophe. Nothing unforeseen could happen in a place governed by a slow natural cycle. Her kaleidoscopic city life, shaken up and reconfigured a million times, was turning into a still life of durable objects. She stepped outside and stood still under a vacant blue sky in an immobile landscape of rocks and straw-coloured grass, the mineral glint of grit on the road the only variable in sight. No man-made sound reached her, except one day, like a warning from another world, the screech of fighter planes passing overhead, likely returning from a training mission to an army base nearby. Laura watched the vapour trail in the sky fade to white. Apart from that, there was no kinetic energy except the wind edging across the land and raising dust that seeped through the windows of the cabin like a sad emotion.

Time seemed endless in the desert, undivided except for day and night, no schedule popping up on a screen, no agenda, nothing to keep Laura from rethinking her life, checking her gallery of friends and those missing from it, the lack of a male friend who could double as a lover, for example, someone like David. His name came up too frequently in the solitude of the cabin to count as random recall. Looking back now at the days of her retreat, Laura saw that it had to end the way it did, in David's bedroom. There was a prescient murmur in her heart even then, an augury in the desert air that she would reconnect with David after returning to the city. David was on her mind, even though she was preoccupied with the exchange engineered by her father: Cereta turning into Laura. Was there a corollary, she wondered. Was she turning into Cereta? She felt a certain levelling had already taken place, in the garage at the airport and later on in Santa Monica. She had become a little more like Cereta.

Her father, she thought, didn't understand the momentous nature of the switch. Giving away one's identity meant nothing to him. He had been named Samuel and was raised as Zoltan. His life was saved by exchanging his Jewish identity for that of a gentile, by switching from the arms of his mother to those of his aunt. After that, identity was perhaps no longer important. He had developed a blind spot to himself, a vacancy in his mind that made him receptive to taking risks, to welcoming life's vicissitudes. He was reckless, a gambler. It occurred to Laura that her father, who had seemed inexplicable until now, was in fact entirely explicable. He was the result of a peripatetic life, from one country to another, from one continent to another, vistas gained and lost, people loved and let go. He had become unmoored. Perhaps that is what drained him of all fear, all compunction, all the feelings other people had naturally. No, drained wasn't the right word. Her father didn't lack feelings. They just kicked in belatedly, after she remonstrated with him, after she put it to him that he *should* have been afraid, *should* have been more considerate, *should* have loved her more. He freely granted her point then and, like a repentant child, asked her forgiveness, took up the wanted emotion, loved her, feared for her, was solicitous for her welfare, but by then it was too late. I shouldn't have asked you to take the risk, he said on the day he left for the Nile cruise with Nancy. I should have taken out a loan to pay for the hospital expenses.

Too late. Cereta had left Budapest by the time Zoltan regretted his plan. She was headed for L.A. and the fateful exchange.

From time to time, in the splendid isolation of the cabin, Laura looked at the poem *anya* had sent her, read the lines, mouthed them, sounded them out, searched her memory for the meaning of those foreign words, but too many gaps remained to tease out even a ghost of meaning. She had to wait until her return to the city, until she could read Cereta's translation.

AS PROMISED, Cereta left behind an English version of "Rape III." It was sitting on top of Laura's purse, car keys, and dry-cleaned clothes from which Cereta's touch and scent had been chemically removed. The translation was the only tangible memento left of their exchange, a page handwritten on a piece of Zoltan's office stationery, as if it was a counselling memo, and perhaps it was. Laura speed-read through the lines, then read them a second time, slowly.

Rape III
Leopold is a manufacturer of waste water treatment
addressing the self-created problem
buying the silence
of those who have been violated
air, water, earth, woman,
or maybe they are willingly silent
because saying the word is too painful
even the memory hurts

Cereta was right. The translation explained nothing.

"I don't understand it, even in English," Laura said to her father. He had handed her the bundle of her possessions and the poem in the close atmosphere of his messy apartment, with boxes of files and clothing still unpacked three weeks after his move, and destined to stay that way for some time, she knew. Her father was an incorrigible slob. I shouldn't have come here, she thought. I should have asked him to come to my place, where the aesthetics encourage organized thinking.

"I'm totally lost," she said to him.

"What did you expect?" he said. "Every translation is an exposition. This is Cereta's take on those lines. Ultimately, you have to interpret them for yourself."

"That's so typical of *anya*," she said, "sending me a mysterious message and leaving it up to me to tease out a meaning. Do you think she is talking about the chemical spill that made Cereta ill? Cereta thought it might refer to the rape of the environment. I even googled waste water treatment companies. There is a large company, F.B. Leopold, a subsidiary of Xylem, with headquarters in Pennsylvania. Maybe that company was involved in the cleanup. And the title: 'Rape III.' Is there a 'Rape I' and 'Rape II?' I should ask Cereta. Or *anya* herself, but I doubt I'll get an answer from her if I write."

Zoltan shrugged. "You want my advice?" he said. "Leave it alone." He looked defeated. By *anya's* poetry? By his own schemes? She had never seen him falter like this.

Out of pity, she said: "Alright." But she pressed on nevertheless with a question she had reserved for him: Was it true that he wanted Cereta to come so he could observe the effect of American life on her?

"Cereta thought you had a clinical interest in her." She gave him a questioning look. "Or should I say, a clinical interest in the two of us as exhibits in a study on Nature versus Environment."

He finished the takeout coffee he had set down on the coffee table and picked at the rim of the Styrofoam cup.

"So what's the verdict?" she said, impatient with his silence. "Have we grown apart, Cereta and I? Has living in America for a month made a difference? Has it changed Cereta?"

He stopped mangling the cup. "I take a clinical interest in Cereta? Is that what she said? That's *anya* talking. I've noticed it before. Cereta is turning into a talking head for her mother. And that's not a clinical observation. It's something that concerns me as a father."

"So you thought you'd give her a break from *anya* and send me in as a substitute, as a temporary slave?"

"I admit, getting Cereta away was a consideration," he said mildly. "But you didn't go to Hungary, and I doubt that you would have fallen under *anya*'s spell in the few weeks you were supposed to stay with her."

"There is always a certain give-and- take when you are in close contact with a person, even for a short time," she said.

He gave her an appraising look, as if she had caught him by surprise, with an unexpected bit of wisdom.

It was true, wasn't it? She thought of the half-hour she had spent with Cereta in the car, driving back from the airport, the give-and-take of words between them, the threat of competition she had heard in Cereta's voice when she said she might emigrate and live in America. "Zoltan will sponsor me," she said. The words had sounded an alarm in Laura. She was afraid of becoming interchangeable if Cereta came to live here. And, she wondered, would the give-and-take involve David as well?

III. NANCY

NANCY EMPTIED A TIN of Purina Friskies into Bébé's dish and wondered whether the horror stories she had read about commercial cat food contamination and the resulting feline urinary tract infections were true, and should she buy a grinder (Cuisinart had the highest rating) and make her own, but it sounded complicated. With or without bones? With or without skin? The thought of trimming excess fat from chicken thighs was revolting, and Bébé looked healthy enough.

She passed her hand over her ermine-sleek pelt. Bébé trembled with the double pleasure of eating and being stroked. Nancy wished for double pleasure in her own life, wished Zoltan would take her out more often, or should she give more parties? But whom to invite? The guest list needed amending, the Wrights were definitely out, he was so crass and had no appreciation for gourmet food, and Loni kept talking about her hip replacement, it was really too much, who wants to hear about titanium hips?

Nancy looked out the kitchen window and saw David backing his car down the driveway, his Karmann Ghia (what year was it again? '78?). He slowed, came to a stop, got out and opened the door for — Laura! No, it couldn't be her! But it was. Laura wearing a dove-grey suit. Maybe she should look into tailored suits for herself, but what was Laura doing in David's driveway, admiring his car? No, not admiring the car, Laura had no interest in cars. It was a romantic kind of

admiration look possibly meant for David. This will complicate everything, Nancy thought, and her heart fluttered. The
Nagys had a knack for intrigue, all of them, Zoltan, Laura,
and Cereta — Cereta was the worst of the lot. They all had
restless fantasies, unlimited what-if dreams. Life was good, but
not good enough for them. They put their improving stories
on life to make it more exciting. Oh, she didn't mean to say.
What did she mean to say? She didn't mean to say anything
against Zoltan. It was heaven to be with him, as spritzy as
a Cristal champagne party, such conversations they had, so
much fun, it was the part where the conversations turned into
action that she didn't like. If she could only keep Zoltan safely
in her backyard, keep all his stories for herself, gather them
up like a bouquet and put them into the living room to enjoy
privately or limit those ideas of his to the sci-fi manuscript.
She thought that's what he was doing, finally, channelling his
what-if ideas into writing a novel, that would be charming,
but there was Laura ducking into David's Karmann Ghia, and
the two of them, David and Laura, driving off. David will find
out eventually, she thought, and it will be trouble all round.

She listened to the beat of her heart. Was she still missing
dear darling Max, of course she missed him, as much as she
should after two years, that's what they say, it takes a month
for every year you were married, and so she felt only a sweet
kind of sorrow now, a cozy nostalgia. It was good to think of
Max, who had been her mainstay all those years. Being married
to Max had been like a refreshing sleep, the REM part, was it
that or the other — NREM? That sleep simile was Zoltan's, mind
you, not hers. Max kept you in la-la land, he said. You've never
really woken up to reality, and in a way Zoltan was right. She
did like to keep reality at bay, at least the unpleasant parts,
there was no reason to dwell on the parts that made you sad.
And why would Zoltan insist on her facing reality while he
indulged in all sorts of caprices that had nothing to do with
reality at all?

Unlike Max, dear Max, who was solidly planted in the here and now, in the big house in Napa which had been home for nineteen years. If life threatened to become too much for her, if reality became too intrusive, there was always the garden to admire: wisteria, heliotrope, lemon tree, pomegranate, hibiscus. And there was Max to save her from dealing with messy situations, who sorted out things with a squeeze of determination and set them up right. She was so grateful to him. He took care of reality for both of them. When he died, she was hoping to find someone, she was hoping that Zoltan — but he wasn't the kind.

You've always preferred innocence to experience, he said. You like living in a dream. Yes, she did prefer innocence. Being jaded was so unattractive, a sort of aging process of the heart and mind. She wanted to stay young within and without. It was different for men. They could handle experience. Max had been almost twenty years her senior, but he aged well. His skin was like century-old silk, and his white hair like a halo. He had dignity. True, he wasn't much of a talker, not like Zoltan, but he was skilled at carrying conversations forward with little nods and approving smiles. And all he wanted in return for his unconditional generosity to the world was being respected and remembered, and there he was in the Timothy J. Chambers portrait (oil on canvas, 42x64), hanging in the study — perhaps it would be better to have it in the upstairs hall. Max looked so distinguished in the Chambers portrait, almost majestic, although she preferred the black-and-white Karsh photo in which he looked gallant and steadfast. With a little pang, she remembered the little solemn rituals that made him so uniquely hers, the cigarette he smoked after dinner, to within an inch and a half of the filter, no more, no less, before he put it out, tamping it, tip neatly folded under, in the Swarovski ashtray. And the intimate gestures — one fingertip raised, just a moment, dear — when the telephone rang, and the post-its, grey, with pencilled notes, pencilled with a freshly sharpened tip

(HB grade) on the bedside table, so he would see the reminders first thing in the morning when he opened his eyes. And his judicious use of proverbs — "what's good for the family is good for the individual," "we make decisions with the mind and implement them with the heart" — the proverbs saved so much time and anxiety when it came to decision-making, they were like so many ready-made conclusions in the orderly file cabinet of Max's mind.

Nancy felt an upsurge of commemorative love and did her best to erase the post-stroke images that weren't fair to Max, that made him look so undignified, the drooling mouth, the twitchy hands, the mangled words, no, no, she waved away those ugly thoughts, rolled over them with a corrective brush, a second take of Max, smiling at her with good-humoured grace. There.

But those lawyer and accountant and stockbroker friends of yours, Zoltan said, and their trophy wives, or even their old wives, so boring! He didn't say "boring," but that's what he meant. Set in their ways, always thinking inside the box, he said. In a way it was true, although they never bored her, and not everybody had Zoltan's intellectual resources. Of course, she understood what Zoltan objected to, the uniformity, the predictability. Everything was pre-planned, Zoltan's words again. Well, what was wrong with pre-planned? Life with Max had been of the ordered kind, serene. The Nagys, when they arrived in '78, gave her a seismic shock. She never thought she would get to like Zoltan, or that he could be so. So comforting? So entertaining? So indispensable to her?

We must see what we can do for the Nagys. They are like family, Max said when they arrived. But it was awkward. They were too colourful. They didn't fit in. Then Zoltan enrolled in graduate school and, when he had his degree, he set up as a therapist. By that time, his accent was quite acceptable, and Laura's practically unnoticeable. Of course, she was just a young girl when she came over. In any case, within two years,

they were presentable, and you didn't have to worry about
social bloopers anymore.

Laura could be troublesome, but you couldn't blame her
for the situation with Jerry. It wasn't her fault. To be fair, the
trouble started earlier, with Jerry changing from the angelic
boy he was at six when she married Max, to the diabolical,
well, no, maybe that was too strong a word, wicked? tricky?
difficult? She was running out of words to describe the teenager
Jerry became. At first he was so delicate, a child saddened
by the death of his mother, Nancy's heart went out to him,
such a beautiful child with that strawberry blonde hair of
his, and those cheeks, like a putto in a Raphael painting,
you expected feathery wings to sprout from his back. But he
lied, oh, he lied, and no matter how often Max talked to him
sternly about fibs, he fibbed again, it was as if Jerry could
not tell the difference between truth and lies, and there was
nothing useful in Maccoby's *Psychological growth and the
parent-child relationship* or Piaget's *Science of Education and
the Psychology of Childhood* or Papalia's *A Child's World:
Infancy Through Adolescence*, or even Gardner's *Children
with Learning and Behavior Problems*. Nancy read them all.
Zoltan couldn't do anything with Jerry either. You'd think
a therapist, but no. He said it ran deeper than fibbing, and
besides, he asked, was imagination really such a bad thing?
You should encourage Jerry to act out his fantasies, he said,
but that's Zoltan for you, that's what he does: act out his
fantasies, and look at the result. It almost spoiled their Nile
cruise. Why, why, why? she said when Zoltan told her, and
he gave her a thousand reasons why it had been necessary for
Cereta to come to L.A., none of which made any sense to her.
It was one of Zoltan's caprices. But in the end, she forgave
him everything. She could never be cross at Zoltan for very
long, it wasn't in her nature, and Zoltan loved her after all
even if he didn't say so, and why didn't he?

But Jerry now, she just wanted everything to be bright and

beautiful between them, she wanted to be a good mother and to fuss over him, and for a while he let her. Max, she didn't like to say it, but he wasn't everything a parent could or should be, it was the one area in which Nancy got no support. Max had to take some blame for the way things turned out. He was too distant, too successful, too authoritative, and there were too many silences. Max was a man of few words. He made it up to her with embraces, but he never touched Jerry. And her Mommy mammoth embraces, that's what she called them, let Mommy give you a Mammoth hug, were not enough, apparently, and no longer wanted by the time Jerry turned into a teenager. He wasn't churlish like the other boys, just slippery, evasive, dodging her embraces, a sneer hidden under his smile. She was afraid to think what he was doing behind her back, she felt helpless. Don't worry, Max said, it's natural in a teenager, but it wasn't natural. And then there was Jerry's whispering, sniggering, touching closeness with Laura. Childish secrets, Max said, except that they were no longer children. Nancy could guess what was going on, she had eyes, she had ears, but the thought was unbearably ugly, she didn't want to catch them out, she didn't want to think about it even, no, it would have been too unpleasant.

When the childish affair between Laura and Jerry survived into adulthood, when it could no longer be brushed off as puppy love, it was too late. Max said so himself. He should have dealt with it sooner. Now they had to let it go. And, she thought, perhaps something good will come of it in the end. Maybe Laura could cure Jerry's unfortunate propensities. And maybe their relationship could smooth over the business of the Liebermann painting as well, the question of who owned it, who had the legal title to it. Cereta kept insisting and insisting, the little snake, insisting on what, for heaven's sake, that Leo Auerperg hadn't been generous enough? And Livia, Cereta's mother, wrote an impertinent letter to Max, telling him to keep his wedding present to Cereta and return the painting instead.

And it all got worse when that woman in New York, Maria Altmann was her name, when she took the Austrian government to court in 1999 over the Klimt painting, the portrait of Adele Bloch-Bauer; 135 million they said it was worth. Every time someone mentioned the Klimt, she and Max exchanged looks, what kind of looks, it was hard to say, she hoped it wasn't guilt that darkened Max's eyes and gave them a mauve shade, she hoped it wasn't fear in her own eyes because there was no reason to feel guilt, Max said, and no reason to be afraid. One time Zoltan was at their house, when Maria Altmann and the Austrian Klimt came up in conversation, and there was something like an electric current running between him and Max, the Liebermann question was in the air, but no one said anything. Laura never brought it up, she was discreet at least, but Cereta was implacable. Or her mother was, Zoltan's ex. The law suit was settled and Maria Altmann got the painting and sold it to a gallery in New York, which made everything worse. Cereta had millions dancing in her head, although Max said the Liebermann painting wasn't worth more than 500,000, and that's what Opa Auerperg likely paid for it, or the 1939 equivalent, or close to. You had to take the circumstances into consideration, the risk he ran, the rush in which he had to come up with the money.

It was so unfair, when you think that Max ignored Livia's impertinent letter and welcomed Cereta in '86, was it really sixteen years ago that she married that dowdy man? Max paid for their honeymoon and welcomed Cereta and her accountant husband, whose English was dreadful, and who wore baggy pants of poor quality and a grey jacket, unspeakably ugly. Max had to outfit him with decent clothes, or he would have been taken for a bum.

In spite of all that, Cereta brought up the subject of the Liebermann painting, very nonchalantly, in her accented English, accented but impeccably correct, grammatically, that is, and idiomatically, she was studying English and was going to teach high school in Hungary.

"I think we should talk about the Liebermann," she said. "Opa Auerperg said he bought it from my grandparents, but the truth is he acquired it after they were deported. He got the painting from Aunt Eva and gave her a pittance for it, but she had to take what she could get. It was blackmail."

Max cut in right away. "Excuse me, Cereta, but I must object to the term blackmail. Where does that come from? Did Zoltan's aunt call it blackmail?"

"I call it blackmail," Cereta said in her brash voice, or at least that's how it came across. Perhaps it was only her Hungarian accent.

"That's *your* interpretation, then," Max said politely.

He spoke softly, Nancy thought, but I could tell he was very, very angry. "And it's a *mis*interpretation," he said. "Zoltan will tell you that my father was scrupulously fair, and I am sure he paid a fair price for the painting. What exactly does anyone know about this business, and why wasn't the question raised when Opa Auerperg was still alive and could have answered it?"

Zoltan agreed with Max.

"You are absolutely right, Max," he said. "None of us knows the particulars. My aunt never mentioned an exact figure. She never said what your father paid for the painting, only that money changed hands, and your father was very good to us, both to me and to Livia. He treated us like family. I will always be grateful to him. I think we should give that Liebermann business a rest," he said, and Max nodded, but Cereta wasn't the kind to give it a rest.

"Gratitude is one thing," she said pertly, "and business is another."

Zoltan does what he can, Nancy thought, but he isn't like Max, he can't or won't control things. He has a soft side to him, something bendable and elastic, he meets you halfway, maybe it's his imagination, he can see your side, he can see everyone's side, he wants to talk things out, which is very

nice in a way, but it doesn't settle things, and it makes me so
unhappy, because the Liebermann painting is part of a whole,
it's integral to, it belongs, it would leave a huge hole in the
the Vienna apartment, it would leave a hole in my heart, I
don't think I could stand losing it. I don't know why I get
so attached — why do you get so attached to things, Zoltan
says — but it's not things, it's patterns, I can't see a beautiful
pattern destroyed, it hurts. Then, thank God, Cereta and her
accountant husband, Laszlo was his name (I wonder whether he
dresses any better now, but I think he has no sense of fashion),
they went back to Hungary, and I thought we had heard the
last of the Liebermann business, especially since it looked like
Jerry and Laura were getting married. They lived together for
two years, I didn't like it at all, it was embarrassing, although
people were kind enough to ignore it, nobody raised an eyebrow, a lot of young people started living together in the '80s,
but why not legitimize a relationship if you are serious about
it? No, not even Max could manage it. In retrospect, it was
just as well, but at that time I thought, things had reached a
certain point, and they should get married. It was the proper
thing to do. And it would have simplified matters a great deal,
the Liebermann would have stayed in the family, but then
Jerry — why do we allow such things to happen? Society has
become so permissive — I still can't bear the thought of Jerry,
I'm just glad he didn't while Max was alive.

When Zoltan wrote his tribute to Max, and read it out at the
Celebration of Life, I cried and cried, surely no one will ever say
anything about the Liebermann painting again, I thought. The
Auerpergs saved Zoltan's life after all, but Laura — Laura of all
people — said it was a maudlin story. If Zoltan wanted to set
the record straight, he should write a proper memoir, put down
exactly what Aunt Eva told him, and what the circumstances
were, and put in the names and dates and places, that would
be something of lasting value, a gift to her and Cereta, a piece
of family history, and Zoltan agreed with her and wrote the

memoir and had it printed, that was the worst of it. I was so distraught because it made Opa Auerperg look like a swindler, and when Zoltan saw how hurt I was, he kissed me and said, Nancy, I don't want you to be upset, I tell you what, I'll pulp all the copies, the whole print run, except for two copies, to leave to the children, because, you must admit, they have a right to closure, and that's what I wanted to give them, a definite narrative. Well, I don't know about that, I said, it's a narrative that makes Opa Auerperg look bad, or casts suspicion on him at any rate, and will only make Cereta dig in deeper and stir up the mud. I could have said a lot more, that it wasn't even the whole story, considering what Max had told me, on his deathbed practically, and it's not wise to stir up the mud, definitely not. But I stopped feeling so desolate after Zoltan said he would destroy the copies, and it was certainly the right thing to do if he loves me, but I kept my copy, because of the pattern, you know, I kept it together with his tribute to Max, it seemed to me that those two pieces needed to be twinned, to show the difference between gratitude and business, as Cereta said, it's one thing to be grateful and another to do business.

And then Cereta almost spoiled our Nile cruise. Or perhaps, I should say, she and Zoltan, I can't absolve him completely, because it was the two of them, they cooked up that scheme, and Laura going along, well, it must be said, unwillingly, no, it wasn't Laura's fault. It was one of Zoltan's theatrical stunts, one of his hoaxes. He told me only after we got to Cairo, and I wish he hadn't told me at all. God, it was high-risk! But it had all blown over by then, and that's why he told me, because, he said, everything was fine, but it's hard to believe that anyone can pull off a stunt like that. I had just begun to relax when Zoltan got the phone call from David Finley.

It was hard enough to relax in Cairo. After some tourists were ambushed, the security at the Hyatt was tighter than at the airport, you had to walk through metal detectors every time you entered the lobby, and there was really nowhere to shop except at the boutiques in the hotel complex, but the fashions were somehow — maybe people in Cairo like that style, the women there tended to be a little too, the makeup, I mean, especially around the eyes, it reminded me of the '60s, and you couldn't walk anywhere because you had to be afraid of twisting your ankle on the cracked sidewalks, and there was construction opposite the hotel, the men climbing up the scaffolding like monkeys, with their jellabiyas tucked into their belts, climbing up the ladders in sandals, can you believe it, no one wore construction boots or hard hats, and on the roof of the building next to the hotel, right across from our room, was a goat tethered to a peg, and all the sightseeing was spoiled because there were always crowds of kids and old men peddling postcards, and touching you, and looking so ragged, and speaking such horrible pidgin English, no, it was a mistake to go to Egypt. The Nile cruise was better because at least we were among ourselves, and the waiters and stewards kept their distance, and the tall men sailing the feluccas were really quite elegant, with their smooth black faces and flawless white teeth and wide smiles, but still, we should have just gone straight to Vienna, which is so much more civilized. In any case, I couldn't enjoy a thing with Laura and Cereta playing that farce, and David Finley getting mixed up in it as well. It turned out he had heard about the so-called mugging and gone to the hospital, it was lucky he'd seen Laura only once, at the party, in soft lighting, so he wasn't able to tell the difference, and a lot could be blamed on amnesia, Zoltan said, but I doubt Laura can get away with this newest twist, going out with David and whatnot, without telling him the whole story, not with David insisting that he saw her in Vienna. I'm positive it was her, he said. I suspect he ran into Cereta. What bad luck, I mean Vienna has two million inhabitants, so what are the odds they'd meet at the Dorotheum — but then he is an art historian, and so perhaps it wasn't so odd that he'd go to the Dorotheum and look at the paintings there. I just hope

Laura won't mention the Liebermann to him because he might take an interest and look into its provenance, complicate things, aren't they complicated enough already?

BUT, GOD, TIME FLIES, Nancy thought. It's already ten o'clock and she had an appointment with Stanley Summers at 10:30, and he was so particular about time, a lawyer's time is money, of course. Nancy understood. She drove up Wilshire, and took the elevator to the third floor. Andrea, Stanley's secretary (did she have to paint her nails blue with little silver stars? but that was probably a Latino thing), Andrea said hello and told her to go right in, Mr. Summers was expecting her, and Stanley in his impeccable Brooks Brothers suit, wool and cashmere blend, striped shirt, but the tie, Koala bears? Isn't that a little? What happened to the Harvard tie? Stanley came out from behind his desk, tall, deferent, came around and shook her hand, he had a bear squeeze handshake, it hurt but it also gave you a solid feeling, like his voice.

"What can I do for you, Nancy?" he said in his rich bass.

"I don't know where to start," she said, sinking into the Loewenstein chair. He should really go for something lighter, but maybe his office was intentionally stuffy, conventional goes with the image of a lawyer. "It's rather awkward, you know."

He waited politely for her to continue. His hand went up to his domed head and planed back the non-existent hair. His eyes glinted at her through the glasses (rimless Silhouettes), he was ready to hear what she had to say, she wished he'd say something encouraging, though, like "take your time, Nancy."

How to put it?

"It's about a painting, Max Liebermann's *Herbstwald*, a painting my father-in-law acquired in 1939 from a neighbour who was deported by the Nazis," she said.

"Acquired — you mean, bought?"

"Bought, yes, that is, money changed hands between him and Zoltan's aunt, but nobody knows how much, and now Cereta,

Zoltan's daughter, the one who lives in Hungary, alleges that my father-in-law took advantage of the situation and did not pay full value for the painting."

"Let me get this straight, Nancy. Zoltan's aunt was the owner of the painting? And your father-in-law bought it from her?"

"No, I didn't explain that properly. Sorry, Stanley. The painting belonged to Zoltan's parents, who were deported and died in a concentration camp. His aunt rescued Zoltan — he was an infant — and sold the painting to Leo, my father-in-law, because she needed money to get away. I suppose she acted on behalf of the owners, or on behalf of the heir — Zoltan, I mean."

"I'm not sure that sort of reasoning would stand up in a court of law, Nancy. The situation, if I understand it correctly, is this: Your father-in-law bought, for an unknown sum, the painting from a person claiming to represent the owners. Now, as to taking advantage of the situation — I do not see how anyone can make that claim if the purchase price is unknown. I can, however, see the heir — Zoltan — claiming that his aunt was not entitled to sell the painting, and that your father-in-law was therefore not the rightful owner."

"I can't imagine Zoltan saying any such thing."

"You'd be surprised what people say or do for money, Nancy. Where is the painting now, if I may ask?"

"In my apartment in Vienna. Max inherited it from his father. And let me assure you, Stanley, Zoltan would never question Max's ownership — not after what the Auerpergs did for him."

"What, exactly, are we talking about here, Nancy? Financial support? Can we quantify what the Auerpergs did for Zoltan? Is this something we can document?"

"Zoltan has put it all into his memoir if that's what you mean by 'document'."

"Let's be a little more precise, Nancy. A memoir — as in a diary? A manuscript? A printed book?"

"A printed book, well, Zoltan self-published it, but he destroyed all the copies because I was so upset — he destroyed them all, he said, except for two, to leave to his daughters."

Stanley raised an eyebrow. She knew what that peaked eyebrow meant, it reduced everything to an alleged thing.

"And I have kept one copy," she said doggedly, as doggedly as she could manage under Stanley's raised eyebrow, "which I can show you. In fact, I've brought it with me."

She opened her purse and brought out her copy of *The Rescue*.

"He says explicitly that Max and his father saved his life," she said. "I don't know whether that quantifies it. You can't put a dollar value on life. Unfortunately, he also says that his aunt — wait, let me find the place, I've marked it — expected more money for the painting than she got, but that she was in no position to negotiate. Here it is. He paid 'less than Eva had expected.'"

"I see. Let's look at two possible scenarios. One: Zoltan's aunt – she is deceased, I take it?" He waited for Nancy to nod yes, before he went on. "One: Zoltan's aunt had no legal title to the painting, in which case the transaction is null and void. Two: She was entitled to sell the painting and sold it under duress, which makes the transaction legally questionable. There are a number of precedents, I'm afraid — judgments reversing such transactions and returning objects of art to the original owners, or their heirs, as the case may be."

"I know. Cereta keeps citing cases. She is a very troublesome young woman, you know. The things she has put me through, just lately, I don't even know whether I should tell you, but I will because I think I should give you the whole picture, so you can advise me what to do."

He leaned forward. "I think I'd have to read the memoir and do some research into related cases, Nancy, if you want specific legal advice from me in this matter. Is that what you want — a legal opinion on whether Zoltan and/or his daughters have an actionable case against you?"

"Perhaps I should tell you about Cereta first."

"If you think it's relevant. I don't want to hurry you, Nancy, but you did book a thirty-minute consultation, and I have another meeting at eleven, so we may have to leave it at preliminaries for today. But do go ahead, and tell me about Cereta, if you think it's relevant."

"I wish you wouldn't hurry me, Stanley. I can't express myself clearly when I'm rushed. And now you're asking me, is it relevant? Well, how am I supposed to know? You are the lawyer, Stanley, not I. Let's just say, I was appalled when Zoltan first told me about the scheme. Cereta, you see — did I tell you, she is Laura's twin sister? Well, Laura always says she herself is the older sister, but that's only by ten minutes. When Zoltan split up with his wife, Cereta elected to stay with her mother, and they moved back to Hungary, don't ask me why anyone would move from Vienna to Hungary. I think the mother was a little, well I don't know, unbalanced, or homesick, or didn't want to learn German, or something like that. Anyway, Cereta studied English at the University of Pécs and afterwards taught high school in Hollókõ, some godforsaken place near the Rumanian border, Zoltan tells me. Some time ago, I can't tell you exactly when, there was an explosion at a local fertilizer factory there, which resulted in a toxic spill. It affected the water supply of several houses nearby, including the house in which Cereta and her mother lived. The factory owners hushed up the accident and offered them compensation. Cereta's mother refused to accept hush money. Both she and Cereta suffered from nausea and dizziness for a while. The complaint Cereta lodged with local authorities went nowhere, and no one helped them because the fertilizer company is the town's main employer. I'm telling you what Zoltan told me, Stanley, so I don't know whether it's true. Anyway, Stanley, I can tell you are getting impatient with me, but I'm keeping it as short as I can. Cereta's kidneys were affected, apparently. By last summer, her condition was acute. No one believed, or wanted to believe, her story. She could not get proper treatment, or not fast enough. That's when she contacted Zoltan."

Stanley looked at his watch. "Nancy, let's get to the point. How is this related to the question of the painting?"

"It's not, but you wanted me to tell you what I've done for Zoltan. He wanted to bring Cereta here, so she could receive proper treatment for the kidney problem. The question was who would pay for it? I wish he had asked me. I would have offered. But he came up with a crazy plan instead: Laura is fully covered for medical expenses, and so, the simplest thing, he said, was for Cereta to borrow her identity for a time."

"Nancy!" Stanley said, scandalized. "That is reckless, not to mention, illegal. I know Zoltan can be over-the-top, but I'm surprised he'd get involved in a scheme like that."

"If he had told me ahead of time, I would have discouraged him. But he only told me after it was over."

She had cried when he told her, on the cruise ship, standing at the rail of the upper deck and looking out into the sluggish water of the Nile, listening to the hollow noise of the ship's engines below. They sounded ominous, like a murmured threat. She cried, even though he said it had gone alright, and she should be able to see the funny side of it. He had his arm around her shoulder and said, Nancy, love, life is generally speaking flat. We need to put a few bumps in the road to keep the driver awake.

Stanley was frowning, but she braved his frown. "What can I say? Zoltan loves hoaxes."

"This isn't a hoax, Nancy. This is fraud. Besides, if his daughter was sick, I'm sure she could have gone to Budapest and gotten treatment there. Hungary isn't on the other side of the moon. They'll be joining the European Community within a year. Their hospitals must be up to international standards."

Nancy nodded helplessly. "I know. Maybe she just wanted to get away from her mother who is crazy."

"Leaving that question aside for the moment, how is all of this connected to the Liebermann painting?"

"Don't you see, Stanley? After I put up with that caper, Cereta can't possibly take me to court. I mean, she'd be afraid. I could report her after all."

Stanley compressed his lips. "Let's not add blackmail to the mixture, Nancy. Two wrongs don't make a right. So, you say, Laura was involved in this as well? I would have thought she was too level-headed to abet a criminal scheme."

"She didn't want to get involved, at least that's what she says. She was furious with Zoltan for setting it in motion, but she felt she couldn't let him down. Him or Cereta. She picked her sister up at the airport, took her to Santa Monica Place, and left her there. That was the extent of her involvement, Laura said. At first, the idea was that they'd do a straight exchange. Cereta comes here, and Laura goes to Hungary, but in the end, she chickened out. She didn't want to spend all that time with her mother, who is crazy, as I said, pathologically depressed, or bipolar, or something. So Laura went to the cabin — Zoltan has a cabin near Twentynine Palms, on a dirt road, I don't know why anyone would want to go there, it's absolutely out in nowhere. Laura went to the cabin and stayed out of sight for the duration."

"Nancy, this is deplorable. I don't know what to say." He looked at his watch again. "I wish you hadn't told me, and I'll do my best to forget the story. My advice — my personal advice, Nancy and I'm speaking as a friend, not as a lawyer — is to do nothing. Forget about the painting until Zoltan, or his daughter, take action, which, as you say, is unlikely in the circumstances. And in the meantime, try not to let it bother you."

That was all very well for Stanley to say, but it did bother her, and she hadn't even gotten to the point of telling Stanley what Max said to her, practically with his last breath. The poor man had carried the burden on his shoulders for years. But her thirty minutes with Stanley were up. She would have to tell him next time, she just wished Stanley wasn't so exacting. If she told him what Max said, she was afraid he'd say you can't rely on the testimony of a stroke victim, Nancy. Do you have anything in writing? Are you sure you understood Max correctly? Well, no, she wasn't sure, and there was nothing in writing, and perhaps it didn't affect the transaction as such if Stanley was right, and it had no legal force after all. But in any case, her time was up.

Stanley came around his desk and touched her shoulder solicitously, or pretended to be solicitous, because Nancy understood, really, he just wanted her to get up and leave. It was the end of the interview.

"If there is anything else I can do for you, Nancy, let Andrea know, and she'll book you another appointment. But as I see it, there is no reason to pursue the question of ownership of the painting at this point in time. I'd put it aside, Nancy," he said, ushering her into the waiting room, where a man in a corporate-style suit, possibly the same Brooks Brother suit Stanley was wearing, put away *The Economist* and took up his attaché case, smiling expectantly.

"Well, thanks, Stanley," she said, turning around to him in the doorway. "I'll think it over and get back to you perhaps another time."

THE TROUBLE WAS THAT, in spite of everything, Cereta had already taken action. It started when Zoltan gave her a copy of *The Rescue* while she was convalescing in the guest house. Why, why, why did he give it to her? Couldn't that have waited? When he said he was keeping two copies for his daughters, Nancy thought he meant for the distant future, a time too far off to worry about, but he gave one to Cereta before she went back to Europe, and so of course she chewed the cud: Leo Auerperg had taken advantage of the situation, the painting was worth a great deal more than he had paid, the Nagys were entitled to compensation. God, what would Cereta say if she knew the whole story, the story Max had kept to himself until the end? That young woman was a minx, and — a horrible thought occurred to Nancy — perhaps Max wasn't the only one who knew. Perhaps Livia was in the know as well and had told Cereta. It didn't bear thinking of, it would be awful because Livia was insane, she could tell when they were introduced in Vienna years ago, and Zoltan said she got worse over the years, that's why he had to get out of the marriage, he couldn't deal with it any longer. Livia had always spooked her. Those eyes, so dark and menacing, as if she wanted you dead already! She was one of those brooding women, you could never tell what went on in her head, Cereta on the other hand was easy to read. She just wanted money, that was the bottom line, and she wanted it *now* because Hungary was joining the European Union. Hungary would eventually catch up with the rest of the world, but that wasn't fast enough for Cereta. She was in a rush to have it all *right now*, was going to divorce her accountant husband and go to Vienna, apply for jobs, and make a brand new start. She needed money to make it all happen. That was the point of the email she fired off to Zoltan, making sure to cc. Nancy.

"Why don't we settle this business once and for all?" Zoltan said when she asked him if she should reply to Cereta? What could she possibly say?

"Let's take the painting to the Dorotheum for an appraisal," he said. "In fact, why don't you offer it for sale at auction with a high reserve, and see what buyers are actually willing to pay for it. Then we can talk."

And so Nancy told the concierge to give Cereta the keys to the apartment in Vienna and allow her to remove the Liebermann painting and have it offered at auction, and there was an empty space now where the painting had hung, it hurt her to think of it, the imbalance that empty space created in the décor of the room. She just hoped Zoltan was right, and the matter could be settled for good. Nancy was willing to pay if it came to that, but, God, this business of offering the Liebermann for sale, yet not really for sale, because she had no intention to part with it, the whole thing was another one of Zoltan's tricks that made her heart go out of sync.

I should have booked an hour with Stanley and told him the whole story, Nancy thought. It's such an awkward business, and why is Zoltan putting me through this, everything would be so easy if he proposed to me, it would be the right thing to do, but he says he's not the marrying kind. Really, that's what it all came down to: It wasn't a legal question. It was a question of love. And perhaps she should talk to Zoltan about what Max said, on his deathbed, devolving the burden on her. She couldn't quite forgive Max for that, but, no, she waved away that thought, so ungenerous of her. Dear Max.

She turned into Wadsworth, and, surprise! Zoltan's black Mini was parked at the curb. But he said he'd come by tomorrow, so why? She left her car in the driveway, too nervous to pilot it into the garage, where the giant garbage bins took up so much space, maybe she should leave them by the side of the house, but that was so untidy, if the colours at least, but black and blue, no.

She went through the garden gate and saw the champagne cooler on the table by the pool, with the top of a Dom Pérignon bottle peeking out, and a tray with caviar on ice, and toast, still wrapped in plastic. The door to the guest house was ajar, which made her think, with a pang, of Zoltan's charade, making her believe that Laura would move in. She thought of everything that could have gone wrong, like now David and Laura, which was sure to lead to complications, and Zoltan talking about bumps in the road to keep the driver awake. She liked her roads smooth, without bumps.

Zoltan appeared at the door of the guest house, spreading his arms wide, giving her a dazzling smile full of promise.

"Nancy-love!" he said, and bussed her on the cheek, deftly avoiding a lipstick smear.

"Zoltan," she said. "Why didn't you phone ahead and tell me you'd come?"

"It's a birthday surprise."

"But my birthday is tomorrow. You said you'd come to-morrow."

"I know, but then it wouldn't have been a surprise, right? Now, close your eyes, love. I have a birthday present for you."

She was a little afraid of Zoltan's surprises, but she closed her eyes obediently, and he took her hand, leading her to the guest house.

"Okay, open your eyes."

She blinked, staring into the semi-darkness of the shuttered room, and there, propped up on the daybed, inexplicably, unframed and obscurely blooming, was the Liebermann painting, no, surely not the Liebermann painting. A copy, a very good copy.

Relief washed over Nancy, because it was a surprise of the pleasant kind.

"Zoltan," she said, "you darling man. You had a copy made for me. And I must say..."

He didn't let her finish the sentence.

"It's the original," he said. He looked at her sideways, waiting for her reaction.

The unease was back. "I never know when you are joking," she said.

"The safe thing is to ask me." He gave her an encouraging squeeze. "Ask me, Nancy, and I'll tell you."

"Is it a joke?" she said.

"No, it's not," he said. "It's the real thing," and her heart started pounding. How could it be the real thing, he must be bluffing because Cereta had taken the Liebermann to the auction house, he had her completely confused.

Zoltan wrapped his arms around her. "I'll explain it in a minute, but first let's drink to your health, wealth, and every-thing your heart desires."

He uncorked the champagne and unwrapped the spread. They clinked glasses, and she sipped, but she didn't enjoy the

Dom Pérignon because she was afraid of what was to come.

"Don't look so worried, Nancy-love," he said, and kneaded her shoulder. "Maybe I should give you a massage first. You are shallow-breathing, love." He kissed her. "*Om-mani padme hum*," he chanted, *om*-ing into her mouth, *om*-ing into her hair. "Say *om*," he commanded.

Om she intoned obediently, and did feel a little better, but she was still afraid it was one of his, she didn't know what to call them, another of his…. "Really, Zoltan," she said, "I'm not up to another of your surprises, your exciting bumps in the road."

"Every hill and mountain shall be made low," he crooned, "and the rough places plain, says the psalmist, although it's the upticks that make life bearable. That's what I tell students when they come to me with their dyspeptic stories. You don't need to inhabit the plains of reality, I tell them. You are free to take flight and leave the earth behind. Be surreal, I tell them, be post-real. Have some fun, for crying out loud. Think Gaudi. Picasso. Koons. Hirst. People pay out millions for their conceits. Sheep in formaldehyde, steel-balloon bunnies, doodles on napkins."

She gave him a distracted look. What did Gaudi, Picasso, Koons, and Hirst have to do with the Liebermann?

"I'm not saying you should allow people to pull the wool over your eyes all the time," he said. "Just occasionally, Nancy-love, give yourself permission to step outside the boundaries of reality and believe in nonsense."

"Zoltan, please," she said, "don't go on like that. You are making me nervous."

"Free advice, Nancy," he said. "Take it. At the Hope Center I charged people two hundred dollars an hour for it."

The long preamble made her anxious. "Alright," she said weakly. "How did the Liebermann get here? Tell me the story."

"Once upon a time…" He saw her dismay at the fairy-tale beginning and changed course. "Okay, in the sixties, Leo complained about the cost of insuring the Liebermann painting. Have a copy made, I told him, and put the real thing into a bank vault. If it's a good fake, no one will catch on, and if you have a craving for the original, you can always go to the bank and admire the Liebermann there."

Zoltan paused and gave her a quizzical look. Was that the punchline? No. Zoltan went on.

"Leo thought about my suggestion. That's one way to go, he said — hang a copy on the wall and lock the original away. Or, I could give the original to you."

Zoltan stopped again, waiting for her reaction, but she didn't know what to say. If you put Leo's offer together with Max's last words, my God! Maybe Zoltan was telling her, in a roundabout way, that he knew the whole story. It would be such a relief if he did, and they could talk about all the ramifications. In the meantime, Zoltan was still waiting for her reaction.

"He actually offered me the Liebermann," he said, prompting her.

She hesitated. "Did he explain why?"

"We never got around to that because I didn't accept his offer. I would have loved to, of course, but it came at an awkward time. Livia and I were talking about a separation. I didn't want the painting to become marital property. She hated it. She called it conventional garbage, bourgeois shit. If we get a divorce, I said to Leo, Livia will insist on selling the Liebermann. In that case, he said, I'll keep it for the time being. I really would like the painting to stay in the family."

"He considered you family?" she said carefully.

"I don't think so. He wasn't a sentimental man. The fact that he supported me and Livia financially gave us no standing in the Auerperg clan. No, I don't think he considered me family. When he said he wanted the painting to stay 'in the family', he meant *my* family, the Wassermanns, the original owners. Perhaps he had qualms about the deal he made with Eva. I don't know. I didn't press the point. But he took my advice and commissioned a copy."

Then Zoltan doesn't know about the situation, Nancy thought, and it is up to me to bring it out. It isn't fair. Max should have told Zoltan. Or —and a horrible thought occurred to her. Or he didn't want Zoltan to know. Could Max have been that calculating? That covetous? No! Why did life present her with such ugly questions?

"I don't know at what point he substituted the copy for the real thing," Zoltan said. "Every time I visited him in the Herrengasse, I looked at the Liebermann and wondered: Was it the original or a copy? Could I even tell the difference? Well, when you and I got back from Cairo this summer, and after I drove you to the spa...." He looked at her admiringly. "Great results, by the way," he said. "You know, Nancy-love, you pretend you don't like hoaxes, but you do. You take a holiday from reality yourself once in a while. You disappear into a spa, you reappear, and ta-da! Forever forty."

"Zoltan!" she said, shocked. "You are not supposed to notice."

"Oh, I'm willing to suspend disbelief, Nancy. I'm willing not to notice. I'm only bringing it up to prove that you, too, love the unreal. You want to hear the rest of the story?"

"Go on," she said, resigning herself to the inevitable slippery slope of contingencies and unanswerable questions.

"Okay, so after I came home from driving you to the spa, I took down the Liebermann and inspected it. It was a copy. There was a card attached to the backing with the name of the painter, Hans Reichard, and the year 1969. Then I had a brilliant idea — if you don't mind me saying so myself — I checked the storage space off the entrance hall, the crawl space, you know, where Leo kept the overseas trunks and the antique photo equipment? I had an idea that he never moved the original to a bank vault, or Max would have known about it. There would have been a receipt among Leo's papers. I was right. I found the Liebermann at the very back, leaning against the wall, wrapped up in a surprisingly flimsy bit of paper and strips of cardboard. Very unlike Leo to treat the Liebermann like that, but maybe he wasn't up to the job. Maybe he had Thea take the painting down and wrap it for him. Naturally, he wanted to keep the exchange private, but that woman, Thea, was in Leo's confidence. He shared everything with her. In fact, if you ask me, he shared his bed with her — well, never mind. *Requiescat in pace.* May his soul rest in peace. "

"Thea was...?" Nancy started.

"Wait, love. Let me finish. I have no idea when Leo exchanged the paintings, or who helped him take down the original. Maybe it was Thea, maybe the man who made the copy, Hans Reichard. He died in 1971. I checked that. So we can't ask him, and more importantly, he can't tell. Anyway, I took off the card with Reichard's name and attached it to the original, in case there was a problem with customs. In fact, I declared it: Gift, estimated value, five hundred dollars. They didn't even ask me to unwrap it."

Then it was probably alright, Nancy thought. The congestion around her heart eased. And Stanley was of the opinion that Eva had no right to sell the painting in the first place so that the transaction between her and Leo had absolutely no force before the law. Zoltan was the legal heir and the owner of the painting, and if he wanted to make her a present of it, he could. She took a deep breath — yes, it was all above board and perfectly legal.

"So do I get the golden seal of approval?" Zoltan said.

"Let me have another look," she said, feeling the pull and subtle seduction of beauty. It was a lovely painting.

Zoltan followed her. "Go ahead, touch it," he said. "Touching is an important step in testing and comprehending reality."

She touched the Liebermann tenderly. She felt a great love rising up in her, a tremor of desire, the passion of the collector.

"But what am I going to do with it?" she said. "Where am

I going to hang it?"

"In the master bedroom," he said, "for your and my enjoy-ment. We won't tell anyone."

She could not take her eyes off the painting. She kept stroking the edges, feeling the charm of its beauty. She was a believer in the healing power of art.

"Above the bed?" she said.

"No, on the opposite wall so that we can see it when we wake up and have the feeling, for a moment, that we are back in Vienna."

"What a lovely idea," Nancy said. It filled her with happiness until she remembered that Cereta had taken the Liebermann to the auction house — the copy, that is. "But what about Cereta?" she said. "The people at the Dorotheum will tell her that the painting isn't genuine."

"That's the point. She — or rather, Livia, because I'm sure she's the driving force behind this campaign — will realize that the painting is of no great value, and that will be the end of the affair. You know, I feel sorry for Cereta. She's just a pawn in Livia's hands. But when she comes back to me with the in-formation about the Liebermann, I'll tell her to forget about it and go after the real money, the money my uncle deposited in Switzerland. I tried that route some years ago, but there was no way of getting at those numbered accounts. The situation is about to change, I understand. The Swiss banks will have to open their ledgers."

"You mean, there is a real chance of recovering your parents' money?" Nancy asked.

"Yes, and I may be a rich man one day. Think about it, Nancy: I might be able to afford you."

"What do you mean, 'afford me?'"

"Take you on fancy cruises and pay my own way."

"Oh," she said. "I thought afford to marry me."

"Nancy-love," he said, "you know I'm not the marrying kind."
But his mind was already elsewhere. He was looking across the

lawn to the driveway and waving to someone. David Finley.

"David! How are things?" Zoltan raised his voice to cover the distance. "Join us for a glass of champagne!"

"What are you celebrating?" David asked, coming into the yard.

"Do we need a reason to enjoy a bottle of Dom Pérignon?"

"I guess not," David said.

Zoltan poured him a glass. "We'll make it a toast to happiness," he said, raising his glass. He eyed David. "You are looking sceptical, David. You don't believe in happiness? Alright, let's toast to the illusion of happiness."

They clinked champagne flutes.

"Speaking of illusions," David said. "Did Nancy tell you? When I was in Vienna last week, I saw Laura. At least I thought it was Laura, but it couldn't have been. She was here in L.A. So it must have been an illusion."

"Well, maybe it was Laura's twin," Zoltan said.

Nancy's heart skipped a beat, but David grinned.

"Oh, really?" he said. "Another manifestation of the Great Systems Theory?"

Nancy laughed helplessly and snatched at Zoltan's hand to keep him from saying more.

"I swear it's the truth," Zoltan said. "As much as anyone can know the truth after Derrida."

"Didn't you tell me the other day that postmodernism is dead, and we are back to certainty?" David said.

"I'd love to follow up on that," Zoltan said, "but it will have to wait because I'm taking Nancy out for dinner. A pre-birthday dinner. And tomorrow, we'll have a birthday lunch. And the day after that, a post-birthday breakfast. It's an old Jewish custom, you know. Like the Twelve Days of Christmas."

"Or the Arabian Nights," David said, and the two men laughed uproariously.

Poor David. He was a good sport but clueless. Well, perhaps if he couldn't tell the difference between Laura and Cereta, he needn't be told.

"You'll excuse me, gentlemen, I have to get changed," Nancy said and escaped into the house. Upstairs, in the master bedroom, she closed her eyes and imagined the Liebermann on the wall instead of the Picasso that was there at present. She always had doubts about the colour scheme, in spite of the interior decorator's assurances. Let's face it, when it comes to personal taste, the advice of an interior decorator, even if he was as famous as Kelly Berman, was worth only so much. Colour scheme apart, the combination of glass and wood was too rough-hewn. It didn't go with the delicate material of the bedspread, and never mind Kelly saying that the juxtaposition was charming. She didn't get it, the glass, and wood thing. It was one of Picasso's sly jokes, Kelly said. And that was the problem. There were days when Nancy wasn't in the mood for sly jokes.

It will be heaven to wake up and see the Liebermann and pretend to be in Vienna, she thought. Just as well that she had run out of time and didn't tell Stanley everything. In the end, the question of ownership had nothing to do with the law. It concerned the family. In which case, she thought, I should talk to Zoltan about what Max told me because I need to tell someone. It's hard to live with ugly truths.

IV. CERETA

CERETA SURFACED FROM THE BLUE ocean of sleep at the sound of her alarm. It took her a moment to realize where she was and why she had set the alarm for this ungodly hour. She was in Nancy's apartment in Vienna. She had set the alarm because she had phone calls to make, to a neighbour in Hollókõ, and to Zoltan, who was time zones away in California.

She got out of bed, brushed her teeth, passed a washcloth over her face and hands, catlick-style, and decided against getting dressed. It was too early. A slice of sky was visible through the gap in the panels of the damask curtains. No rosy dawn. Drizzle, it looked like. She padded into the hall barefoot, picked up the Liebermann — the pseudo Liebermann, as it turned out — from where she had left it on the floor, leaning up against the wall, and brought it into the study.

She turned on the desk lamp, and in the yellow ring of light, saw the empty spot above the old desk, a square where the wallpaper had faded, the contour of a ghost painting. She took the Liebermann out of its protective wrapping and hung it in its old place.

The last of a series of bad decisions, she thought. I hope it's the last.

She sat down at the desk, crouching a little, looking up at the painting from below, the way she had seen it as a child sitting at the desk with Opa Auerperg, leafing through his books or listening to his stories.

That's how she remembered him: In her peripheral vision an old man, in her ear the creak of his chair when he leaned forward to point at the pictures in the book, in her nose a scent of patchouli. And all over a feeling of coming first, holding the # 1 spot in Opa Auerperg's heart, at least for that afternoon.

The chase after the painting, *anya's* campaign, had been going on for as long as she could remember. It had started with hints and innuendos. She remembered listening to the arguments that went on between *anya* and Zoltan, the angry voices coming from their bedroom when she and Laura were children.

He stole it, she said. Don't be ridiculous, Zoltan said. He has no right to it, she said. Even if he didn't pay full price, Zoltan said, he's made it up to you and me, many times over. He is a criminal! *anya* said. It was a soap opera recitativo, overheard by Laura and Cereta and stored up for later use in a skit, "The Case of the Stolen Painting." The skit was never performed because a new, real-life dialogue took over: Who will go with Zoltan to America, who will stay behind with *anya*?

Laura was the lucky one. She left, quit midway through the dramatic season, deserted their stage. No more plays after she was gone. There was no one who knew the secret lines, the blinks, the special looks, no one who understood the rules of their game. *Anya's* game was different, for adults only. She waited for Cereta to grow up, groomed her carefully for the role she had in mind for her as the lackey, the translator of her poems into action. *Anya* had a keen sense of occasion and how to spoil it. She rewrote "The Case of the Stolen Painting." The play opened on the day of Cereta's high-school graduation. Instead of kisses and congratulations, *anya* offered her daughter a poem, a monologue on Leo Auerperg, the thief, the criminal. She celebrated Cereta's graduation from university with another poem on the same theme. And Cereta's wedding was the signal, to launch a new production of the same old show.

"The Liebermann never belonged to Leo Auerperg," *anya* said, standing in the door of their shabby living room, watching

Cereta and Laszlo pack for their trip to America, paid for by Max — his wedding present to them.

"Ask Max for the Liebermann painting," *anya* said. The crusading spirit was in her eyes, a trumpet flourish in her voice.

"The family heirloom? The one Leo Auerperg finagled out of your aunt?" Laszlo said, raising his head and sniffing the air for money. He had picked up on "The Case" by then, and his accountant's mind was on the alert.

"Keep out of this," Cereta said to him.

"Yes, that's what I'm talking about," *anya* said ignoring Cereta's objection and answering Laszlo's question over her head. "The one Leo Auerperg got from Eva under false pretenses or worse."

"Worse? What are we talking about here?" Laszlo said.

Cereta glared at her mother. "*Anya*, can we talk about this another time? In private?"

Laszlo stuffed a pair of socks into the corner of his suitcase and straightened up.

"You want me to leave the room, Cereta?" he said. "Okay, fine. I'll wait in the kitchen. I'll leave the two of you to discuss this in private." He gave Cereta a tight smile before pulling the door shut behind him.

She turned to *anya*. "So what *are* you talking about?"

"Rape."

"Please, *anya*, try to make sense. You are saying Leo Auerperg raped Eva, and in return, she gave him a valuable painting?"

"He demanded sex *and* the painting before giving Eva the money she needed to get out of Vienna."

"How would you know?"

"I just know," she said with a breathless rush that made objections impossible.

"And you want me to confront Max with that magical knowledge of yours and demand the painting back?"

"I already did. I wrote to him. I told him to keep his wedding present and give us back the Liebermann."

"You didn't! *Atkozott*. That was a crappy thing to do. He pays for our trip, and you bring fantastic accusations against his father."

"I didn't accuse him or his father of anything. I simply asked Max to return the painting. I didn't need to explain it to him. He knows the transaction wasn't legal. Eva gave the painting to his father under duress. She needed the money. She had to get out of the country."

"And did Max answer your letter?"

"He wrote back and said he wasn't going to fight with me over the painting."

"You mean he is willing to give it to you?"

"Or compensate us for it. You go and tell him: I want that painting appraised by a professional."

Cereta felt a spasm of shame when she remembered the scene she had made on her mother's behalf. She faced Max with the dizzying confidence of someone fighting for a just cause, *anya's* cause. She argued with him, and after his death, with Nancy until she agreed to have the painting appraised and put up for auction to see what it would fetch. It wasn't *anya's* letters or Cereta's word power that persuaded Nancy to go along. You couldn't get a handle on that woman. She had such a smooth finish that words slid off her. Zoltan must have talked her into it, made her see some advantage in the procedure because Nancy wasn't as stupid as she pretended to be. That giddy laugh of hers, with the emphasis on breathing in, that wide-eyed look she gave you as if poised for immediate flight — those were poses, Cereta thought, to trick you into thinking she was a silly goose. When she agreed to have the painting appraised, she knew exactly what she was doing — making nice with Zoltan. She was after him, that much was clear, and she was ready to sacrifice the Liebermann if there was a chance of getting Zoltan in return.

Cereta tried to imagine her as Mrs. Nagy and Zoltan as her husband, the two of them in Nancy's immaculate house in Santa

Monica. Impossible. Perhaps Nancy would banish Zoltan to the cabana, restrict his messy habits to the backyard.

In any case, the painting wasn't valuable after all. The appraiser had warned her right away. "As you wish," he said in the flat voice reserved for difficult clients. "We'll list *Herbstwald* at 400,000 euros, pending authentication."

"I don't think it's an unreasonable price," she said. "I've done a little research." She saw his lips contract. He could barely disguise his disdain for lay opinions, but she continued. "Liebermann paintings have sold for considerably more than that, closer to one million euros in fact."

He looked at her over the top of his rimless glasses and nodded, as if he had expected to be drawn into foolish arguments.

"You realize of course that potential buyers will raise questions about the provenance," he said, shuffling the papers on his desk to indicate that it was pointless to continue their conversation. It was just too obvious. "We know that the artist sold the painting to Samuel Wassermann in nineteen thirty-two. That much is documented. But there is no record of a subsequent sale to Leo Auerperg. You say the transaction records were lost during the war…"

He paused discreetly, as if to say: You understand, don't you? Samuel Wassermann died in a concentration camp. How do we know Auerperg acquired the painting legally?

In the end, the question of provenance became moot. A more thorough examination of the painting revealed that it was a copy.

Cereta had a sense of relief, as if she had dismantled a booby trap that might have exploded and torn her to pieces. She took a deep breath and allowed herself a laugh. It was a little crazy to be laughing in Opa's study all by herself. Was *anya's* craziness contagious? If you are exposed to madness day after day, does some of it flake off on you, or was the madness in her blood, a genetic liability? Maybe it was a matter of entangled particles. That's what Zoltan called the phenomenon in one of his impromptu performances, playing the joker at dinner on their last night together in Irvine.

THEY HAD SPENT that last night in his apartment, surrounded by moving boxes, a cardboard stockade, as if they were under attack and needed protection, and perhaps they did, against the rays emanating from the dark mysterious core of *anya's* mind, which threatened their sanity.

Zoltan hadn't bothered to unpack in his new place. He uncrated only the essential furniture: a table, two chairs, a pullout sofa, a futon. The rest was stacked up against the walls. The fridge and the kitchen cupboards were empty. They were eating take-out food from paper plates, using plastic cutlery, drinking Chardonnay from Styrofoam cups. Zoltan seemed content to live a temporary life.

It was the evening before her departure, the end of the charade. She was once again Cereta, although Cereta reborn. For a month now she had tried to patch herself together, taking bits of Laura, bits of her early self before things started to go wrong, and bits plucked from her surroundings. She was waiting for something good to emerge, a new persona. She lay in the hospital bed in a cold sweat of thought, sticky with the effort of beginning a new life, more exhausted by the labour of starting over than by her illness. At last, under the benevolent eye of David, under the quirky direction of Zoltan, she began to take on a discernable shape, but the skin holding it together was still new, thin, and transparent, as if the old slavish Cereta could break through at any time. And now she was afraid of exactly that happening on her return to Hungary, on breathing in the old air, taking in the old sights and sounds. She was afraid *anya's* first word would pierce her skin, and leave her deflated, her delicate new persona collapsed in a wet heap of old habits.

Over Krispy Kreme doughnuts, she said to Zoltan: "I don't want to go back to Hungary. *Anya* is crazy, and she is driving me crazy, too." At the same time she thought: Why do I even bother telling him? He knows. That's why *he* left her and got a divorce. He and Laura got away. Me, I have no choice. I don't have the option of staying in California. It was childish to say, "I don't want to go back." It was wishful thinking. Maybe that's why Zoltan put on a song and dance routine, a little after-dinner entertainment to go with her fantasy of breaking out of *anya*'s prison of guilt, of never returning to her.

"A crazy person can do that to you — teleport qubits of madness across the room," Zoltan said, pulling his face into a lopsided smile. "Did you know that qubits can travel as far as a mile? It's a principle of quantum mechanics first explored by Charles Bennett in 1993."

He pushed away the plate with the crumbly remnants of his doughnut and leaned back in his chair with a sly grin, which suggested that qubits were something he had made up on the spot, that he expected applause. Although you could never tell whether or not Zoltan was joking. He was full of obscure bits of information that sounded fantastic and turned out to be true after all. She would have to google Charles Bennett to be sure. When she was a child, she always fell for Zoltan's jokes. He was a stand-up comedian in those days, but the number of his performances had tapered off, she noticed, as if he had run out of stage material. He is getting old, she thought. He is turning into a practical man. And this was good because she had business to get through after dinner, family business. She needed an answer to a question *anya* wouldn't answer.

She brought out the "Rape" poem and the English translation she had made for Laura.

"*Anya* gave me this poem for Laura, and I made a translation for her," she said. "Could you look it over? I don't know if I got it right." It was hard for her to figure out the elaborate system of pulleys and levers that made up *anya's* mind, but Zoltan had a blueprint, she knew.

She saw the alarm go on in his eyes when he read the title.

"'Rape III.' One of her crazy poems," he said.

"What do you think it means?"

He read it through and shrugged. "Your guess is as good as mine."

"No," she said. "You are ahead of me there. *Anya* told me the poem was a sequel. She wrote 'Rape I' and 'II' years ago. For you. To warn you, she said, but you refused to listen. You read her poems and ripped them up."

He sighed. "They were nonsense."

"And this one is nonsense, too?"

"Look," he said. "For some reason, Livia hated Leo Auerperg. She wrote the first poem after she came to Vienna in fifty-nine She said Leo was a rapist. I asked her: What do you mean? Is this a metaphor? It's a fact, she said. Do you have proof, I said. I have no letters or photos or bloody sheets, if that's what you mean, she said. I can't offer you material proof. I just know."

"You never told me about that," Cereta said. She had noticed it before. He didn't talk much about Livia, and Livia didn't talk much about him. They were protective of their life together, even after the divorce. They were secretive about their past. They spoke in code. Zoltan used jokes, *anya* used poetry. The effect was the same. It made the past unreadable for others.

But now, Cereta had been initiated into the subterranean story. There was a set-piece dialogue, she realized. It went like this:

A: Leo is a rapist.

B: Do you have proof?

A: I have no proof. I just know.

Cereta had played that scene with *anya*. Like Zoltan, she had asked the question and received the answer: "I just know." But what about the rest of the dialogue? Did *anya* tell Zoltan what she had told Cereta: "I read it in Eva's eyes?"

"I don't know why she hated Leo," he said. "Leo was very kind to us. He did everything he could to help us. Without him pulling strings, Livia wouldn't have gotten an exit visa. But she didn't consider that a favour. I never asked to come to Vienna, she said to me. I came because you begged me to come."

More subterranean stories. "You begged her to come?" Cereta said. "You put pressure on her?"

"Pressure? I was lonely, and I was naive. I thought everyone wanted to leave Hungary and make a better life for themselves in Vienna. But she said, no, it wasn't a good move for her."

"She was trying to make you feel guilty," Cereta said. "She does that to everyone."

"I don't know about making me feel guilty. She was unhappy. There were problems from day one. Leo and I went to pick her up at the train station. I expected — what did I expect? — smiles, embraces, gratitude. No, she gave us a frozen look and pulled away from Leo when he took her suitcase as if she was afraid of touching him accidentally. And in the car, on the way to Leo's apartment, she didn't say a word. Not a single word. I thought she was shy in Leo's company, didn't want to bring out her faulty German, but it wasn't a language problem." He paused. His mouth worked as if he was trying out descriptions of Livia's silence. "Like hiding from the enemy," he said at last. "Livia was holding her breath, waiting for Leo's next move, or planning her next move — that kind of silence."

The silence of the trenches. Cereta had experienced it as well. She understood what Zoltan was saying. They looked at each other like two survivors from a war, from an experience no outsider could understand: living with *anya*. Now that Zoltan had put it in words, Cereta, too, remembered the watchful, breathless silence *anya* kept in Opa Auerperg's presence. When they were invited to his apartment for *Kaffee und Kuchen*, Livia came along unwillingly, coaxed by Zoltan. She did not refuse the cup of coffee Thea served her, but she did not drink it. Cereta could see her lift the cup to her mouth, careful not to let her lips make contact with the rim, and set it down again, untouched. She saw *anya* poke her fork at the piece of cake on her plate, break it up, crumble it, and move it to the side without taking a bite. She took it all in, for later use in their pretend games, but *anya's* movements turned out to be too subtle for drama. How do you execute the almost imperceptible recoil when Leo put out his hand to her to say goodbye at the end of the afternoon?

"I know," she said to Zoltan. "I've seen that hostility many times. If she hates someone or something, it is irreversible. She has — how do you say it? — a one-track mind."

"You are right. You can't change her mind. She declined Leo's offer to stay at his apartment until she found work. No, thanks, she said in that brittle voice she brings out when she hates something. So where will you stay, Leo said. With Zoltan, she said. I was sharing an apartment with three other students at the time. Leo knew I couldn't put her up. There was no space. But you will have no privacy, he said to Livia. I don't mind sleeping on the floor, she said. I'll make my own privacy."

"That is one thing *anya* is very good at: making her own privacy, shutting everyone out. Except when it suits her to call them in, when she wants them to do her a service."

"Leo ended up paying for a furnished room, just for Livia,until she got a job. But she never did, had no intentions of getting a job, never applied for one. You know how she felt about German. She refused to speak German."

Yes, Cereta remembered. *Anya* left their apartment only when necessary, went shopping in one of the few supermarkets that had opened up in the city, so that she could pick what she wanted without talking to anyone. She didn't want visitors, went out reluctantly, sat mutely in the company of Zoltan's friends, preferred to stay home in her room and write poetry in her native language.

"So Leo kept on paying for her room until I graduated and got a job, and Livia agreed to marry me. To end her financial dependence on Leo, I suspect."

"I thought people married for love in those days," Cereta said.

"And divorced because they fell out of love?"

"Something like that."

The pause that opened up between them came with a freight train of thought moving from the question at hand to other questions better left unasked, questions about her own failed marriage, her breakup with Laszlo. She was grateful for Zoltan's silence. She wasn't ready to do a post-mortem on her relationship with Laszlo. One failed marriage at a time, she thought.

"It didn't take long for us to realize that we'd made a mistake," he said. "We should never have married. Livia knew it all along. I came to the same conclusion eventually."

"And having children was a mistake, too?" Cereta said.

"Why are you asking that question, Cereta? Because I haven't told you often enough that I love you? I know it's a problem I have. I'm working on it. I wanted children. I can't speak for Livia, but I don't think she regretted having children. In fact, she said you turned out to be more interesting than she thought. I had hopes that she might say the same thing about me one day, that I was more interesting than she thought at first, but she didn't change her mind about me."

"Or about Opa Auerperg?"

"Or about Leo. It was a fixed idea. She couldn't get it out of her system. I tried to reason with her. I told her: Write it out of your head, Livia. Paint it out, if that's your mode of operation. But you need to understand that it's a figment of your imagination. Leo is no criminal. He certainly is no rapist. She flicked me off. She insisted it wasn't her imagination...." Zoltan waved away the rest of the sentence. "Eventually, I gave up. She had no rational explanation."

That's what *anya* said to her as well, giving her a dark concentrated look, like an animal at feeding time: "It's not my imagination."

"She said she read it in Eva's eyes. Leo's crime, whatever it was."

"In Eva's eyes?" Zoltan said and gave her a searching look. "I think there was something like that in the second poem, 'Rape II.' She wrote it after Leo died and left us money. She wasn't going to touch Leo's money, she said. It was blood money. You can do what you want with your half, she said to me, but I don't want any part of it. He is a rapist. I saw it in his eyes." He looked at Cereta, with a helpless shrug of his shoulder. "She put that line into her poem: 'I saw it in his eyes.'"

"In Opa Auerperg's eyes?"

He nodded glumly. "She squandered her half of the legacy, went out and handed wads of Leo's money to beggars, left large bills at playgrounds and in the lobby of hospitals, dropped them into the Danube from the Donaubrücke, threw them over the wall into the exercise yard of Steinhof, an institution for the mentally ill — that one made the papers. They all reported on the 'prank.' The inmates had a ball, according to the papers. IT'S RAINING MONEY IN STEINHOF, one headline said. I showed the headline to Livia. She laughed. A terrible laugh, like an attack of whooping cough."

He looked up. His eyes were wet, as if he had been whipped by a gust of wind.

"That's when I knew I had to get out," he said. There was no comedic breath left in him. He had taken off the clown mask and showed her the pasty face of a man exhausted from years of cheering up his audience.

"That's why *I* want to get out too," Cereta said. "Because *anya* is crazy."

Everything Livia said was subject to multiple interpretations. Nothing was literal anymore. *Anya's* voice was stuck in the poetical register. She found her words by reading people's eyes.

"I agree. You should get away from her, move out, leave Hollókő. Why don't you go to Vienna?" he said, attempting a comeback smile, a happy ending to the story. "You could apply for an EU passport. You were born in Vienna. Your grandparents were Austrian citizens. That should be sufficient."

"Or I could just wait until Hungary becomes a member of the EU."

"But that won't happen for another year — a whole year out

of your life." He gave her another smile, rawer this time, as if he was letting her in on a secret. "But I guess that's an old man's take. At my age you can't afford to waste a year. You know you are running out of time."

"Okay," she said. "I'll find out what is involved in applying for Austrian citizenship or a work permit at any rate. I'll check the job postings on the web." She noticed he hadn't offered to sponsor her for American citizenship. Perhaps he had enough of the father-daughter confidential. Perhaps the process was too complicated and involved lawyers and money he did not have. In Hungary, she had always thought of Zoltan as a rich man, but that was an East European cliché: "All Americans are rich." She had to let go of that kind of thinking, get over her breathless admiration for the West. There were poor people here, too, like the drifters she had seen on the boardwalk, the people living in vans parked on side streets, people at the warped core of American life. Zoltan wasn't exactly poor, but he was too careless with money ever to be rich. Easy come, easy go. He really should stop sending money to *anya*, she thought, or send it to me instead. But she didn't have the nerve to bring up the subject at their farewell dinner.

"I'm glad Laura didn't go to Hungary," he said, "and the two of you had a chance to touch base."

"So I could give a more convincing performance as Laura?"

"No, I didn't think you needed cueing. I assumed playing Laura would come naturally."

"It wasn't easy. We've grown apart, you know."

"Interesting," he said. "Studies of identical twins have shown that, on the whole, genetics trump environment, but perhaps *anya* is a force of her own. She has a warping effect. That's why it's important for you to get out. I thought role-playing might help. Stepping away from your Self for a time and looking at your surroundings from the perspective of another person — I thought that would have a therapeutic effect. I wish I could do more for you, Cereta, but the next step in creating your own space is something you have to do on your own."

The exhaustion she had seen in his face earlier was gone now, replaced by the professional mask of Zoltan Nagy, therapist.

The next day, when they said goodbye at the airport, they were careful not to break the surface calm. She kept her voice level. No more childish cries of "I don't want to go back!" He gave a creditable performance as father, squeezing her shoulder in a tactile show of regret at seeing her go. It was as if they had scripted the farewell scene together and kept to their lines. No impromptu sighs or tears. No spontaneous breakouts, no mad anguish. She allowed herself only a twinge of regret at what might have been had she stayed on in America. A walk on the beach with David, perhaps. A moment when she would take his arm and tell him her name, and he would call her Cereta.

SITTING IN THE room that had been Opa Auerperg's study, in his chair, at his old desk, looking at the fake Liebermann, Cereta no longer worried about her solitary laugh. It wasn't mad. It was merely circumstantial. She had no one with whom to share her relief at being done with chasing after the painting. She wished David was with her. He was such a sensible man, the antidote to *anya,* unless she had overlooked something — his penchant for poetry perhaps? Could that cause trouble? His reluctance to answer the phone — there was something odd in that, but it was a minor foible. His failure to raise her pulse rate? That could prove lethal to a relationship in the long-run. Perhaps David was too pleasant, too sensible for her. Still, she shouldn't have run away when she saw him at the Dorotheum a week ago — unless the sighting was a mirage, a manifestation of her congenital or acquired madness, because David's appearance at the Dorotheum was inexplicable. A case of qubits being teleported? She shook that thought out of her head. I refuse to go crazy like my mother or turn into a joker like my father, she thought. But someone looking like David stopped in his tracks the moment he caught sight of her at the auction house. She saw a current of recognition move across his face, and when she turned around at the exit and looked back, she saw him coming after her. She should have stopped and talked to him. But she panicked because she couldn't think what to do next: Keep on playing Laura or confess to David? If it had been David.

A celebratory laugh was justified at any rate, even if she had no one with whom to share the good news: The hunt was over! No, a whole phase of her life was over, the phase when she felt caught in some preordained misery, thought she couldn't help it, like the coin-toss that decided who was going to go to America with Zoltan, or like the watermark on the wall of *anya*'s house, a permanent blot on her life. Now she knew: It was possible to escape and start over.

Sitting at the desk, looking up at the pseudo-Liebermann, she started the remedial process, allowed Opa Auerperg to slip back into the place he used to occupy in her heart. He was no longer the man who had tricked Eva into handing over a valuable painting, whose eyes spoke of rape. He was once again the splendid old man, her stand-in grandfather of whom she was impossibly proud, who looked down on her from his great height, shining on her the light of his benevolent eyes. She could allow herself once more to love Opa Auerperg.

The Liebermann folly, she promised herself, was the tail end of a series of bad decisions that began with her loyalty to *anya*, continued with the move to Hungary and her marriage to Laszlo, and culminated in the quixotic pursuit of a fake painting.

How did everything go so wrong? She thought Laszlo would provide the orderly life, the normalcy she craved, but instead of order, he gave her boredom and routine. She thought love would redeem her because she was in love with his lazy smile and his soulful eyes, with his fleshy lips and fluttering kisses. Who knows what he saw in her, but he didn't love her enough, and she moved back into her mother's madhouse. After that, the chemical spill was just another accident bound to happen in the natural progression of things, an event linked to her wrong choices like cause and effect, like sin and punishment, like destiny. She had to escape the noxious air of *anya*'s house, and to her surprise Zoltan understood. He gathered what was wrong from the few words she said to him on the phone, from a sigh perhaps, or from a certain inflection. His understanding wasn't paternal. It was the diagnosis of an experienced therapist. He knew: In America, away from Laszlo, away from *anya*, she could break through the clouds and see the lie of the land, make out the pattern of her life, and plan her escape route. A bridge was needed to get from one side to the other, an in-between space where she could try out versions of a new life, staging it, blocking out the steps. It was unfortunate that David showed up at the hospital and spoiled the scene, made her want to be herself prematurely.

It's me, she thought, not Laura, who should have gone to the cabin in the desert. Trying out a new life is the stuff of a monologue.

And now the time of acting was over. End of play. Beginning of new life. Thank God the Liebermann had turned out to be a fake. Cereta had a sense of redemption, of second chances. Zoltan was right: playing Laura had had a therapeutic effect, almost like a holiday, the strenuous kind that involved survival training or an expedition into the Amazon Basin. Now it was back to work. In fact, she had an actual job offer, to work as an event planner in Vienna. Would living in the West close the gap that had opened between her and Laura and make her more like her sister? Could she appropriate Laura's dry voice and make her spare, stripped-down, intellectual look her own? Perhaps it wasn't even a matter of "could she." That is how she would have turned out if she hadn't lived with *anya,* if she hadn't taken all those wrong turns, making decisions for all the wrong reasons. I opted to stay with *anya,* she thought. Why? To enjoy a moment of moral superiority over Zoltan and Laura. I moved to Hungary with *anya*. Why? Because I felt sorry for her and didn't want her to feel lonely. I found out too late: *Anya* is never lonely. She doesn't need people. She uses them. She gave me a pitying look when I said I would stay with her, but she accepted my sacrifice. And I married Laszlo, God knows why, in spite of the warning signs, because no better man had come along, or just to get away from *anya*. And the Liebermann painting, why was I chasing after it? It was *anya*'s pet project. She wanted the painting. Not because she liked it — the Liebermann was bourgeois shit in her opinion — but because she wanted to right a wrong. *Anya* was always on a crusade, always mobilizing. She needed a crew to man her galley.

But the crusade was over. The next step was to draw a solid line under that episode. Make sure it's over.

Cereta picked up the phone and called Mrs. Kertesz, their neighbour in Hollókő, a call that needed to be timed exactly, after Mrs. Kertesz had gotten out of bed and before she went off to work. *Anya* always made things more complicated than they had to be. This refusal of hers to have a phone in the house, or a television, or a washing machine wasn't a matter of money. It was because those things were "perversions of nature." *Anya* wanted a simple life, she said, but her life wasn't simple. It made her dependent on the goodwill of Mrs. Kertesz, who had to drop whatever she was doing, eating breakfast most likely, and go next door to fetch *anya* while Cereta was waiting on the phone.

"It's me, Cereta," she said when Mrs. Kertesz picked up. "Sorry to bother you again. Could you get my mother on the phone? I really appreciate it."

"No problem, girl. I'll get her for you. So how's it going?"

"So-so. Thanks."

She imagined Mrs. Kertesz putting the receiver down on the counter and walking to the door, groaning softly — she had a bad back and a habit of sighing whenever she straightened up or bent down. For a while, there was silence, then Cereta heard the muffled opening and closing of a door, some steps, a rustle, a perfunctory exchange of pleases and thankyou, her mother taking up the receiver.

"Cereta?" she said in her hollow what's–the-use-of-talking voice, as if she didn't trust the phone to convey her meaning, as if nothing of substance could ever be discussed using that unnatural medium.

"I got the appraisal," Cereta said. "It turns out the painting isn't an original. It's a copy."

"A copy? Are you saying that Leo Auerperg…"

"I'm saying it isn't worth fighting over, so listen: I'm letting this whole thing go, *anya*. Don't ask me to do anything else about the painting. That's the end of the Liebermann business as far as I'm concerned, you hear?" She braced herself for a defiant reply, but it didn't come.

"I see." *Anya's* voice was porous, momentarily weakened by defeat, but she recovered quickly. "Alright," she said, her voice filling with new purpose. "I'll go back to my poetry then."

Her rape poems. "If that's what you want to do. Just don't ask me to read them." No more poetic innuendos, Cereta thought and took a deep breath. "And another thing, *anya*. I have a job offer. I'll stay in Vienna."

Her mother didn't ask what kind of job, was it well-paid, was it permanent? She said: "Running away from me, are you?" And after a pause. "But you can't run away from yourself."

"I'm not," Cereta said. "That's the whole point of my staying in Vienna. I want to be myself."

She listened to her mother's breathing, a wordless incantation, or perhaps it was only static. No, she was still there, exhaling silent accusations.

"Goodbye, *anya*," she said and hung up.

It was goodbye to Hollókõ as well. She felt a generous sense of experimentation. Free to be herself — the words seemed too tawdry to describe the rush of desire she felt to start over and pass into the realm of the untried, to call on friends and amaze them with her transformation from a woman made in Hollókõ to a new and improved Cereta put together from original ingredients. Except that there was no one to call on in Vienna, no friend, no acquaintance on whom to practice her incarnation, no one who had known the old Cereta. She thought of the chance meeting with David at the Dorotheum. She'd like to start with him, let the truth come out, confess everything and meet him over again as herself. She had seen the flickering interest in David's eyes. She listened for an inner echo, an increased heartbeat responding to his name, a warming trend at the thought of her new self together with him, but it was hard to read the internal gauge with nothing to go on except the memory of a casual touch of hands, an American-style kiss on the cheek. She had no tactile memory of David's body. She had no idea how he felt up close, flesh against flesh. Would there be sparks when she met him again as Cereta? Would they reach the melting point and come to an elemental fusion? She had only words and looks to go on, and they were mixed up with Laura's name. Her name had intruded on every conversation with David. "Why don't we read Brecht, Laura?" "Would you like to come over for dinner, Laura?" It was hard to think of herself as Cereta meeting David when she had been on stage playing Laura, when Laura's name hung at the end of every sentence.

She opened her laptop and began typing an email: "Dear David, are you still in Vienna? Are you wondering about the woman you saw at the Dorotheum? You may have guessed it by now. Laura has an identical twin: me. My name is Cereta. The woman you visited in the hospital and with whom you read Brecht was me, impersonating Laura."

She wasn't sure how to go on. David was the only one at hand — if he was still in Vienna — the only one to appreciate her new self. But perhaps he wasn't the right man to start with. Her hand hovered over "cancel" and moved on to "save draft." I'll decide later, she thought. First, she needed to figure out, was David the right foil for her new self? He was pleasant. But what if mild pleasure was all he could give her? No, she thought, I want desire to run through my body and throb in my head. I haven't had enough passion in my life. And now that I'm starting anew, why settle for mild pleasure? I should run risks, find someone core-shaking. Perhaps David is too tame for me, too gentle, too bookish. I need someone wild to start life over with, someone to add momentum to the next phase of my life.

In the glow of the Viennese job offer, California was beginning to pale. The West Coast was no longer golden, and David moved to the periphery, a possibility if other things didn't work out.

She checked her watch. I'll make a decision later, after talking to Zoltan, she thought, and picked up the phone again.

V. ZOLTAN

IN NANCY'S BACKYARD, Zoltan looked at the caller ID. Cereta. He picked up the phone. "Yes" he said with an extra breath, charging his voice with the energy needed to get through a conversation he feared would be difficult.

"Zoltan," she said and paused as if she wanted to make sure she was talking to the right person. "About the painting…"

"How did the bidding go?" he said. He could hear the waver of bad conscience in his voice. Could she hear it too? Suddenly, he felt tired of playing games to keep everyone happy. It was a zero-sum equation. There was only so much happiness to go around. If you gave it to one person, you took it away from another.

"There was no bidding," Cereta said. "It turns out the painting is a copy. The people at the Dorotheum asked me to withdraw it from sale. If we want to go ahead, the painting will have to be relisted in their catalogue as a copy, in which case it won't fetch much. A few hundred dollars, perhaps."

She is keeping her temper under control, he thought. She doesn't sound angry. Maybe she doesn't care, and it's as I thought: Livia is behind the whole thing. Cereta only does what Livia tells her to do.

"It's a copy!" he said, trying to sound surprised. "Maybe that's what Eva meant when she told me she got less money from Leo than expected. Perhaps he had doubts about the authenticity of the painting as well."

"Could be."

She still didn't sound angry.

"I guess we'll never know," Zoltan said carefully.

There was a pause. Then she said: "I put the painting back where it was, above Opa Auerperg's desk. It makes no sense selling it in the circumstances."

He didn't know what to make of Cereta's calmness. He had expected fireworks, furious explosions.

"That's the bad news," she said. "The good news is that I got a job offer as an event organizer in Vienna."

"Congratulations," he said. So that's what took the sting out of the bad news. A job offer. "I'm sure you'll make a go of it. As far as the Liebermann is concerned, I agree with you. No sense in putting it on the market if it's a copy." He felt relief that his gamble had paid off. "To tell you the truth," he said. "I'm glad this whole business is over. It was a hassle."

"It may be over for you and me," she said. "But I don't know about *anya*. She won't let go. She has made it her mission to set the record straight, whatever the record is in her head."

"She'll want to carry on, I know." He dreaded talking to Livia about the painting. "I'll let you break the news to her," he said, knowing that it was a cowardly thing to do, but Livia wouldn't expect anything else from him. She knew he was a coward. She had told him so.

"I told her already," Cereta said. "I phoned her before I phoned you."

"And?"

"She said she'd go back to writing her poems."

She won't let it go, he thought.

"Say hello to David from me," Cereta said. "I'm thinking of writing him an email explaining...."

"Leave him alone, Cereta."

She laughed. It came over as a raw, threadbare sound. "Thanks for the advice, Zoltan. I'll take it into consideration, but from now on I'll make my own decisions."

"Has anyone ever kept you from making your own mistakes?" he said.

"No," she said. "Unfortunately not. You let me stay with *anya*. You should have taken me along to California."

"Oh, I don't know," he said. "You have a heroic streak. You needed to stay with *anya*. You had to prove something, no?"

"I cut off my nose to spite my face. Is that the correct idiom?"

"It is," he said. And you enjoyed your gesture of defiance and the unbelieving look on our faces, he thought. But he didn't say that aloud. "Alright then. Talk to you later."

She said goodbye, allowing him to escape. That's the feeling he had. She let him off the hook.

He tucked the phone into his back pocket and did a synopsis. Liebermann back above Leo's desk. Livia knows. More poems. Cereta has job offer. His need to recap a conversation was turning into a compulsion. I'll have to work on that, he thought. What's the purpose? To wind up. Wind up what? Cereta's call. But in a way Vienna was still on the line. A line stretching back to 1956, he thought, memories without an "end conversation" button.

He remembered Leo Auerperg picking him up at the refugee centre in Vienna and taking him home. Leo, he thought, with his lean commanding face, raw dents beside his nose when he took off his glasses and wiped them with a monogrammed handkerchief. His sharp appraising eyes took me in and held me fast.

Leo drove a Mercedes. So that's the type of car rich people own, I thought when he picked me up. And, as we drove into the city centre: so that's what a Western city looks like, with a lot of traffic, late-model cars, store windows lit up and displaying an abundance of goods, well-dressed shoppers. There was a look of prosperity everywhere. When we got to the Herrengasse, I thought: So that's where rich people live. And in Leo's apartment when I saw the Liebermann and recognized it from Eva's description: So that's the painting she sold to Leo.

What was I feeling at that moment, looking at a painting that used to belong to my parents? I must have felt something, but I didn't know what to call it. I could only store up what I saw for later analysis. I was already doing the compulsory recap, a synopsis of my impressions: Mercedes, city centre, Herrengasse, Liebermann painting.

Leo asked me about Eva. I told him she had died the day I fled Budapest. He didn't say much. Sorry to hear it. Some polite phrase like that. He didn't know she had cancer. His own wife had died of breast cancer, he said, but there was no empathy in his voice. He spoke coldly, as if he took only an academic interest in death. Then he asked me a series of precise, factual questions. Was I with Eva when she died? Was she conscious when I saw her last? Was she talking? I would have expected him to ask, Did she suffer a great deal? But then Eva hadn't talked about suffering either. She talked about dying, and that her death might come too soon, before my eighteenth birthday. She was ready to die, but she fretted about a public guardian taking control of my life if I was a minor at the time of her death. What's the law in Austria? I asked Leo. Do I need a guardian? I'm almost eighteen. My birthday is in May. I'll look into it, he said. I was worried in case the Communists returned to power and demanded the repatriation of minors. Not to worry, he said. By the time the diplomatic haggling is over, you'll no longer be a minor. Then he came back to Eva again. Was that the last thing we talked about, the business of the public guardian? She mentioned your name, I said. Did she ever tell you about the night when your mother was arrested? he asked. What was he after? Gratitude? Admiration? Eva told me about that night many times, I said, but not at the hospital, when she was dying. She was too weak to say more than a few words. She said your name. And Livia's. I think she was worried about her. That I would stop the support payments? he asked. I don't know, I said. That Livia would be lonely, maybe. And you? he said. Will you be lonely here without friends? I'll miss Livia, I said. I didn't know how to tell him that I was in love with her, that I needed her, but he seemed to understand. I'll see what I can do about bringing her to Vienna, he said. I asked her to come with me, I said, but she wanted to stay, to be part of the revolution, and she couldn't do any writing in Vienna, she said, surrounded by German sounds. She is a poet, you know. A poet? he said. Ah, yes. She sent me a poem once, in Hungarian. I had it translated by someone here at the university, but I'm afraid it was rather obscure. I wish I could ask her about its meaning.

Livia's bleak and impenetrable poems.

ZOLTAN POURED THE REST of the Dom Pérignon into his glass and watched a Coast Guard helicopter loop inland, hover noisily and sweep back out into the bay. In the pool house, he could see the Liebermann resting against the back of the sofa. So that's done, he thought. A birthday present for Nancy, to level the playing field, because he couldn't go on taking her money, letting her pay for things like the Nile cruise. He wasn't sure why Nancy spent money on him, what she wanted to buy: pleasure, company, love? He was perfectly willing to give them to her free of charge, but apparently they all involved places he couldn't afford. Nancy wanted her life gilded. She was happy only in a beautiful world made possible by the money she had inherited, the combined fortunes of the Goodwell and Auerperg families.

Poverty must be hard on lovers of beauty, he thought. Unless they are relentless minimalists like Livia, who needed no tokens of existence, believed in the pristine beauty of absence, the austere grandeur of nothing, the divine beauty of plain ugliness.

Lovers of conventional beauty who lacked the means of living in a beautiful world had to do the gilding in their heads. At least that's how it was, he thought, before Hollywood took on the task of reconfiguring life for the needy, providing them with sweet love, passionate sex, action, suspense, and laughter,

supplying whatever they needed, on screen, with the oral satisfaction of popcorn in a hushed room with the lights dimmed
to keep the real world at bay. All that was required now was
a mind receptive to fantasy. Nancy was receptive to fantasy,
luckily, and she had Zoltan, stagehand extraordinaire, upping
the reality quotient of her dreams, because sharing your dreams
with a sympathetic listener makes them more real.

The problem was that Nancy wanted more from him than a
casual sharing of dreams. She wanted a formal arrangement:
vows, rings, witnesses, signed registers, a change of name.
So far, Zoltan had balked at marriage. He didn't mean that
marriage was out of the question. He could be persuaded to
go ahead and indulge Nancy.But first he needed to clarify his
own feelings, and that's just what he couldn't do, not even if
he recapped their conversations, or pretended that the Nancy/
Zoltan relationship was a case he had taken on as a therapist,
not even if he applied the relevant factors into the object rela-
tions theory. Psychology failed to provide an answer to Zoltan's
most urgent question: Did he love Nancy?

Throughout his childhood, this deficiency — his lack of emotional intelligence — had gone undetected and undiagnosed. It
wasn't obvious like nail-biting, or annoying like a facial tick,
or boorish like reaching down to your crotch and rearranging
your balls. It was an inconspicuous problem. No one ever
pointed it out to Zoltan, no one questioned him about it. On
the contrary, people thought he was cool. They admired his
sang-froid, his nonchalance, his black humour.

He first became aware of his blind spot as a teenager. Experiences didn't register until someone played them back to him.
It wasn't a memory problem. He had no difficulty recalling
faces, names, dates, events, but things just stayed things. They
signified nothing. They didn't generate love or hate, didn't
console or frighten him. His experiences were like the tiles of
a Scrabble game. Someone had to assemble them for him and
turn them into words: love, hate, desire, aversion, fear. It was

as if he lacked the enzyme necessary to digest life, to boil it down to emotions. It wasn't a lack of empathy either. Other people's experiences weren't a problem. He understood very well what his patients felt, for example. And he envied them. They had in excess what he lacked. They felt their emotions keenly.

Zoltan needed someone like Livia, who could read a person's eyes. She was the only one who understood his predicament. He remained her patient for years, trusted her to explain the inexplicable to him. She was his analyst until she crossed the line from inspiration to madness.

Livia had noticed his blind spot at once and confronted him with his lack of understanding when they met at youth camp in the summer of '54 — youth camp, that great initiative of the Communist regime, ostensibly all about health and hygiene, an ingenious way of getting young people to interact and betray their non-regulation, non-Communist thoughts, or just a way to discipline their bodies until they were too exhausted to think. That's where he met Livia or rather found her again.

They had met before, when he was twelve and his aunt took him to visit the Orbans, Livia's foster family. Until Eva took him along, "spending an afternoon with the Orbans" was a phrase without content, words with a vague association, something women did privately, like buying underwear or having their hair dyed. The Orbans stayed on the periphery of Zoltan's awareness, although something in Eva's voice when she spoke of them, a glassy, skeletal quality caught his attention and suggested that there was a hidden meaning to those "afternoons with the Orbans." Eva visited them once a month. It was a charitable errand, Zoltan concluded, because she always took gifts, and perhaps he was a gift too the time she took him along as an afternoon companion for Livia, a playmate, someone on offer. He remembered feeling uneasy, or that's what Livia told him when they met again at camp. You were uneasy, she said, when you came to visit. Eva had had her first intimation of mortality, had been diagnosed with cancer and felt vulnerable. She was afraid of death, Livia said, and you sensed that. You thought she was lining you up with a foster family. You were afraid your aunt was going to leave you behind and you would have to stay with the Orbans.

That is how it began, Zoltan thought, with Livia telling him what he felt, and as soon as the words were out of her mouth, those feelings suddenly came up from his core, and he became conscious of them. Livia was a year younger than he. How could she be so wise? They had sneaked out of their tents at night and met by the edge of the water. A wind had blown up. The waves travelled across the dark water, white crested, fast moving as if they were carrying an urgent message. Or perhaps the urgency was inside Zoltan's head. He wasn't in the mood for reminiscences. He was there for the present, for Livia, her lips, her breasts, the nipples visible under her T-shirt, which was imprinted with the slogan *Mens sana in corpore sano,* A Healthy Mind In A Healthy Body. All he wanted was to feel her healthy body, thin with wiry strength. He had to satisfy the animal before he could ascend to the anima and drift into memories. She was there by the dock for the same thing, to slake her thirst, to cool the fever. She led him along the narrow, pebbled beach into the darkness of the pine forest. There was no coyness or pretense about her. She walked ahead purposefully, knowing exactly what she wanted, what he wanted, an expert in intimate knowledge even then, a genius at reading emotion.

When Livia told Zoltan about himself, about what he had felt that time when they first met at the Orbans, her description was quiet, systematic, intricately detailed, like her love-making later on. Don't you remember, she said and repeated to him what he said that afternoon at the Orbans, and what she herself said in reply, and what they did when they were alone, on the balcony. He asked her a lot of questions, she said, questions she too had asked her foster parents: Why was Eva visiting so often? Was she a friend, a relative? They compared the answers they got. They differed. A distant relative, Eva told Zoltan. A friend, the Orbans told Livia. Clearly one party was lying. You have no relatives, the Orbans told her. You were a foundling.

A foundling like Moses in the basket, hidden in the reeds, Livia said to Zoltan. She laughed when she said it. "Foundling" was such an old-fashioned word, he thought. It belonged in a holy book or a fairy tale, but it suited Livia, who seemed to him a mythical creature with the power of extrasensory perception.

"So who found you?" he asked.

"Eva. On the steps of a shuttered house pocked by grenades, a wartime ruin, where someone had left me bundled up in a blanket. Eva took me to the foster agency. Later, she came to visit the Orbans, out of a bad conscience."

"Why did she have a bad conscience?"

"Because she had not kept me herself."

Livia had a perfect ear for emotions. She needed to hear the tune only once to play it back without a single mistake, fingering all the right keys. That's why Eva kept visiting, Livia said. She felt guilty about giving me away. She felt guilty enough, Livia said, to find me a sponsor in Austria, a friend of hers, Leo Auerperg, who pays the Orbans a monthly stipend or salary or something. I am supposed to get a lump sum from him when I turn eighteen, she said, to set me up in life. The Orbans don't know what to make of that. They are so ignorant, so dull. That's why they treat me the way they do, she said. That's why they keep their distance from me because they know I'll be gone the day I turn eighteen and I won't look back. They'll never be my parents in any sense, I'm too different from them. They can't figure me out, so they keep their distance from me.

"Don't you resent that?" he asked.

"Resent what?" she said. "Being a foundling, you mean?"

"The whole thing."

She shrugged. "That's just how it is," she said.

"It doesn't bother you at all?"

"Oh well," she said. "Sometimes, when I'm in the dumps and need a lift, I write poetry. I look at the shape of the lines.

Long lines draw me out, short lines pull me back, until I'm in good shape again."

They were sitting on a rock under the pines that night at camp when she described the lines of her poetry. She was rocking back and forth in a kind of davening, a worshipping of poetry. "Long, short, long, shot. They balance out eventually," she said, and stopped the rocking motion. "Then I feel steady again. Sometimes, instead of writing poetry, I fantasize about Eva. I pretend she's my mother, and that she abandoned me because she wasn't married to the man who got her pregnant. I confront her, and she admits it. There's a thrill in a nicely managed pretend game, don't you think?"

"I don't play pretend games," he said. "I prefer reality."

"You want your real mother?"

He considered her question. "I don't know," he said. "She's dead. I have no memory of her. I can't tell whether I'd be happier with my own mother than with Eva."

"You don't understand anything, do you? You can't tell whether you're sad or happy. It's a mystery to you, right?"

He had to admit it was a mystery.

"I could tell right away that afternoon when Eva brought you along," Livia said. "I knew you were dumb as far as emotions are concerned."

He remembered being sent out of the room. Go and play with Livia, they said.

"They wanted to get rid of us so they could have their adult talk, about your aunt's cancer."

They played on the balcony. It was small, with a cast-iron railing that rattled when you touched it. Zoltan was afraid it would give and drop to the courtyard below, where a woman with a kerchief tightly wound around her head was beating a carpet, dust flying. Nah, Livia said and rattled it on purpose. You are scared, she said and laughed.

Livia had a kitten, which followed them out on the balcony, mewling for attention. She picked it up and held it over the balcony railing. It is scared, too, Livia said. The kitten clawed the air frantically and cried like a baby, and for a moment he thought she would drop the animal. He was frozen, fascinated by her cruelty, could not move even a finger to prevent the kitten from falling, but she didn't drop it. She put it down, finally, and quickly pulled back after she released her hold on it. The kitten flew out of her hands, a furry ball bouncing on the balcony floor and hiding behind a broom and dustpan leaning in the corner. Livia herself was bouncing rhythmically against the railing, rocking it, and the woman below stopped beating the carpet and looked up, giving Livia a warning glance. She stopped bouncing, slid down the railing and sat on her haunches, facing him. She was no longer interested in the kitten. She was watching him.

You had the hots for me even then, she told him that summer at camp, moving close to him in the pine forest, under the night sky. I opened my legs, she said, and you looked up my skirt. I did it on purpose to see what you would do. I made it easy for you to touch me, but you were a coward. I had to take your hand and make you do it, and I could read it in your eyes: You were afraid. You thought I would tell on you later on.

The moment she said it, Zoltan remembered his twelve-year-old self, and that same desire rose up in his crotch with teenage furor. He pawed at Livia there, in the pine forest, as her eyes turned the colour of night, and she didn't object. She talked dirty while they were doing it, describing what they were doing, in that deliberate way she had, a slow crescendo, giving him for the first time in his life instant feedback and instant understanding of what went on inside him.

I was hooked on Livia, Zoltan thought recalling that night, hooked on living in the moment with her help, and of course she knew it. She shrugged back into her T-shirt and pulled up her pants after their teenage lovemaking, looking at him with calculating eyes. He was afraid she would be as cruel to him as she had been to the kitten on the balcony.

Once he was able to name his deficiency, to use clinical terms — loss of neural synchronicity, alexithymia — it was a case of doctor heal thyself. Perhaps that's why he studied psychology in the first place, to learn how to manage his disease. Because there was no cure. He learned the necessary tricks to compensate for his shortcomings. He recapped his experiences. He wrote them down and read the words back to himself aloud, or he listened to himself telling his experiences to others. Absorbing the information in that way allowed him to identify his emotions, but those tricks didn't always work, and they didn't slake his desire for direct living.

After making love to Livia that time in the pine forest, he dutifully kissed her and said, "I love you." He didn't know whether he loved her, but he thought that was the default ending for such scenes, that's what he was supposed to say.

She turned away from his kiss. "No," she said, "you don't love me, Zoltan. You are just horny, that's all."

He knew she was right the moment she said it. She had read him correctly. But later I did come to love her, he thought, although he wasn't sure because she never said, "You love me, Zoltan, don't you know?" And Livia's feelings? He knew better than asking Livia, "Do you love me?" because that was something he could tell, the feelings of others. Livia, he realized, did not love him, couldn't love anyone, he suspected, because she knew too much about feelings and couldn't stop knowing. Such clarity was sure to deaden the heart, the part not connected with any tissue. "Soul" was perhaps a better name for it than "heart." It's bad if you know too much about your soul. Or too little.

THE CLOSEST THEY came to love was in 1956 during the chaotic days of the Revolution in Budapest. The chaos helped, he thought, the suspension of ordinary rules of engagement, the abandon that came from sensing danger, the joy of last things in the face of death, although the death that registered most on his mind wasn't caused by gunshots. Eva was in hospital during those October days. She was dying of cancer. Zoltan visited her every day, and every day he was trying to sort out his feelings. He got no help from Eva. They didn't talk much. She was pumped full of morphine. She wasn't lucid enough to sort out even her own feelings. Is this the end, she asked him once, or is there something else, something that comes after death? Should I be afraid? Imagine her asking him, a teenager, who knew nothing of death. But the question was urgent, and she had no one else to ask. She suffered from the loneliness which suspicion inflicts on people in a closed society, the constant fear that someone might betray them. Don't ask. Don't tell. Someone might report you. Zoltan was the only one she could trust. You are the only one I have, she said, and there is so much to tell you. About Leo Auerperg, she said. About him and me. But she didn't have the strength to go on and sank back into a morphine dream.

On a day in October, Zoltan came back from the hospital, made himself a makeshift dinner of sausage and boiled potatoes, and choked it down with water. Afterwards, he did his homework, huddling in the kitchen close to the hotplate, which still gave off a faint residue of warmth. He wasn't going to light the stove. He was trying to save on coals until it got really cold. There was no money for a luxury like coal. He decided to do his reading in bed, keeping warm under the duvet. He was gathering up his books when there was a knock on the door. It was too late for any of the neighbours to come by, and he hadn't heard any opening and shutting of doors in the corridor or steps going up and down the stairs. A weightless being, he thought, a ghost. When he opened the door, he saw Livia standing in the hall. In the dim light, in the mysterious gloom of the thirty-watt bulb, she looked like a maenad, a mythical madwoman. Her black hair was loose and wind-ruffled, streaming down over the shoulders. She pushed by Zoltan and closed the door behind her, leaning against it, as if to keep out the dark forces.

Have you heard, she said, breathless with excitement, her eyes unnaturally bright. Heard what? he said. The revolution, she said. Turn on the radio! But there was only classical music, sombre strains, an orchestral warning. Livia fiddled with the dial, moved through aural glitch, gave up, grabbed Zoltan's arms, and made him sit down on the only chair in the kitchen, standing before him as if to deliver a lecture.

"Listen," she said. "There was a demonstration in front of the radio building. Students, workers — we were all yelling slogans. 'Rákosi must go!'; 'Russians, go home!' Then somebody said, 'But what do you want?' We had a list of demands, but no one dared to speak up. They didn't know what to do next. So I said: 'I'll read the demands.'"

"You did?" he said, wondering at her courage. Wasn't she afraid of the secret police? "The AVH will come after you," he said.

"I don't care," she said, "but I didn't get to read it after all. A student climbed up on a table some people had dragged into the middle of the street and read out the demands. They want Imre Nagy to become president. Someone from the radio station promised to broadcast the demands, but he was lying. All that happened was Ernö Gerö going on the air and calling us traitors and enemies of the nation."

He took Livia's hand, as if he could read the pulse of his own feelings by touching her. He looked into her eyes, trying to discover: Was he in favour of the revolution?

"Can I stay the night, Zoltan?" she said, casting a covetous look past the door leading to Eva's bedroom, a room of delicious privacy. Livia had no private space at the Orbans. She had to share a bedroom with two other girls in their care. There was little private space anywhere and for anyone. All the flats in Zoltan's building were shared by more than one family, except Eva's, which was too small even for one family. It consisted of a galley kitchen, where Zoltan slept on a narrow couch, and Eva's room, closet-sized, cramped, but hers alone, a little square. It was where she read magazines after she came home from her factory job —Western magazines in English or German, contraband smuggled into the flat, hidden between the folds of *Szabad Nép,* the daily paper put out by the regime.

"Will Eva mind?" Livia said. "Where is she anyway?"

"She's in the hospital, dying of cancer."

"Then you'll let me stay," she said unmoved by what he said about Eva, not even bothering to say something conventional like, Oh, I'm sorry. Livia was innocent and hard-boiled, both. What did she — or he — know about death then?

"But what about your folks?" he said. "Won't they be worried if you don't show up?"

"Oh, fuck the Orbans," she said, her breath hot with revolutionary fire. "They are bourgeois pigs. They suck up to the regime. They'll be the first to denounce me to the AVH if they find out that I went to the demonstration. They are shitting their pants already. They found my poetry, you know. They got their dirty paws on my notebook and read it with their dirty eyes and ripped up the pages. 'If anyone reads this,' they said — understanding nothing, you know, absolutely nothing — 'if anyone reads this,' they said, 'the AVH will take you in for questioning, and us too.' That's what worries them, what the AVH will do to them, not what happens to me. So now they don't have to worry anymore. I'm not going back to those scumbags. I won't let anyone shut me up, not the AVH and not people like the Orbans who kiss their asses."

She dug her fingers into his arm, keeping him down on his chair. She wasn't through with her story, with the events of that evening. From the radio station we marched to Városliget, she said, to the Stalin monument. Someone put a steel cable around his neck and pulled him down. Only the boots are left standing, she said and laughed.

They slept in Eva's bed that night, sharing body heat, sleeping chastely, because Livia wasn't a teenaged minx that night. She was a seeker after the revolutionary truth. The next morning, she turned on the radio and listened to the news bulletins.

And when Zoltan returned in the evening from his visit to the hospital, she said: "I kept the radio on all day." She didn't ask him about Eva. She didn't ask. How is she? The revolution was all that mattered to her, but by that time Zoltan himself had seen it and understood that the wave was unstoppable.

It will sweep everything away, Livia said. Everything is going to change now that Imre Nagy is prime minister. That night she was still political and untouchable, but the next day they stayed in. She rewrote her poetry, as much of it as she could remember, on the blank back pages she ripped out of Zoltan's textbooks. She read her poems to him aloud — clashing, dissonant, chaotic cadences, polyrhythmic mayhem, which made his blood boil. Only then did the carnality return to Livia's eyes, and they made love to the background music of solemn radio announcements and the Soviet tanks rolling into the city. They made love in the rumpled blanket cave of his narrow couch in the kitchen. Because I don't want to do it in Eva's bed, he said, and Livia laughed wildly because she thought he was a fool or because she was high on sex and radio announcements, a convergence of lines that made her burst into animal joy.

Later that evening, a young man knocked on the door of the flat. He was going door to door, he said, looking for empty bottles. The Russians were firing at the freedom fighters, he said, and they needed bottles to fill with gasoline, to make Molotov cocktails to throw at the Russians.

Livia rummaged in the kitchen cabinets, and found the tomato paste Eva had made and bottled in the fall, enough to last them through the winter. But Livia poured the red paste down the sink and handed the young man the empty bottles to the hollow echo of gunshots.

The next morning, they went out into the pockmarked streets. You go to the hospital, Livia said, I'll get us some food. On the way. they saw bodies hanging from lampposts. Members of the secret police, someone said. They saw bodies stomped on, spat on, half-naked bodies hung upside down. Livia wanted to stop and look, but he wouldn't let go of her arm. He dragged her away. Let's get food, he said, and she turned away reluctantly and joined the queue at the butcher's. He walked on, stepping over corpses of Russian soldiers, their limbs awry, their uniforms clotted with blood. Someone had sprinkled their faces with chalk to avoid the spread of disease, but no one buried them. A man was crouching beside a burnt-out Russian tank, his bicycle leaning against the twisted steel. He was painting over the red star and the hammer and sickle, covering them with the Kossuth coat of arms, in red and white.

Zoltan spent the day at the hospital, sat on the edge of Eva's bed in the noisy ward. There was no chair for him to sit on. Every available space had been filled with cots to accommodate people wounded in the street battles. He sat on the edge of Eva's bed, holding her hand, waiting for her to die, measuring the length of her breaths. He was afraid she would ask him what he thought about her condition, and he would have to lie and say there was hope for recovery, would have to enter into the conspiracy of lies expected from bedside visitors, but she was wrapped up in her own aura of thoughts, in a morphine haze. All he was expected to do was listen to her rambling voice. He watched and listened, with no one to help him understand what he was feeling as he watched her, no one to tell him, was he sad, was he afraid when she opened her eyes. She came out of her dreamlike state and told him she was sorry, she had tried to hang on until he was eighteen, to stay alive until May, to save him from a court-appointed guardian, but she couldn't. She felt death coming on, and she couldn't stop it.

"There is so little time left to talk," she said. "Have I told you about Leo Auerperg?"

"Yes," he said. She had told him about the man who saved his life and who became Livia's sponsor. "I met him two years ago," he said, embarrassed that he had to remind her. "I met him when he was here on business."

Leo had been staying at the Hotel Gellért, the epitome of wealth and elegance, a suitable place for a distinguished visitor from the West.

Eva was supposed to meet him there and introduce him to Zoltan and Livia, but at the last moment, she backed out. I've got a killer headache, she said to Zoltan. Why don't the two of you go on your own? You can translate for Livia. It sounded like an excuse, but why wouldn't she want to see Leo Auerperg again, after all he had done for them? Zoltan at any rate wanted to meet him. It was a chance to show off his German — good for something after all. Eva had brought him up bilingual but there wasn't much opportunity in Budapest to use such a skill.

Zoltan met up with Livia in front of the Géllert. She stood with her shoulders hunched forward, engaged in a pissy argument with Mrs. Orban. When she saw him, she straightened up.

"Nobody invited *her*," she said and gave her foster mother a withering glance. "She just tagged along."

"I want to make sure you behave," Mrs. Orban said.

"You want to see what it's like to have coffee in a posh place."

"Hold your tongue," Mrs. Orban said and marched them to the entrance of the hotel. Her shoes creaked. They were brand new, Zoltan noticed.

She smoothed out her angry face and put on a syrupy smile for Leo, who was waiting for them in the Géllert Cafe. After the introductions, they sat stiffly around the table. They were unused to napkins and white tablecloths and gold-rimmed coffee cups, and intimidated by the waiters who bowed and scraped and treated them with the deference reserved for foreigners.

Livia kept her x-rays-eyes trained on Leo, and he regarded her with the same fixed look. They were inspecting each other. The conversation was halting. Livia took advantage of Leo's ignorance of the language and said in Hungarian: I don't like him. Mrs. Orban covered her mouth to stifle a gasp, alerting Leo that something was up.

"Do you speak German?" he asked Livia. "I understand you have been taking lessons."

"*Ja, ich spreche Deutsch. Wie geht es Ihnen?*" she said in a smirking parody of Lesson One in the manual the Orbans had pressed on her for the occasion.

Leo faced her solemnly and continued the textbook conversation, politely asking after her health in turn: "*Es geht mir gut. Und Dir?*"

No doubt, he expected her to go on in the approved fashion and tell him that she was well, but Livia bucked the standard dialogue and denied her well-being:

"*Nicht gut*," she said.

He asked why she was not well.

She deliberated, then shrugged. "*Ich kann es nicht sagen auf Deutsch*," she said. She didn't have the words to say it in German, but she smiled and continued in Hungarian. "Because I don't like living with the Orbans."

Mrs. Orban bit her lip and looked down on her lap. Leo looked at Zoltan, waiting for a translation.

He stumbled over the words and caught himself. "She would prefer to have real parents to live with," he said.

Leo nodded. He stretched out his hand as if to pat Livia, but she flinched, and he retracted his hand. Mrs. Orban saw that the crisis had somehow passed and took a sip of her coffee.

"*Sehr gut*," she said with a gurgling rush and a burst of social laughter, exhausting her German. It wasn't clear who or what was "very good" — the quality of the coffee or the way Zoltan had defused the situation.

When they came out of the hotel, Mrs. Orban wanted to know what he had said to Leo, and he told her. Livia was furious. You call that translating? she said.

The elegant hotel and the moneyed visitor awed Zoltan. His admiration, kept in check by Livia's sarcastic smile while they were at the hotel, broke out and bubbled over when he came home. He looks like a tycoon! he said to Eva. She gave him a weary look. Tycoon? she said. He's a wheeler-dealer with aristocratic manners. Her voice was disparaging, full of submerged meaning. You don't like Leo Auerperg? he said, surprised. What do you know about likes or dislikes? she said. She did not often speak sharply, and he wondered what he had said that made her angry, but later he thought the rebuke was deserved. Really, what did he know about likes and dislikes? He thought he was in love with Livia, but she only shook her head and laughed. No, you want me, she said. That's different. He knew that already. His body told him so. He could read his body even if he could not read his soul.

So what did you and Leo Auerperg talk about? Eva asked him. He didn't tell her about Livia's pert remark and Mrs. Orban's embarrassment. He made it a good-news report. But lies have no staying power. That's why he had to remind Eva now, at the hospital:

"I met Leo Auerperg at the Géllert. You stayed home because you had a headache, remember?"

"A headache," she murmured, lost in thought, slipping away into the past.

They sat in silence. She hadn't noticed the commotion in the ward, was deaf to the intrusion of nearby voices. She didn't ask Zoltan about the moans of the wounded, the crying women and children, the clattering bedpans and IV lines, the confused rush, the exhaustion of the nurses and doctors and interns. She didn't notice, as he did, their heavy tread, the way they dragged their heels and allowed their shoulders to slump or alternatively hugged themselves for warmth, all those gestures of hopelessness. She didn't ask what was going on, and he didn't tell her about the events outside, the revolution, because he thought the time she had left was too short for politics. The future could be of no interest to Eva now, he thought. The cancer was spreading through her veins, a rich oxygenated red, as he pictured it, discolouring her internal organs, and morphine lay on her brain like a grey apron of lead.

IN THE EVENING he went home, storing away what he had seen at the hospital without saying anything to Livia. There was no room in Eva's mind for the future, and there was no room in Livia's mind for anything but the future. She had no place for words like "cancer" in her narrative. She had room only for revolutionary words. That's all she talked about as they lay in bed side-by-side. *Szabadsag*, freedom, was the last thing he heard as he dropped off and fell asleep with her mouth against his cheek, still forming revolutionary words. Sometime during the night, but it must have been early in the morning, Livia turned up the volume of the radio, which had accompanied their sleep like a lullaby, a low murmur, and Imre Nagy's voice came on and announced a second Russian invasion, the end game to topple the new government. Our troops are engaged in battle, Imre Nagy said.

They got dressed. I have to go to the hospital, he said. Yes, go, go, Livia said impatiently, refusing to waste words on Eva's unrevolutionary condition. What if they attack the hospital, he said, but Livia waved him off. They won't. There are international conventions, she said briskly. I know, he said, but what if they ignore those conventions? They won't, she said again, her voice brassy now and impatient with the fate of individuals.

"Can I borrow Eva's boots?" she said. "I need shoes with decent soles. Mine have had it. They are shredded. I stepped on glass yesterday, and the shards came right through. Can I borrow her coat, too?"

"Stay in, Livia," he begged her. "You'll get hurt." But she only bared her teeth at him.

"I'll go out as soon as it's daylight," she said.

It was still winter-dark when he stumbled downstairs to the sound of peepholes opening and closing, wary neighbours keeping an eye on him. Everyone else here is staying indoors, he thought, sitting out the revolution. At the corner, someone hawked black market goods, or so he thought, but he was mistaken. The man wasn't hawking tins of corned beef, as he had expected. Boys, who wants a machine gun? he said, touting his wares to passersby. Zoltan shook his head and rushed on. Livia would have taken the man up on his offer, he thought, but she had already told him: You are no fighter, you are a coward, Zoltan. So he knew how he felt about guns, and he averted his eyes from the young men passing him on the street, ammunition belts slung around their necks and carrying Kalashnikovs. The sun came up, as he passed the Horizon Bookstore on Lenin Boulevard. The large plate glass window was shattered. Torn books lay in a heap out front. People were going through the blackened pile. He was tempted to join them, but he thought of Eva and pushed on, climbing over the rubble on the sidewalk, skirting people who lined up for food. They were going through their everyday routine in a calm way that struck him as bizarre. They stopped to gossip, queued for pretzels at a cart, inspected the handbags a woman had laid out on a piece of cardboard.

When he got to the ward, he saw that someone else was occupying Eva's bed. She has died during the night, he thought, but a nurse pointed him to the hall. They had pushed Eva's bed out into the corridor, as if she was beyond human help and taking up space needed for more hopeful cases.

"Auntie," he said, leaning over her.

Her eyes fluttered open. "Did you bring Livia?" she said.

He was confused. He hadn't told her that Livia was staying with him at the flat. How did she know?

"You wanted me to bring Livia?" he said, irrationally afraid of pronouncing her name and giving away the fact that they were lovers. Was it right to make love at a time of death?

Eva rallied. "I no longer make sense, do I?" she said with surprising energy. "My mind is wandering." She held his hand

and apologized for her wandering, misaligned words. "I can't think straight with all the medication they pump into me, you know. I meant to ask you to look up the Orbans. Tell them I won't be seeing them at Christmas, I don't think so. Ask them how Livia is doing in school." She closed her mouth and looked thoughtful, paying the Orbans a visit in her mind. "I worry about Livia," she said. "She's such a precocious girl. She sees and understands more than is good for her, more than she can handle at her age."

Zoltan pressed Eva's hand. In his head, he tried out comforting words: I'll bring Livia with me tomorrow. She is at our flat. She has run away from home. But those weren't comforting words.

"I could ask Livia to visit you," he said, but he had missed the moment of lucidity. Eva was rambling again.

"Have I told you about Leo Auerperg?" she said, asking him the same question she had asked him the day before.

"Yes, you have told me about him."

She shifted uncomfortably, dribbled haphazard words, sentence fragments.

"You have told me many times," he said, stroking her hand, massaging her fingers. He didn't know how to comfort her.

"I haven't told you everything," she said, her eyes suddenly focused and clear. She paused for breath. "I've pushed it down for too long," she said.

"Pushed down what?" He tried to make it easier for her, to prompt her, to coax out of her whatever it was she wanted to tell him.

"Am I making sense?" she said. "I can no longer tell. The words come and go." There was another long pause, in which her breathing changed, became noisier. "Have I told you about Leo Auerperg?" she began again, as if there was no other way to get to the core, as if the question was a gateway to everything else.

"You did," he said patiently. "He is Livia's sponsor, I know."

"Her sponsor?" she said. "Yes. The other thing I wanted to

tell you, no, I mean Livia. Is she here? I need to tell her." She closed her eyes, exhausted by the effort to concentrate. "It was wrong. I did it because I was desperate. I needed someone. And then I found I was…" Her hand reached out, and he took it, but he wasn't sure the pressure of her fingertips was for him. It could have been for someone else whose name was on her lips, Leo or Livia, a name starting with an "L." The word was too soft to be audible. It came out as an elongated sigh, Leo or Livia. What will I do when I come here tomorrow, and Eva's bed is no longer in the corridor, he thought, but he didn't have to wait for tomorrow. She tried to sit up, desperately gripping his arm, then released him and sank back. There was a shift in dimensions, he realized, the distance between them had become wider. He flagged down a nurse. Strange, he thought, how easy it is to recognize the arrival of death, even if you've never seen a dying person before, like a shadow shutting out the light of life.

The nurse may have said something consoling to him when she pulled the sheet over Eva's face, but he didn't hear her. Coldness crept into his head, barred his hearing and his vision, putting him into a frozen daze. He could barely follow the directions the nurse was giving him. Go to Office 201, she said, they will look after you. There, in a room with green walls and a counter that ran the length of the room, a woman looked up from her desk and without rising from her chair asked what he wanted. She reminded him of the secretary at school, same dirty blonde hair, same dark blue smock, same disinterested expression, neither helpful nor peevish, closed in on herself, an expression saying that he was unimportant, there was nothing important going on in this room, just the boring routine that had to be gotten through every day. She got up with a sigh when he told her why he was there. She stepped to the counter, reached down and brought out a folder and several forms for him to fill out. She wrote "Eva Nagy" on the outside of the file with an old-fashioned flourish and handed him the forms. Sit down over there, she said, pointing to the wooden chairs along the wall, and fill out the papers. He sat down obediently, but all he could see were the scuff marks on the linoleum floor by his feet, and the places on the chair legs where the varnish had come off. He tried to read the papers in his hand. He went as far as looking at the first few lines, the name and address lines, but he didn't think he could hold on to a pen or shape letters, and so he stood up again. He expected to be held back, told that he couldn't leave without filling out the forms, but the woman was on the phone now, had turned away from him, was paying no more attention to him. He walked out of the room, unhindered. Once outside, he stood on the steps of the hospital, the forms still in his hand, without a clue to his feelings. I am sad, surely, he thought, looking down at the documents which he would have to fill out eventually and sign and return. And then? He thought of other government offices he would be obliged to visit, the lineups, the sullen faces of clerks. Would they come after him, or did he have to apply for a public guardian? He was a few months short of turning eighteen. But perhaps no one would worry about that now, he thought, suddenly aware of a beehive murmur around him, the crowd in the street, dense like after a soccer match.

The winter sun had come out, and people were carrying their coats folded over their arms. No, they were carrying more than their coats, they looked like travellers. Was everyone on the move, on some sort of pilgrimage? From the steps of the hospital, he looked down on the crowd clogging the pavement, a steady stream, street-wide. He saw a familiar face bobbing up, Andras, and was reminded that there were schools and classes somewhere with teachers and classmates like Andras, who hopped off his bike, stood at the bottom of the stairs and shouted:

"Hey! Zoltan! Are you going?"

"Going where?"

"To Austria, idiot." He saw Zoltan's blank face. "What's the matter?" he said. "Are you brain-dead?"

"My aunt just died," he said.

"Oh," Andras said. "Well, sorry. But even so. The borders are open, nobody knows for how long. We are going. My uncle thinks he can organize a van."

Zoltan woke up to the possibilities of life after Eva's death. "I'll come along," he said, starting to breathe freely again.

"I don't know if there's room for one more," Andras said. "I don't know if my uncle can take you. You can't bring any luggage, that's for sure."

"I won't bring any luggage," Zoltan said. Why would he? He wanted to leave this life behind. No, wanted to leave death behind.

"Come by before noon, then," Andras said.

"What about Livia? I can't go without her." He couldn't possibly.

"Livia? That morose little shit? You screwing her or what?"

"She's at my place," he said.

Andras shrugged. "It's up to you. But my uncle won't take two people, I can tell you that much."

Andras ducked back into the stream, and Zoltan, too, forded the human river flavoured with smoke and sweat and dirty underwear, shook off hands trying to push him, hands with black-rimmed fingernails and orange nicotine stains. He held his own in the jostling crowd and was cast up finally at his apartment building.

He ran upstairs two steps at a time, jangled the keys impatiently, pushed open the door, suddenly afraid that Livia would no longer be there, had left without him, but she was there, sitting at the table, writing, giving him a triumphant look, as if she had just found the perfect word to describe the day.

"The borders are open," he said to her. "Let's go to Austria."

"I'm not leaving," she said.

"Why not?" he said lamely. I should be kissing her, he

thought. I should take her into my arms and overwhelm her, but he looked into her pale face and knew he could not change her mind with words or embraces.

"Because I don't speak German," she said.

"So what? You'll learn."

"No, you don't understand, Zoltan," she said. "It would interfere with my poetry. I couldn't write in German."

"You don't have to. You can keep writing poetry in Hungarian."

"I couldn't with everyone around me speaking German. You can't have two kinds of rhythms in your head. Besides, why would I want to leave? This is where it's happening. Right here. Right now. The revolution."

They looked at each other.

"Do I need to explain everything to you, Zoltan?" she said. She used body language on him now, gestures and stares, flapping hands, a skittering sideways step. "Don't you understand anything?"

No, he was helpless. He couldn't make head nor tail of his emotions. He moved closer, looking hard into Livia's face, looking for clues in the landscape of her flesh, trying to get at the quintessence of her thoughts, seeing at last how it was. Livia had taken him on as a project, but now she had better things to do than telling him what he felt. She had a new project: the revolution.

"You are in love with the revolution," he said.

"So you got that straight at last. I just hope Eva will let me stay with her."

"Eva died this morning."

"I see," she said. "So that's why you are leaving."

"Come with me," he said, hopeless, because he knew he had no words to persuade Livia, and nothing to offer her in compensation for her services as a translator of his emotions. She didn't even answer his plea.

"Start packing," she said. "You can take the food that's

here and leave me your money. You don't need forints where you're going."

"And what will you do? Someone will requisition the apartment now that Eva is dead. They'll throw you out," he said as he put on a triple layer of clothes because Andras had told him to bring no luggage, and he wasn't even sure that his uncle would take him along with or without luggage. He might have to make it on his own. And Livia would have to make it on her own, too. "They'll throw you out," he said again in the vain hope that she might change her mind and go with him if she had no place to stay in Budapest.

She shrugged. "Nobody gives a fuck about requisitions and allocations right now. The old guard is on the run. When the revolution is over, we'll see who gets to live where. I won't go back to the Orbans."

When he saw that she was determined to stay, he asked her for one of her poems. "As a souvenir," he said. He meant as a talisman, something to hold on to since he couldn't hold on to Livia.

"You are a sentimental shit," she said, but she gave him a poem. "Don't read it now," she said. "There is no time."

He threw his arms around her and tried to kiss her, but she turned away. He thought he would remember that moment forever, that last awkward embrace, but when he arrived at Andras' place and saw an old man in a cracked leather coat get into the driver's seat of a van, he forgot everything. He started running, slipping on the pavement, kicking up slush and yelling Andras' name. His shout stopped the movement of the old man's arm, displaced all thoughts of Livia, and even wiped his aunt's face from memory. The only thing that stayed in his brain was his chance to get away. As he passed the front of the van, he saw Andras' mother sitting in the passenger's seat frowning down at him, and Andras waving to him from the back, shouting, Get in. The old man wrinkled his brow and looked at Zoltan darkly, but he did not prevent him from climbing into the back and hunkering down with Andras and his sister. They sat wedged between boxes and kitchen stuff, holding on for balance to each other and to battered suitcases as the van moved out into the street. Zoltan reached into his pocket and pulled out Livia's poem. Three lines.

"*Freedom is everything.*

A revolution.

Coming into my own."

"What have you got there?" Andras said. "A love letter?"

He snatched at the paper, but Zoltan elbowed him away.

"An address," he said. It was true. On the reverse, he had written down Leo Auerperg's address and phone number. "Someone in Vienna, a friend of my aunt's."

"You got a contact in Vienna?" Andras said. "You lucky bugger!"

They reached the outskirts of Budapest and the open country. They passed people pushing bicycles or strollers piled with possessions. They saw, through the square window in the back of the van, others lugging suitcases or carrying bags slung over their shoulders, and where the road curved, tanks, army trucks, armed infantry carriers. They saw farm buildings with shattered windows and gaping holes in the walls, remnants of barricades...

HE SAW NANCY coming out of the house, crossing the lawn, creating a force field that swallowed his Hungarian memories and replaced them with the image of the moment, Nancy dressed in Birthday Beautiful, a white linen dress that deepened the innocence in her eyes. He gave her a smile of appreciation, but for some reason Nancy did not smile back.

"Has David left?" she asked.

"Gone home to read Derrida," he said lightly.

Nancy gave him an uncertain look. "All that talk about philosophy," she said.

She is worried, he thought, because of what I said to David earlier on about the Cereta/Laura mix-up. That's what's dampening her mood. But you have to start somewhere, and David is bound to find out one day that he was tricked into holding Cereta's hand for a couple of weeks. He may find out very soon if Cereta gets in touch with him and spills the beans. Or if Laura decides to confess now that they were seeing each other. At least, that's what Nancy told him. David had looked pathetically happy when they toasted the illusion of happiness. Zoltan felt sorry for the man. He wanted to pat him on the back and say: Listen, David, I know. Reality is a bitch, and life is complicated, but hey! Lighten up. Take it one day at a time. You are going out with Laura now? Good. Enjoy.

"Ready?" he said to Nancy, and without waiting for an answer steered her across the backyard to the gate.

"I've been thinking, Zoltan," she said, putting her hand on his arm, slowing him down. "We should be more honest with each other."

Sounds like the beginning of a confession, he thought. What can Nancy possibly have to confess? And how did we get here from there? He tried to connect Nancy's confessional voice to what came before — the two of them sipping Dom Pérignon by the swimming pool, the unveiling of the Liebermann, David coming over, their toast to illusion. What was Nancy's point of reference?

"I thought we *were* honest with each other," he said. All those sliding doors and secret passages he had come through to present Nancy with the Liebermann! She had no idea how hard he worked to please her.

"I mean..." she said and trailed off.

I should ask her about those apologetic elisions one day, he thought, and find out exactly what those half-sentences mean.

They were standing in the driveway. She had stopped beside his car and was waiting for him to open the door.

"Let's walk," he said. "It's only a few blocks. I like the fact that there are places here you can walk to. Unlike my neighbourhood, which is all strip malls and four-lane highways."

"That's the nice thing about Santa Monica, isn't it? All those little boutiques and cafés. They remind me of Vienna," she said.

Okay, he thought, we've sailed past the honesty question, but perhaps we should return to it and talk about the degree of honesty we can afford without making each other unhappy.

"I'm thinking of taking German lessons," Nancy was saying, "so I can talk to people the next time I'm in Vienna. A course at the Goethe Institute perhaps. I always let Max do the talking for me. I depended too much on him, I think, but he liked it that way."

Zoltan raised his eyebrows. Was Max, that dear and perfect man, coming off the pedestal? "You mean he *kept* you dependent?"

"Not in any negative sense," she said, flustered. "It's just that Max liked to take charge, and I was such a child when we got married. Eighteen. Nobody gets married at eighteen anymore. All my friends warned me off at the time because Max was twice my age. He was *sooo* old." She dragged out the syllable and smiled. "That's how we thought of anyone over thirty."

"Perhaps you were looking for a father figure."

He put a tease in his voice to let her know it was just a talking point, the analyst playing analyst, but she picked up on it eagerly.

"Yes, that's what I wanted, a mentor, someone to provide me with guidance. My own father was too mild-mannered, you know, too polite to correct anyone."

"Maybe you were the perfect daughter and didn't need correction."

"I was a good child, yes," she said and smiled up at him. It wasn't ironic. Nancy wasn't capable of bent talk.

"And then you grew up," he said, "went through a belated teenage rebellion and slept with me."

"I'll never forgive myself," she said earnestly.

"You have long ago forgiven yourself, Nancy. That's why you are still sleeping with me."

"Oh, but that's different," she said. "We are both free now. And I wish you wouldn't put it so crudely."

Yes, why was Nancy putting up with a schmuck like him, who put things so crudely? What a comedown after Max, who spoke the refined language of diplomacy and had inherited his father's aristocratic bearing. Mind you, life in California was erosive. Even Max was not entirely immune to its levelling effect and subsided into communal pleasantness toward the end of his life.

They got to the boardwalk. Nancy reached up to protect her perfect hairdo. "I should have brought a scarf," she said. "It's always blustery down here. Where are we going anyway?"

"I've made reservations at the Casa del Mar."

"Oh good," she said. "I hope they'll seat us by one of the windows, so we can watch the sunset."

"We can watch the sunset from here," he said. "We've got lots of time." He bent down and unlaced his shoes.

She watched him, disconcerted. "We aren't going to walk in the sand, are we?"

"What's the use of living a block from the beach if you don't get your feet into the sand?" he said.

She looked down at the delicate straps of her sandals and at her cranberry red toenails and back up at him for a solution to her dilemma. "But I can't walk on the sand like this."

"Why not?" he said. "Just take off your sandals."

She slipped them off and gave him a look of patient love. See what I'm doing for you? She reached for his hand as they waded through the mounds of soft dry sand. When they reached the water's edge, she started in again on the topic of their adulterous affair.

"Your conscience never bothered you, Zoltan?" She had to raise her voice over the pounding surf.

It was a murky question he didn't want to look into. Not

because he didn't want to acknowledge his guilt but because he couldn't tell whether he felt any. In any case, remorse wasn't productive. He had written *The Rescue* as an appreciation of what the Auerpergs had done for him — that was enough atonement if atonement was needed. But wasn't his affair with Nancy a kind of rescue as well? Her delivery from the prison-like cocoon of her marriage to the halfway house of his arms, her final release into the wilderness pending. So, was there a need for bad conscience, or not? It was one of those situations when he missed Livia, the old Livia, the interpreter of his feelings, who would have settled the question of guilt in a flip second. But why raise the subject of adultery now when Max's death had made it obsolete?

"I don't know whether I have a bad conscience," he said. He realized the disclaimer sounded phony, especially coming from an analyst.

Nancy picked him up immediately.

"How can you say you don't know?" She leaned in close. "You don't want to admit it."

He gave her an amused smile. It *was* an amusing twist to their relationship, this attempt of hers to analyze him. It should be the other way round, shouldn't it?

"How can you be sure?" he asked.

"You aren't that difficult to read, you know."

Maybe Nancy had hidden talents. He had never considered her as a reader of his emotions.

"You and Jerry," she said. "Especially Jerry. I could usually tell what was on his mind."

"Then why did you come to me for help?"

She thought for a moment. "Because it is your field of expertise, and Max was of no help at all. He was in denial. That's why I turned to you."

"But you didn't take my advice."

"I know. I thought you were too liberal when you said it all had to come out, but you were right. I realize that now. There was nothing we could do about Jerry's orientation. Nothing."

She gave him a stricken look. Jerry had tasted the forbidden fruit and driven them all out of the Garden of Eden. It was the end of her perfect family. Thank God for sunsets. They remained eternally beautiful. Nancy stopped and drew an admiring breath.

She took Zoltan's arm, and together they watched the sun drop into the sea, West Coast style, with a blaze and sudden loss of light. Only the Ferris wheel on the pier remained, a spinning halo, an afterimage of the sun, tiny green lights blinking on and off.

Nancy's dependence on Max. Bad conscience. Jerry. "And how does all this tie in with your new quest for honesty?" he said.

"Oh, but I didn't mean..." It was the start of another of her *oh but* half-sentences, only this time she got past the hyphen. "I meant, honesty up to a certain point."

"The point where it becomes ugly?"

"Yes, maybe that's what it is. I want to close my eyes to ugliness. There were a lot of things Max and I never talked about because they were too, you know, too..."

Ugly, she meant, but he refused to complete the sentence for her.

"It would have been better to talk before Max had the stroke and everything became so complicated," she said, and gave him an exhausted look. "But let's go up to the restaurant. I hate shouting into the wind. And I probably look a fright."

I guess we're through with the honesty topic, he thought, and it's back to nice and easy.

Dusk had robbed the Casa del Mar of its third dimension and turned it into a movie flat, the ideal set for a Great Gatsby scene. Zoltan didn't think he was up to it, but this evening was for Nancy, and she could easily slip into the Daisy role. She wasn't as careless as the Fitzgerald character, but she had that golden girl quality, and was living in a pink cloud.

They took the Art Deco staircase up to the restaurant. All the tables on the window side were taken. But it didn't matter, Nancy said. There was nothing to see now that the sun had set.

The ocean had gone a deep midnight blue, and she looked melancholy. Thinking of Max, post-stroke?

No. Halfway through the hors d'oeuvres, Nancy eased into the subject of birthdays. That's what made her melancholy. Too many birthdays. Elision points before segueing into more pleasant thoughts. The Liebermann painting. What a lovely present.

"And, by the way, Stanley thinks the transaction between Leo and Eva had no legal force whatsoever."

"You consulted Stanley about the Liebermann painting?" Surprising initiative. Nancy was nearing emancipation, getting ready to be released into the natural habitat of American society. He felt almost sorry that his rescue efforts had been so successful. He would have liked to keep her close a little longer.

In any case, Nancy said, she had no more qualms about the Liebermann business now that she knew Leo had offered the painting to Zoltan. It was all in order, wasn't it? What a relief. But. She had one more question.

"He offered you the painting, and you declined. But was that the end of your conversation? You know, Zoltan, I think you are holding something back."

Bingo. How many more days to full emancipation?

"And you think we need to be more honest with each other?"

"More open, I mean. Talking of Leo, for example."

"Why don't you start us off?" he said. "Because I'm not sure where we are headed."

She sighed. Was the assignment so difficult? Should he have asked her an easier question?

"I was always a bit afraid of Leo," she said. "He had something imposing about him, or what's the word I want? Regal? I think it was all those generations of Auerpergs going back to the Holy Roman Empire. That's why I'm asking. What did you think of Leo? You've never told me about the time when you came to Vienna and stayed with him."

Vienna 1956, again. A tricky time. When he had lost the interpreter of his feelings.

"There isn't much to tell," he said. The reluctance in his voice carried across the table. Nancy looked at him attentively. She was on the alert now.

"Maybe it wasn't a happy time for you," she said, "but Leo helped you out, didn't he? He took you in for a while. He saw you through university. I thought you'd put that into *The Rescue*, that he was your benefactor, I mean, but you don't say much about your relationship with Leo."

Of course, she couldn't guess the reason for his reticence — that he didn't know what sort of relationship it was. He was helpless without Livia, without a guide, blind, tapping a white cane to sound the depth of his emotions.

"I didn't think it was relevant to the purpose of the pamphlet," he said. "And I'm not sure I have a great deal to say about Leo. He and I were never close. His charity wasn't a personal thing. It was more like a duty to society." He thought of Leo's face, a handsome mask, an expression of ennui perfected over generations. Every gesture, every look was designed to keep him in place, to keep him at a distance.

He could see that Nancy wanted something more. "I guess that doesn't answer your question," he said. He put on his funny pompous voice, the one he used to put patients at ease when he touched on an uncomfortable subject. Only in this case, he needed to put himself at ease. "Okay. Full disclosure. In the spirit of our new motto — let's be honest with each other. I haven't talked much about my relationship with Leo, because I can't tell how I felt about him. I have no emotional memory."

Her eyes widened. "I don't understand. What do you mean you have no emotional memory?"

"It's a blind spot, a flaw in my makeup. I find it hard to say what I'm feeling now. And I can't remember what I was feeling then."

Nancy looked uneasy, and he was afraid that the disclosure had been too much for her, that he had said the wrong thing at the wrong time, putting obstacles into the path of their relationship and of Nancy's flight to freedom. There was a pause while the waiter cleared away their empty plates and served the next course. He thought Nancy would take advantage of the pause and veer off topic. But she stayed on track. Perhaps she had been on track all along, and it was he who couldn't see the thread, the connection between honesty, father figure, and Leo.

"That's odd," she said. "I mean about your blind spot. It explains a lot, though. Why you never say you love me, for example. Maybe, you can't tell. But don't they...I mean, psychology is your... Isn't there a way to overcome that?"

"A coping mechanism? Yes. I relate my experiences to others and listen for an echo, a clue to my feelings. That's how I process life. Or else, I rely on other people to extrapolate my feelings and play them back to me."

"But why haven't you told me before?" Nancy said. "I could have helped you."

Helped him identify his feelings?

"I know exactly what you are feeling, Zoltan," she said. "Now, at this moment at any rate. I don't know how you felt about Leo in fifty-six. But *right now*, you are feeling pressured. You don't really want to remember Leo. I suppose you didn't like him, but it would be so helpful to me to know why. So, please..."

"I don't think it was a matter of dislike. He baffled me. When I arrived in Vienna and told him that Eva had died, he put me through a kind of interrogation. He practically gave me the third degree. He asked me: 'What exactly did she say when you last saw her?'"

"But, Zoltan, last words *are* important. What did Eva say?"

"She was barely conscious. She said a few words. They didn't make much sense. She mentioned Leo's and Livia's names."

The conversation with Leo made a staccato comeback in his mind.

"Did she talk about me?" Leo had asked.

"She did," he told him. "Not at the very end, but she talked about you earlier, that you helped her escape from Vienna, that you bought a painting from her."

Leo was waiting for more.

"She said she didn't get as much as she expected for the painting," Zoltan said.

A steepled furrow appeared between Leo's brows. "You have to consider the circumstances," he said. "We had to stay under the radar. I gave Eva as much money as I had on hand."

Last words. Escape. Leo's furrowed brow. Money on hand.

Nancy interrupted the flow of his synoptic memories. "Then you don't know," she said.

Zoltan forced himself to pull away from the past and concentrate on Nancy's words.

"Don't know what?" he said.

"I'm trying to tell you, Zoltan. But it's so difficult." She bent over her salad and poked at the leaves. "Max only told me after he had the stroke. Sometimes, I think I misunderstood him. It was hard to make out what he was saying. Guesswork, really, but perhaps you can help me sort it out."

"Nancy," he said patiently. "I thought we were having a pre-birthday dinner, but this is turning into a therapeutic session."

"I'm not asking for your help because you are a therapist, Zoltan. I'm asking because we are…"

Another of Nancy's half-thoughts.

"Lovers?" he suggested.

She lowered her eyes. She can't get herself to acknowledge our unregulated relationship, he thought. It was one of those disturbing things that needed exorcising. Nancy longed for the exorcism of a wedding ceremony.

"Because I want us to be open with each other," she said.

"I don't know what you are getting at." Their conversation was adrift. "What exactly did Max say to you?"

She took a deep breath. "He said that Leo and Eva. That they. He…"

Zoltan waited for her to get over the hurdle of the elision points.

"…fathered a child with Eva."

Zoltan's breathing stalled. A cranial storm blew up in back of his head, Livia's Rape poems flashed through his mind like lightning, exploding his thoughts, leaving him wordless.

Nancy dabbed at her mouth with her napkin and looked at him, waiting for him to explain things away.

"I see," he managed to say, falling back on his couch-side manner to cover up the tempest. He tried to sound calm, to play down what she had said. "And why was it so difficult to tell me about an indiscretion that happened long ago? Or is there more to it?"

"More? How can you be so matter-of-fact about it, Zoltan? It reflects badly on the family. On Leo and Eva at any rate. But, yes, there is more. The child. That is the difficulty. Max said…" She reached for her glass to take a sip, changed her mind, took a reinforcing breath instead, something to take her to the end of the sentence. "Livia is Leo's daughter."

The truth unfolded in Zoltan's brain with a churning motion, the untold story, half-told in a spill of words, in the dying minutes of Eva's life. The pressure on his ears and eyelids was tremendous. His eyeballs were going dry.

"I wonder why Eva never told me," he said. He could hear himself speak, an external voice, on automatic pilot. But perhaps Eva did tell him. His thoughts curved into space. With sudden clarity he remembered her last words: *I was desperate to hold on to someone. It was wrong.* He felt surprise at his sudden understanding, or was it shock? He felt something, it occurred to him, something vaporous but surprisingly close to the surface. A feeling. He could almost put a name to it.

"Do you think I misunderstood Max?" Nancy was saying with a glimmer of hope.

"No, I'm sure you are right," he said. "It all makes sense now. Eva's last words. The fact that she mentioned Leo and Livia together." He added to the list of his proofs: Eva's visits to the Orbans, Leo's sponsorship of Livia, Leo asking Laura and Cereta to call him Opa, Livia fantasizing about Eva being her mother. And Livia's "Rape" poems inspired by what she had seen in Eva's eyes, confirmed by what she had seen in Leo's eyes.

"Maybe that's what Eva was trying to tell me when she coupled their names," he said to Nancy. "That they were father and daughter. And the time frame is right, too. Livia was born in June of nineteen forty"

"But if it's true," Nancy said, "how could they? At a time like that, with the Gestapo dragging off Eva's husband. I can't understand it."

"You can't?"

Nancy blushed at her inability to understand Eva's adultery. "In those tragic circumstances, I mean. Max said they did it 'in a moment of abandon.' But I still don't understand."

"In a moment of desperation," he said, trying to cut through the wad of clinical terms for abnormal behaviour, the vocabulary of psychopathology lodged in his brain. When you care for someone, it is cruel to speak of hyperdopaminergic foundations and critical levels of stress. You look for the consolation of familiar terms. "When you are in despair," he said, "behavioural norms don't apply." Still too clinical. "When they took away Joseph, Eva must have been desperate, but to save me, she had to act unconcerned. When you suppress your feelings, they are transformed…" He tried to find the right words for Nancy. Transformed into what? A suffocating cloud of grief? A pulverizing rage? A searing need to press your body against another, to know you are not alone? But somehow those words seemed to be rooted in his own memory and couldn't be plucked to describe Eva's case. He could only give a generic description to Nancy. "Suppressed feelings cause a disruption of the soul," he said.

Nancy listened breathlessly, but not to his explanation, it seemed to him, because the reflection he saw in her eyes wasn't a reflection of his words.

"You say you have no emotional memory," she said. "And you've just explained why. Because you went through a disruption of the soul."

My God, Nancy had put her finger on it. And now he could feel it, too — a lingering despair deep down buried below jokes, capers, and hoaxes — the unmooring effects of violence, of being trapped in the labyrinth of terrifying events. "Yes," he said. "I've had a brush with that kind of despair." Subconsciously perhaps, when I was a small child, and later during the Revolution when I saw men lynched and people spitting on the dead bodies of Russian soldiers, and my aunt dying, her bed shunted into the corridor as if she no longer deserved a place among the living. "I felt it the day Eva died. I needed to hold on to someone, I needed the warmth of another body to shield me from my own chilling thoughts. I went home, and there was Livia."

Nancy sighed. "And when Eva went back to the apartment in the Herrengasse, there was Leo. I accept that explanation, Zoltan. At one level, I do, but in here..." She put her hand on her heart. "I still don't understand."

She never would. Nancy believed in beauty. She refused to regard evil as more than a temporary aberration. She wanted the world to be as it had been Before the Fall, perfect. It was naïve of her. Silly even, but I love her for it, he thought, taken by surprise when the word floated up like a speech bubble, an emotion identified in real time. Perhaps there was hope for him yet.

"I love you, Nancy," he said and carefully listened to himself as he said the words. They rang true. "I'm sorry I haven't told you before."

"You don't look sorry," she said. "In fact, you look happy."

Right again.

"What you see is anticipation."

Nancy waited for Zoltan to slip his credit card into the folder with the bill and for the waiter to take it away before she said:

"What are you anticipating?"

"Burying the past."

Her smile, kept largely in abeyance during dinner, made a comeback. "You mean, we needn't tell anyone about this? That Livia is... And that crazy business about Laura and Cereta switching identities? The whole..."

"The whole genealogical soap opera?"

Too flippant for Nancy's taste. Her mouth straightened. "The whole thing," she said weakly. "The past, as you say."

"Let's hope Cereta will leave the past alone as well. She threatened to confess all to David, you know."

"Oh, Zoltan," she said. "You shouldn't have told me. Not on my birthday."

VI. ALL TOGETHER NOW

D AVID SAT AT HIS COMPUTER DESK which was still in its old position, angled toward Nancy's backyard. He could no longer remember what it was that irritated him about the view. The swimming pool? Why? The rippling surface was rather pleasant to look at. Zoltan's presence? There was a time when Zoltan annoyed him, but that was last summer when everyone and everything annoyed him. There had been a sea change since then. Zoltan was as loopy as ever, but David was back on track, had recovered his balance in time for the fall term. His lectures were going smoothly. He had been afraid of a relapse into moroseness, but the first day of classes passed and gave him only a dull headache, no worse than a hangover. It was October now, and he was still coping, staying on top of his lectures and seminars, posting assignments on time, making a convincing show of interest at department meetings. He answered his phone, checked his email, and replied within a reasonable time. He even started watching the news again without experiencing adverse reactions. It was the soothing effect of Laura's company. Certainty had returned to David's life. Laura had the gift of explanation. She was able to lay out the world for him in a grid that was solid at the centre and intuitive at the edges, a layout that accommodated even Zoltan's wildest plan, his latest caper -- the Laura/Cereta exchange. The way Laura explained it left only a mild surprise in David's mind, as if he had always suspected it, had been minutes away from discovering the illusion for himself. It almost made sense even if it was legally questionable. A kind of historical truth was shaping up, with events proceeding in a straight line. All facts checked out. There were no obvious contradictions.

He logged off. Time to go next door. Nancy's party was getting under way. From his desk, he saw people milling around on the patio. It looked like a big do. The invitation, which had arrived by snail mail two weeks ago, was printed on cream-coloured stationery with a lacy ribbon tacked to one corner, mimicking a wedding invitation, but the occasion for the party was: "Zoltan has won the lottery." David wasn't sure what to make of that. Another example of Zoltan's wacky sense of humour?

"What's the party about?" he asked Laura when the invitation arrived. "Zoltan didn't really win the lottery, did he?"

"No idea what's going on," she said. "The bit about winning the lottery could be a coy reference to the progress his lawyer has made with inquiries in Switzerland. Maybe he's finally tapped into the Wassermann accounts. I no longer ask any questions of Dad. I can't get a straight answer from him. Ever."

Through the window, David could see Nancy doing the round of the guests, touching shoulders, and pecking cheeks. The caterers carried trays of drinks and bite-sized food that looked like something from the florist's, tiny flower arrangements in cups. People popped them into their mouths. They were edible at any rate.

He didn't see Laura. She must be inside, he thought, and doing the audio. Nancy had put her in charge of streaming the music. She had a timed playlist. It was a party with a musical theme, apparently.

David put on his jacket and walked across the driveway, past the two valets chatting on the sidewalk. Their work was done. The guest cars had been parked in a lot on Neilson Way. He had his hand on the latch of the gate, but the occasion looked too official for a casual entrance through the back, and he walked up to the front door. Right. A rent-a-maid checked his name off the guest list. He walked through to the patio, and in passing noticed the black-and-white photo of Max Auerperg, which had been on the second floor, was now hanging in the downstairs hall. Had he been demoted? Or were there specific stages of grieving, involving the gradual removal of keepsakes from the intimacy of one's bedroom to more public spaces like the upstairs hall, then the downstairs hall, and from there into storage? He wondered what Nancy had put in place of Max Auerperg's portrait. He stopped at the staircase and looked up: Ah, the Picasso was there now. It had been in Nancy's bedroom, right?

Then he saw the feet. Laura's feet in strappy sandals. She was sitting on the floor in the corridor, knees pulled up, head resting on her knees, face hidden behind the shiny black curtain of her hair. Sick?

He bounded upstairs.

"Laura?"

She looked up, pale and beautiful even when she was upset.

The door to Nancy's bedroom was ajar, and Laura said, "Look at this!" pointing to a landscape painting. The disputed Liebermann, he realized, even before Laura said it.

"The painting that used to hang in Opa's study in Vienna."

"The painting that turned out to be a copy?"

"No, the copy is back above Opa's desk, according to Cereta. I'm totally confused. The one in Nancy's bedroom is definitely the painting that hung in his study when I was a child. I know, because when I was about six years old, I picked off a small paint chip and swallowed it."

"You did what?"

She laughed, a nervous hiccup of a laugh. "I know it sounds crazy. I guess I wanted to make the painting mine, claim my legacy. Something like that. I checked the painting in Nancy's bedroom. That paint chip is still missing. You can see the weave of the canvas where it was."

"Well, let me take a guess," David said. "The story goes something like this. Leo Auerperg has a copy made of the Liebermann. He puts the copy on the wall and gives the original to his son, who stores it away. Nancy inherits the original with the rest of her husband's assets. When Cereta demands the return of the Liebermann, Nancy tells her to go ahead and have the painting in Vienna assessed. Cereta finds out that it is a copy and decides it isn't worth fighting over. The end. What do you think?"

Laura shook her head, and David realized that his story was incomplete. It didn't explain why Nancy had brought the original out of storage. Was Zoltan behind that move? Was this a lead-up to another of his hoaxes?

"So what's *your* explanation?" he asked Laura, but she had no time to give him an answer. Cheers went up outside. Someone came rushing into the house and called: "Laura, where are you? Come out here, or you'll miss it!"

"Miss what?" Laura said, as they went downstairs.

Nancy and Zoltan were standing poolside between two giant planters with elaborate, porcelain-like flower arrangements, the kind you see in the foyer of five-star hotels. The sunset tinged the scene dusty rose. A distinguished gentleman in a black suit was making a speech. No, holding a sermon. No, officiating.

"This better not be a hoax," Laura said.

Nancy was pinning a corsage on Zoltan's lapel now, and Zoltan, with an apologetic glow in his eyes, placed a kind of bird's nest on the bride's head, with feathers arcing out and trembling in the breeze that had sprung up.

"A fascinator!" Laura said. A laugh escaped her, and she covered her mouth. "Oh my God," she said, "I was supposed to…" She rushed back into the house, and by the time the man in the black suit was asking the bridegroom to kiss the bride, "*Morning has broken…*" floated from the loudspeakers over the lawn. The guests whooped and applauded and swamped the couple with congratulations. For a moment, they froze and radiated in the flash of cameras, then Nancy opened her arms wide and said she was just so thrilled for them all to be here. Her voice was Oprah-esque with joy.

As the event photographer moved on to blitz the guests, David thought: There will be an explanation for all of this. Laura will come up with the missing part of the story, put it in place, and complete the Nagy family puzzle. But maybe that was impossible, even for Laura who was good at that kind of thing.

ACKNOWLEDGEMENTS

I wish to thank first of all Luciana Ricciutelli, Editor-in-Chief at Inanna Publications, for giving a voice to the marginalized, disadvantaged, emotionally damaged, or merely odd characters who people my fiction.

Many thanks also to my friends who patiently read through the various drafts of my manuscripts and gave me advice on how to improve them: Gisela Argyle, Roberta Johnson, Karin McHardy, Jim Ryder, and Howard Katzman.

And finally, thanks to my copyeditor, Adrienne Weiss, for her careful and close reading and her suggestions and corrections. I am very grateful to all of them.

Erika Rummel has taught history at the University of Toronto and Wilfrid Laurier University, Waterloo. She divides her time between Toronto and Los Angeles and has lived in villages in Argentina, Romania, and Bulgaria. She is the author of more than a dozen books of non-fiction, and has written extensively on social history. She is also the author four previous novels, *Playing Naomi, Head Games, The Inquisitor's Niece,* and *The Effects of Isolation on the Brain.* She was awarded the Random House Creative Writing Award, 2011, for an excerpt of *The Effects of Isolation on the Brain. The Painting on Auerperg's Wall* is her fifth work of fiction.